Hollister drew up the car sharply and was about to stop when there came the sound of a shot, sharp and terrifying. Melissa cringed in the back seat and thought of screaming for help, but the car lurched forward so suddenly that it threw her to her knees, and she had to struggle to get back in the seat before Henry, her back seat companion, fell on top of her.

She glanced at him and was horrified to see him looking at her intently. "Hello, Beautiful!" he said, bringing his unpleasant face nearer to her own, his sickening breath of alcohol pouring into her nostrils. "Where'd they find you?" he said thickly, then suddenly he brought his lips down on hers. Melissa frantically pushed him away and screamed, not just an ordinary scream but a shriek that echoed piercingly through the woods.

Almost at once they heard another shot and the rumble of an approaching motorcycle . . .

Tyndale House books by
Grace Livingston Hill
Check with your area bookstore
for these bestsellers.

COLLECTOR'S CHOICE SERIES
1 *The Christmas Bride*
2 *In Tune with Wedding Bells*
3 *Partners*
4 *The Strange Proposal*

LIVING BOOKS®
1 *Where Two Ways Met*
2 *Bright Arrows*
3 *A Girl to Come Home To*
4 *Amorelle*
77 *The Ransom*
78 *Found Treasure*
79 *The Big Blue Soldier*
80 *The Challengers*

CLASSIC SERIES
1 *Crimson Roses*
2 *The Enchanted Barn*
3 *Happiness Hill*
4 *Patricia*
5 *Silver Wings*

Grace Livingston Hill

THE CHALLENGERS

LIVING BOOKS®
Tyndale House Publishers, Inc.
Wheaton, Illinois

This Tyndale House book
by Grace Livingston Hill
contains the complete text
of the original hardcover edition.
NOT ONE WORD
HAS BEEN OMITTED.

Printing History
J.B. Lippincott edition published 1932
Tyndale House edition/1988

Living Books is a registered trademark of Tyndale
House Publishers, Inc.

Library of Congress Catalog Card Number 88-51435
ISBN 0-8423-0362-6
Copyright 1932 by J. B. Lippincott
Reprinted by permission of Harper & Row, Publisher, Inc.
Cover artwork copyright 1989 by Steven Stroud
Printed in United States of America

2   3   4   5   6   7   8   9   10   93   92   91   90   89

THE room was cold. Phyllis shivered as she took her hands out of the dish water to reach for a pile of plates that stood on the inadequate little table behind her. The table was inadequate because there wasn't room for a larger one. Everything in the tiny dark hole that passed for a kitchenette was cramped. One had to turn around carefully lest something be knocked over.

Phyllis tossed her head to get a refractory lock of hair out of her eyes, and failing, pushed it back with her elbow; then shivered again. The apartment was supposed to have heat in it, but the radiators had been stone cold all day, and when she tapped on the door of the landlady's room down the hall there was no answer, although Phyllis was sure she was there. She had heard her scolding her baby but a moment before. But of course, that was because the rent wasn't paid. When Phyllis remembered that, she beat a hasty retreat back to her cold room. She had no desire to bring down upon her lonely young self a tirade such as her mother had had to endure the evening before, just because she had told the old skinflint that she would not be able to pay the rent for another week.

Unbidden, a great hot tear rolled down her white cheek and dropped into the dish water.

The dish water was cold too. Phyllis had tried to heat some water because the dishes were greasy, left over from last night to save heating dish water twice. But the gas had flickered and gone out under the kettle before it was more than luke warm, and Phyllis had not another quarter to put into the meter to start it again. That meter was always eating up quarters. This cold dish water in the cold room, with the greasy dishes, seemed just the last straw, and another tear followed the first one.

But Phyllis Challenger was not a crying person, and with the upper part of her sleeve she wiped her eyes defiantly and applied a little more soap to the greasy plate she was washing, setting her lips firmly. Things did look pretty black but she was not going to let a mere greasy plate in a cold room conquer her. Mother had enough to worry her now without having any one of her family give way to weakness. If they were all going to starve to death, she resolved that at least she, Phyllis, would die smiling.

When the dishes were done and the clammy towels hung up to dry, she scrubbed away at the ugly sink with a worn old sink brush.

"How I hate you!" she said aloud to the rusty iron sink that the landlady had bought for fifty cents from a junk man when she bungled her rickety old dwelling over into a so-called "apartment" house.

She washed her hands in clear cold water from the spigot many times. She must not waste the soap for mere hands. Thank goodness there wasn't any extra charge for water at least. Of course there was a water meter in the house but the landlady looked out for that. She took a good drink of water to still the empty feeling in her stomach and cast a wistful glance in the bread box. Nothing but half a loaf of mother's home made bread left. It had been hoarded carefully, and was as dry as could be, but it would soak in hot water, if she only had a quarter to start the gas with to heat hot water. But dry as it was how good a little piece of it would taste! Only if she took a piece now and it should just happen that mother was not able to get any money yet, perhaps this half loaf would be all they would have for the whole family for supper. She measured the loaf with her eye. Cut in thin slices there was barely enough for a portion each, Mother, Bob, Melissa, and Rosalie. Lucky thing Stephen wasn't at home or it never could be made to go around.

Home! As if anybody could call this a home!

Phyllis slammed the bread box shut, took another drink of water, and went into the little front room which was both living room and Bob's bedroom. The squalid apartment contained only one other room, a small bedroom, nearly full with its two beds, a bureau and chiffonier. They could just barely crowd around between the furniture. One had to sit on the side of the bed to open the drawers of the bureau. Phyllis and Mother slept in one of the beds, and Melissa and Rosalie in the other. It was just like berths in a sleeper. Phyllis sighed. Would they ever go on nice long vacation journeys in a sleeper again? Would they ever have a car like other people and drive away to the shore for week ends and trips?

She went to the window and looked out on the dismal little street, sordid and grimy. It was a narrow street with rows of two-story brick houses facing each other across uneven old brick paved sidewalks where on certain days one had to pick one's way between garbage pails and ash cans. Such a terrible place for the family of a college professor to have to live, even for a little while! Would Father ever get well, and be able to come out of the hospital? Would he ever be able to get back to teaching, and they all live in a respectable house again? Low down, that was what this was! Just plain low down and disgusting, like drunkards' homes. That was what Phyllis thought. Her experience in drunkards' homes had been limited however. There really were worse streets than Slacker Street, even in that city.

She continued to gaze out of the window, hoping against hope that she would see her mother coming. It had begun to rain, steadily, drearily, which only seemed to accentuate the coldness of the room. The window panes had bias trickles like tears, so that it was hard to see out, but the girl continued to press her cheek against the pane and gaze wistfully up the street. If mother would only come and bring some good news, somehow!

There were patches of dirty snow in the gutter here and there, and across the road in a narrow passage between two houses, one of which was unoccupied, a drift of snow was banked untidily against the two walls where no one had passed in and out since the winter months.

A gaunt gray cat streaked warily across the road and disappeared down the alley. A little wet mongrel dog hurried down the sidewalk as if on some special errand. A woman under a bent cotton umbrella with a large basket on her arm walked painfully by on the opposite side. She was lame and she was wearing a man's shoes which were too large for her. She made slow progress. Her long untidy skirts sloshed drearily about her ankles, drabbling into every puddle she passed. What a sordid thing life was! Tears threatened again and Phyllis turned with a shiver back to the dreary room casting an anxious eye about. If she only could do something to make it look a little more cheerful when Mother came back. She would be wet and tired and cold. How wonderful it would be if they could have a fire, an open fire! But the high wooden mantel-piece only sheltered an inadequate little old-fashioned register up which nothing was coming now but cold air. The landlady had gone out for the afternoon evidently, and the fire must have gone out too.

Phyllis went and put on her old sweater, then she opened the hall door cautiously and listened. There was no sound anywhere, neither baby nor landlady. A queer time to take a baby out in a rain like this, but either that or they were both asleep which was not likely at this hour of the day. Dared she?

She tiptoed to the woman's door and listened, tapped softly again and listened, but there was no sound save the noise of the landlady's little dog thumping his tail in a friendly way on the floor, whining gently. Yes, they surely were gone and had left the dog in the house to guard it.

Phyllis had never been in the cellar. It was not a part of their province. But she was going now. Love for her mother gave her courage.

With a defiant look toward the closed door of the householder, she grasped the knob of the cellar door and opened it cautiously, looking down into the forbidding shadows below the steep winding stair.

Cautiously she ventured down a step or two and peered again. There seemed to be no place to turn on a light. Perhaps a gas jet somewhere, but how was she to find out its location? Could she do anything in the cellar without a light? She remembered a short end of candle and hurried back to her kitchen for it, a little anxious about having to use it. She must save even a candle and a match if possible. How terrible life was! There were only nine matches left. She had counted them that morning, but she must use one to light the candle for she could not do a thing to a strange furnace in the dark. Perhaps she could not anyway. She had never made a furnace fire in her life. She had never had to. But now she had to, and what one had to, one always could do, she firmly believed.

With her candle casting flickering shadows before her she descended at last into that awful cellar. One dismayed glance she cast about her at the dirt and disorder, and then walked straight over to the grim rusty object that must be the furnace.

The door stuck and she had hard work to get it open, but after much tugging it gave way, and revealed a dark cavern inside with just a spunk of fire winking as if it were about to expire. No wonder the house had been cold! And that woman had taken her baby and gone out, and left the house cold on purpose! That was probably the truth. She had done it because Mother had not been able to pay last month's rent last night when she had promised!

Phyllis' cheeks burned hotly even while she shivered. To think that they, the Challengers, had come to this, to have a common lodging-house keeper punish them because they could not pay the rent on time. But of course, reasoned the honest child, even through her indignation, the woman perhaps needed the money, and it was right that she should be paid. Oh, the shame of being in a position like this, they who had always had plenty and to spare for others!

But there was no time to philosophize. This fire must be made. Even if she had to break up some of the furniture to make it the room must be warm when Mother came home! And besides, she must hurry. No telling what Mrs. Barkus would do to her when she returned if she found out she was daring to enter the sacred precincts of the cellar and make a fire in her absence.

She held the candle high and looked around. There were some old newspapers piled in one corner, but they looked damp, for there was water on the floor of the cellar. No wonder such a musty smell came up the register!

There were a few old boxes and crates scattered untidily around, and a rusty ax lay on the floor. Dared she?

She put the candle carefully down on the floor and lifted the ax gingerly. She approached a box and brought the ax down on it with a crash, and exulted in the splintering ruin that ensued. The box didn't look very substantial. It was perhaps an orange or peach crate but the splinters would be just the thing to catch fire from that spunk of brightness just winking out. She laid down the ax and gathered a handful of splinters stuck them carefully down into the fire and was heartened to see them catch and blaze up. She applied a few more and had a neat little blaze going. It was interesting coaxing a fire into being, but how fast it ate up the fuel! She seized the ax and attacked a heavier box, finding it not so easy to break up.

While she worked she wondered what Mrs. Barkus or her grouchy husband would say when they found their kindling wood all gone. Could they arrest her for a thing like that when she was cold? When—but of course their rent wasn't paid. Still, it was only a month behind. Well, she would get a job and pay for the kindling wood herself.

But her heart sank as she remembered how she had spent her whole morning until two o'clock trying to find a job, and had stopped only because she had come to the end of the advertisements she had cut out of the paper that morning. It wasn't easy in these hard times for a girl to find a job, especially a girl who had never been trained for a job.

But she had never been trained for a fireman, that was certain, and she found it a back-breaking job before she finally got a good blaze, juggled with the queer dampers and doors, and got the coal to catch with a little licking blue flame that promised smartly to accomplish some real heat pretty soon. But at last she closed the cellar door on her efforts, extinguished her candle and went up stairs, just in time, for she heard the front door key rattling in the lock as she turned away from the cellar door, and she had to beat a hasty retreat to get inside her own room before the door opened.

It was not Mrs. Barkus as she had feared, but her own sister Melissa, looking pale and tired and pretty, and carrying a dripping umbrella.

Phyllis had retreated to the kitchenette and was entrenched behind the table when Melissa entered bearing the umbrella to the sink.

"Mercy!" said Melissa crossly. "What's the matter? What have you been doing? You've got a smudge all across your nose and cheek and you look as if you expected an army with banners."

"I did," laughed Phyllis with relief. "I thought you were Barkus the Belligerent, and I was about to defend myself with the iron spoon."

"But what have you been doing, Phyl, that you should

have to defend yourself? She hasn't dared to come down on you for the rent, has she?"

"Not yet," said Phyllis solemnly, "but she may. When she finds out what I've been doing she may turn us out of the house before night. Or worse than that perhaps. She may have us all arrested. Lissie do they ever arrest people for making fires in other people's furnaces?" she asked with mock solemnity.

"Oh, Phyl, you haven't been making a fire! How did you dare? Does she know? A fire! How heavenly! I'm frozen to the bone. I didn't know it was so cold or I'd have worn my old sweater under my coat, but I did want to make a good impression!"

Phyllis cast a quick anxious look into her sister's face and saw the sudden overshadowing of trouble as she spoke.

"Did you get the place, Lissa? You didn't! Oh, *Lissa!*"

"Of course not!" said Melissa crossly, stumbling over the rocker of Rosalie's small chair. "You didn't expect I would, did you? I told you not to expect anything. I thought you'd just go and do that thing, be disappointed! That's why I hated to go. It's almost worse than getting turned down to have to come home and tell it."

"Oh, Lissie, dear! I didn't mean to seem disappointed. I really am only disappointed for you because I saw you were counting on it so."

"I wasn't counting on it!" snapped Melissa. "I'm not fool enough to count on anything any more. Somebody's got it in for us, what's what. I guess God wants to destroy us the way he did some of those old fiends in the Old Testament."

"Don't, Lissie! Don't talk that way. You know that's not true. That's not like you. You're a good little sport!"

"Sport nothing!" glowered Melissa. "I mean it. Somebody has. It couldn't be just happening, all this to come to one perfectly good respectable family!"

Phyllis shuddered involuntarily at the hard tone her sister used.

"But don't, Lissie," she pleaded again, following her sister into the living room. "It only makes it worse to take it that way. Tell me about it. What was the matter? I didn't see how you could possibly fail with that wonderful letter from the provost, and Miss Waring the librarian being an old friend of Mother's."

"Oh, *friends!*" sneered Melissa taking off her beret and shaking the drops from it into the sink, "Now look! I've got my only good hat wet, and all for nothing."

"But what was the matter, Liss, didn't you even *see* her? Didn't she read the letter?"

"Oh, yes, I saw her, after waiting hours. She was in some kind of conference. She read the letter of course, and smiled her sweetest, and said she was so sorry, but they had about decided on an assistant librarian. 'And anyway,' and then she looked at me as if I were some kind of merchandise she was rejecting, 'and anyway, are you through college, my dear?' and when I told her no, I had had only one year, she shook her head and said, 'Well, that would settle it. We're giving the preference to college *grad*uates now. You know almost *every* young girl goes to college nowadays.' As if I were staying away from college to play parchesi!"

Suddenly Melissa sank into the one big overstuffed chair that the room contained and putting her head down on the worn old arm, broke into heartbreaking sobs that shook her slender shoulders.

Phyllis was on her knees beside her in a moment with an arm about her shaking shoulders.

"There, Lissie dear, don't cry. There's probably something a lot better for you. Don't feel so bad, dear."

"Well, I do feel bad," said Melissa suddenly sitting up and pushing her hair up from her forehead wildly. "Here I am a great big girl and just as able as any college graduate to be assistant to a librarian, you know I am. You know Father has trained us all about books, and I had that library course be-sides, and I *can't get in!* Not even with that wonderful letter from the provost. The old grump! I wouldn't have felt half so bad if she hadn't smiled so much! Just smiled and called me 'dear'! I wanted to smack her hypocritical old face. Do you know what's the matter? I heard it just after I got there. Another girl that had applied for the same job sat next to me and talked awhile. She said she had heard that Miss Waring wanted to keep the job for her young niece who is graduating from college this spring, and she has turned heaven and earth to get a pull with the trustees and get her in. And they say that even if one got the job now it would last only till spring because she is determined to get that niece in."

Phyllis patted her sister's hand and looked troubled.

"Didn't she say anything at all about Mother, and us, and that she was sorry, or anything?"

"Oh, yes," snapped Melissa, "said she was sorry all right, honey and almonds all over her lips when she said it. She was *surprised* that Professor Challenger was *willing* that his daughter should go to work before she had finished her college course. Said she should think he would have *insisted* upon that at *any* sacrifice. Said if it was a question of *money* that *money* could always be *borrowed*. Said if there was *anything at all* she could do for my mother to be *sure* to let her know. Was Mother quite well? She had always been *very fond* of Mother! Pah! The old hypocrite!"

"The idea!" said Phyllis getting to her feet indignantly. "Father! Poor Father! Didn't you tell her he was sick and didn't know that you had come back from college? Didn't you tell her Mother was having a terribly hard time, and you needed that job even if it was only for two or three months? But no, of course you didn't. You couldn't. I understand perfectly, Lissa. Now don't think another thing about it."

"But I can't help thinking," said Melissa with trembling lip. "It was going to be so wonderful earning all that money. We could have had all we wanted to eat every day, and, Phyl, I'm *hungry* right now. Is there anything in the house to eat?"

Phyllis turned her head quickly away and swallowed hard,

trying to control the shake in her voice, trying to answer cheerfully. Though she was the younger of the two sisters it had somehow always been her aim to keep Melissa happy. She could not bear to see Melissa's blue eyes clouded with tears, or to know she was suffering in any way. She had adored Melissa since they were babies together.

"There's—just enough bread—for supper—I think—in case Mother doesn't get her money."

"Oh, but surely she'll get something won't she?" asked Melissa looking up with new anxiety in her eyes. "Didn't she say that Father had some government bonds put away that were only to be used in an absolute emergency? And didn't she say she was sure he would consider that they had to be used now. Surely she would be able to get money on them right away."

"I don't know," answered Phyllis doubtfully. "Perhaps it takes time to get government bonds cashed. Maybe she wouldn't be able to get the money until to-morrow. I thought we ought to save what there is for supper so everybody would get something in case—" her voice trailed off into anxious silence.

Her sister looked at her sharply, noted the blue shadows under the brown eyes, the pinched white look around the sweet lips.

"I'll bet you never ate any lunch yourself, Phyl. Come own up. Did you?"

"Well, I didn't have time, really," evaded Phyllis. "You see I had to make that fire. I was out all the morning myself hunting a job, but everything had been taken before I got there of course."

"And so you came home and washed the dishes and didn't eat a crumb. Why didn't you at least make yourself a cup of tea? There's quite a lot of tea, isn't there?"

"Well, not a lot, but you see the gas went out before I got the dish water heated, and I didn't have a quarter to put in the meter."

"Mercy!" said Melissa getting up from the chair and walking back and forth frantically like a caged lion, "Isn't this awful! To think of us all hungry, and not a cent to get anything with! I spent my last nickel going down to that library. I had to *walk* home. I think God is just awful to treat us this way! Yes, I do Phyllis! You needn't look so horrified! We're hungry! We'll starve pretty soon if this keeps on! Oh! I'd give anything for a good thick juicy beefsteak!" And she ended with a choking sob of desperation.

"Oh, Melissa, don't!" wailed a small sweet voice from the doorway.

The two girls turned and there stood Rosalie their little sister, blue eyes troubled and fearful, gold curls dripping with rain, little cold fingers gripping her school bag, the water squashing out of a crack in her rubber.

2

BOTH girls were filled with compunction at once, but it was Phyllis who sprang to her and took the heavy school bag from her.

"Why, you're wet, darling! Where is your umbrella? Your hair is simply dripping. And your clothes are wet through to the skin. Didn't you carry an umbrella this morning to school?"

"Yes, but somebody took it," said Rosalie, troubled. "I think it was that Sara Hauser. Some of the other girls have missed things. I'm so sorry. It was Mother's silk one. She *made* me take it this morning."

"Never mind Rosy Posy," soothed Phyllis, "it isn't the worst thing in the world."

"No, I guess not!" murmured Melissa from the window where she had retreated and was looking out on the dirty street with unseeing eyes.

"Why does Lissa talk that way?" asked Rosalie, turning troubled eyes on Phyllis.

"Oh, she's just a little upset because some one else had the job at the library. But she'll get another pretty soon," explained Phyllis. "Take off your wet shoes, Rosie, quick! You'll get tonsilitis again."

"H'm! Another job! Fat chance!" grumbled Melissa.

Rosalie submitted to being dried off and wrapped in a blanket by the register, from which a good rush of heat was now issuing, but her eyes were still troubled as she watched her oldest sister driving a pin hard into the window sill, her very back eloquent with desolation.

"Why does Lissa talk that way, Phyllie?" she asked again. "I heard her say she was hungry. Haven't we anything left to eat, Sister?"

"Well, we've got a little left for supper. Are you hungry too?"

"A little," owned the small sister, "I shared my apple with Anna Betts. She's the colored girl from down on the flats. She didn't have any lunch at all to-day. Her father broke his leg yesterday and they're awfully poor."

"You darling child!" It was Phyllis who said it and there were tears in her voice.

"It's just awful!" burst forth Melissa.

But Rosalie suddenly broke forth into a joyous little squeal.

"Why it's hot, Phyllie, the register's really *hot!* I didn't know it *could* get hot like that. It's only been kind of warm before."

"Yes," said Melissa whirling around, "This room is warm for the first time this winter. You must have made a wonderful fire, Phyllis. Maybe the house is burning up."

"It is getting hot isn't it?" said Phyllis. "Isn't it wonderful? Perhaps I ought to go down and shut something. It will all burn out."

"I guess you ought. Hurry and I'll watch the street and see if Mrs. Barkus is coming, and warn you. You don't want her to find you down cellar at her old furnace."

"No," gurgled Phyllis, "let her think she made her own fire and it has lasted. Let her see how nice it is to have the house warm for once, even though she did go out all day to save coal on us." Phyllis hurried down cellar, and back again as fast as she could without meeting any menacing landladies.

"There!" she said triumphantly, closing the hall door, "I shut something down below, and turned a little handle in the back of the pipe that opened something. I guess it's all right. Anyway it stopped roaring. And I put some more coal on, too, so she can't put the fire out to-night any more unless she pours water on it. I guess I did everything I ought to have done."

"Well, it's good to get warm anyway," said Melissa who had come over to the register and was warming her feet.

"Yes," said Rosalie smiling, "It's nice isn't it?"

"Now," said Melissa after she had basked in the comfortable heat for a moment, "our next need is food. What are we going to do about it? Shall we make a raid on the Barkus larder and really be put in jail, or would it be better to starve to death?"

Rosalie giggled, but it was easy to see that her laughter was near to tears.

"Seriously, Phyllis, what is there in the house? Mother will be hungry too when she comes. We ought to have whatever there is ready, oughtn't we?"

Melissa had a way on occasion of rising to a situation that she had been leaving to her younger sister as if she had been working hard and Phyllis doing nothing, but Phyllis was too genuinely troubled by the facts of the case to mind just now.

"Liss, there isn't a thing but the large half of a loaf of bread! Honestly! Oh, and a little tea. There isn't even hot water unless I go down and boil it on that furnace."

"Mother will have a quarter for the gas meter when she comes won't she?" said Melissa thoughtfully.

"Maybe. But she hadn't but a dollar and five cents in her purse when she went away. If she couldn't get the money cashed to-day she might have had to spend that for something for Father."

There was silence in the room for a moment and then

Rosalie looked up with a sacrificial expression.

"I've got a quarter. It's the one that Mother gave me when I won that contest in school. I was saving it to get her a birthday present. But I guess perhaps she'd rather have tea ready when she gets home."

"I'm afraid she would, Rosy Posy," said Phyllis, stooping to kiss the sunny hair, and hide her own tendency to tears. "Suppose you lend it to us on interest, a cent a month, how's that? I'll promise to pay as soon as my ship comes in."

"Oh, Phyl, how funny!" said Rosalie, "I don't want any interest," and she pattered over to the bureau drawer where she kept all her small belongings and rooted out the quarter from underneath her most precious things.

"It seems wicked to use it," said Phyllis as she held the quarter in her hand as if it were a jewel.

"Don't feel that way, sister," said the little girl, "I'm so glad I have it just now when we need it. Put it in quick and I'll get the table set. Can't we have soaked bread? I love that. Lots of butter and salt and pepper and parsley and an onion, mmmmm-m, it's good."

"But we have hardly a scratch of butter," said Phyllis sadly, "just salt and a little pepper."

"Isn't there even an onion?" asked Rosalie. "I love onion in it."

"Not even an onion, nor so much as a sprig of parsley," said Phyllis. "I wonder where Bob is. He might have raised a penny or two and we could send him for an onion."

"Why yes, he is late, isn't he? Perhaps he hasn't got done his paper route yet. But he doesn't get his pay for that till tomorrow."

"Well, we'll have to do the best we can. Lissa, you cut the bread up and put it in the yellow bowl. Rosalie you get your shoes and stockings on and set the table quick. Mother is liable to be here any minute and we want it to look cheerful. Put the little geranium pot in the center, there are three buds on it almost open. It will look real festive. We'll pretend we're going to have a banquet. We ought to be very thankful that you had that quarter so we could get that gas going! It's uncanny to be without hot water."

"There's a little sugar for mother's tea," said Rosalie lifting the lid of the fine old china sugar bowl.

"Isn't that great!" said Phyllis with forced gayety. "Things aren't anywhere near as bad as they might be."

Melissa finished cutting up the hard bread with a sniff, and went into the other room in the dark to stand by the window and glower.

"Oh, come on back, Lissa, and let's sing something. Things won't seem half so bad if we sing, and besides Mother'll like to hear it when she comes in," called Phyllis.

"I can't sing!" snapped back Melissa. "I tell you I'm hungry, and I don't think it's fair, so there!" and she flung herself down on the old davenport that was Bob's bed at night, and they could hear a choked sob.

Rosalie was laying the knives and forks carefully on the table, and her face was very serious. At last she said in a whisper to Phyllis:

"Phyllie, do you think it would be all right to pray for just an onion?"

Phyllis felt her own tears near the surface again, but she tried to keep her voice steady and cheerful as the answered:

"Why, I can't see it would do any harm, dear. Unless—"

"Unless what?" asked the little girl anxiously.

"Why, unless you'd get your hopes all up and then if it didn't come you'd be so disappointed."

"No, I won't," said the little girl. "I thought about that, but you see, if it didn't come I'd just think God had some other way He wanted to do. He mightn't think it best for us to have an onion now."

Phyllis looked at the earnest little face wonderingly. What a sweet simplicity there was in a child's faith. She sighed, for in her own heart there was stealing a fierce resentment against something, some one, that all her dear ones should have to suffer so. She could not quite put it into words as Melissa had done, and blame God, but it did seem that God, if there really was a God, had forgotten the Challengers.

Rosalie had slipped away into the big clothes closet and closed the door.

Phyllis salted and peppered her dry bread cubes, laid on top of them a little wisp of butter that had been left over from the morning meal, carefully hoarded, then lifted the steaming kettle of water and poured it over the bread till she was sure she had just the right amount, covering it tightly with the biggest plate to let it steam till mother came. The sight and smell of even that steaming, unbuttered bread made her sick with faintness, and she turned away, blinking back the tears.

The tea was ready in the tea ball, the gas turned to the minimum under the kettle, the cups ready. Everything was done. If there was only cream for the tea, and butter for the bread, plenty of butter, and an onion! How many things it took to make just plain, simple, palatable food, and how much money it took for them all! Yes, life was very horrid!

She wandered into the other room and dropped down beside Melissa on the couch, her hand on the pretty head among the pillows.

"Don't get down and out, Lissa, it makes it so hard for the rest of us!" she pleaded.

"I won't!" said Melissa meekly, sitting up and brushing back her tumbled hair. "You're a darling. You never get down and out, do you? I don't know what we would do without you. But honestly, Phyl, I'm all in. I didn't eat any breakfast this morning. I'd kind of set myself not to eat till I got a job, and it sort of made me woozy."

"You dear precious old goose!" said Phyllis catching her in her arms and kissing her, "You're going to have a cup of tea at once. There's plenty of tea at least for to-night. Why didn't you tell me before. You must be famished."

"No, I don't want any tea now," said Melissa, "I'd rather

wait till Mother comes. I couldn't bear myself after all this fuss if I took anything before the rest of you did. But where do you suppose Mother is? She always gets here sooner than this. It's perfectly dark, Phyl, and she's always here before dark, don't you know? Every time she has been to the hospital."

"Well," said Phyllis anxiously getting up and going to the window, "You know she may have had to go down town afterwards to get those bonds cashed. It may have taken some time. I don't know much about bonds, do you?"

"No, not much. I have a hazy idea of having studied them in math, but it doesn't mean a thing to me now. You don't think anything has happened to her, do you, Phyl?"

"No, of course not," said Phyllis briskly with an assurance she was far from feeling. Then suddenly she turned swiftly away from the window.

"She's coming," she said, and hurried back to the kitchenette, and there was in her voice something anxious mingled with the gladness, for she had seen a droop to her mother's tired figure as she walked past the street light in the gloom of the evening, that filled Phyllis with a sudden alarm. Could anything have happened? Was Father worse? Was there some new menace? Phyllis had an almost uncanny way of divining the truth just before it occurred.

Rosalie had heard and came out of the closet with a sweet radiant look upon her face. She went to putting the napkins around and drawing the chairs up. Phyllis was pouring the boiling water over the tea ball, and just a second before the front door opened Melissa struck up with her clear flute-like voice, that nevertheless quavered a little unnecessarily:

Be it ever so humble, there's no place like home—

and the other two slid into harmony from the kitchenette,

Home, home, sweet, home—

Mrs. Challenger closed the door and paused a second in the hall to get control of herself as the bravery of the music struck into her harrowed soul. Then she opened the hall door and stepped in, and they were upon her at once.

"Where have you been, dearest?" carolled Phyllis seizing her wet umbrella and bearing it to the sink.

"We've been scared to death lest you had been run over," put in Melissa unbuttoning her raincoat. "Why, Mother, you're wet to the skin! This raincoat has gone bad. And look at your feet! You didn't have any rubbers! Now, if *we* had done that! In this driving rain, too!"

"My dear, the soles of both rubbers gave out and they flopped so they impeded my progress, so I took them off and threw them in the gutter!"

Mrs. Challenger was trying to laugh flippantly, but the girls could see a bright glitter of tears in her eyes.

"Oh, I'm glad you've come, Mother precious!" said Rosalie, putting up her face for a kiss.

"Sit right down in this chair, Mumsie," said Phyllis, "and get those wet shoes off this minute. That's the way you make us do. Hurry! The tea is all ready, and you are to sit here and get warm and drink yours first before you come out to dinner. Gaze on that hole in the wall called a register. Did you ever feel a heat like that come out of it before in all your experience?"

Mrs. Challenger sank into the chair that was pushed up for her and stretched her numbed fingers to the grateful heat.

"Oh, Phyllis! How did you manage it? What have you said to her?"

"She doesn't know a thing about it, Mumsie," exulted Phyllis, "she went away for the day; took the baby, locked up, left us without a spark of fire; and I went down and made it up. Do you think she'll put us all out, or send us to jail or anything?"

"*You* made the fire, dear? Oh, my dear Phyllis!"

"But isn't it wonderful?" said Rosalie dancing around and clapping her hands.

"But I didn't know you knew how to make a furnace fire," said the mother, who had never had to do such a thing in her whole life.

"Neither did I," laughed Phyllis, "but it's warm isn't it?"

"But—hasn't Mrs. Barkus come back? What did she say?"

"No, she hasn't come yet. It's all dark over on her side of the hall. There! There's some one turning the front door key now. Perhaps she has come!" said Phyllis in sudden alarm, and they all stood breathlessly still and listened. Then the front door shut with a bang that only a boy could give it, and an eager breathless boy at that.

"It's only Bob!" said Rosalie, "Oh, I'm glad he's come!" and she rushed to open the door for him.

"Oh, boy!" said Bob, rushing in and thumping down a big basket on the floor, "whaddaya think I got? Guess!"

Rosalie stood with her hands clasped under her chin, her eyes fixed upon her brother's face, and a look of breathless radiance.

But Bob could not wait for them to guess.

"A beefsteak!" he shouted. "A real beefsteak, thick as yer foot and big as they make 'em. It's all red and juicy. Oh Boy! Lead me to it. All I had t'-day is one banana! Who's goin' ta cook this spread?"

"A beefsteak!" breathed Rosalie with starry eyes.

Phyllis received the precious brown paper bundle, soft and damp and looked down at the basket which was still fairly full.

"What else is there, Bob?" asked Melissa stooping down. "Where did you get them all? These things must have cost a lot of money. You didn't go and charge anything did you?"

"Naw, I didn't charge anything, Funny-face! Where'dya think I'd find anybody ta charge things to, I'd like ta know? I *earned* 'em all righty. That's why I'm sa late. I donno what all's there. I told him ta put in a lotta things, p'tates, and t'mates, and cheese and crackers. I guess there's onions there too, an' parsley—"

"Onions!" exclaimed Rosalie, her face aflame with joy, "Oh, onions, Phyllis!"

"But how did you get them, Bob?" asked Phyllis, "You couldn't have sold enough papers to buy all those things."

"Sold enough ta get a pound o'butter," said Bob indignantly. "Had Tom's route and mine both ta-night. And then when I went ta Brady's ta buy a pound a butter he asked me could I do him a favor. He'd just had a phone call from a good customer of his wanted an order sent away out in the country where somebody was sick, and wanted it sent right away, and his boy was gone, and he couldn't leave the shop, so I said course I'd go. I hadta take a trolley and change twice and Gee, I thought I'd never get back! He didn't say what he'd pay me. I thought it might be a quarter, but Boy! When I got back, didn't he have this basket all fixed up for me to take home, and a whole dollar besides, and he said he'd never forget it, because it was late and this was an awful good customer, and he wanted ta please her, cause she buys a lot and she was awful anxious ta get the things there ta-night."

"There's a glass of jelly, and some olives," announced Melissa who had been rooting in the basket.

Then suddenly as they all stood gazing at the wonderful basket, the mother dropped down into a little heap by the fireplace, and in dismay they turned their attention to her.

"Quick! Melissa! Put her on the davenport!" commanded Phyllis. "I'll get her a cup of tea. She's done out! Oh, we shouldn't have let her wait so long. She's had nothing to eat all day!"

"Oh, Gee! Wait!" said Bob as he saw the tea being poured, "I'll run and get a bottle of milk and some cream. I've got money enough left for that."

"Yes, go," said Phyllis, "but I can't wait for that. We must get something hot into her stomach at once. Or wait, Bob.

See if she revives. We might have to send for a doctor you know."

"Oh Gee!" said Bob in awe and dismay and hovered anxiously at the edge of the group.

But the first drop of hot tea that passed her lips brought the mother back to her anxious little family again, and Bob went whistling out across the street to the drug store to get some cream and a whole bottle of milk.

When he came back his mother was propped up with pillows on the davenport and Melissa was feeding her spoonfuls of tea. The color was coming slowly back into her face, and from the kitchenette came a most delicious odor of broiling beefsteak.

It was not till then that Rosalie came softly around the little table to the gas stove where Phyllis was broiling the steak, and whispered in an awed tone full of wonder and delight, and a kind of sweet shame, almost as if she were half frightened at what she had done.

"Oh, Phyllis, what do you think? It was a *beefsteak* I prayed for! Wasn't that wonderful?"

Phyllis looked at her little sister with an almost startled expression.

"You did!" she said thoughtfully, "That was very strange! Yes, I guess it was wonderful."

They were just about to sit down to their wonderful meal. Phyllis had lifted the plate from the soaked bread put in a generous chunk of butter, with chopped onion and parsley, and its savory smell mingled with the heavenly smell of that wonderful steak, steaming there on its platter. The glasses were brimming with milk, a mound of jelly was quivering in the center of the table, and the teapot with a fresh supply of tea was ready. The mother was just insisting that she was entirely able to get up and sit at the table now that she had been revived by the tea, and everybody was cheerful, and hungry to the last degree. Then suddenly they heard a door slam on the other side of the hall, and a heavy step came down the hall, that ominous Barkus footfall that had grown familiar through the last bitter months of their sojourn in Slacker Street. Everybody stopped short and listened to the menacing steps and Phyllis almost dropped the carving knife she held, a look of fear coming into her face. This surely was swift retribution coming to her for making the furnace fire! She looked at Melissa and Melissa shrank visibly, as they both looked at their white-faced little mother. What could they do to prevent a scene? What might not happen to Mother if she had to go through another such tirade as they had endured last evening?

Then the heavy footsteps halted at their door, and a thunderous knock came, resounding enough to wake the seven sleepers. In shocked silence the five hungry Challengers stood and listened to that knock and looked at one another.

3

JUST that instant they stood listening. Then Phyllis laid down the whetstone and the carving knife she was sharpening, and walked swiftly over to the door.

"Don't you go, Phyl," whispered Melissa, putting out a frightened detaining hand, "I'll go."

"No," said Phyllis summoning a fleeting grin, "It's my job," and she swept the door open bravely.

Mrs. Barkus was short and square, with a large head covered with coarse black hair, always untidy. Her eyes now as she stood under the flickering hall light of the old gas jet, looked like battle axes, and her nostrils were wide spread like a war horse who snuffs the battle from afar.

"Where's yer ma?" she asked sending a sharp glance into the room beyond.

"Mother is lying down. She's just come in and she's not feeling well. Is there anything I can do for you?"

"No, I guess she don't feel well. I guess that's a convenient way to get outta her obligations," sneered the Barkus lumbering a step nearer. "Well, that don't make any diffrunce ta me. Step aside. I wantta see yar ma."

"Please!" said Phyllis stepping in front of the woman as she made to enter the room. "Mother fainted dead away when she came in and we've just been able to bring her to. Won't you talk a little more quietly, Mrs. Barkus. Mother really is feeling very unwell and I'm afraid she may faint again."

"Oh, yes, I suppose she can do it to order any minute. She's prob'ly had lots of experience. But ya can't put that over on me. I'm not a spring chicken. I'm going ta see fer myself. Get outta my way!" She thrust Phyllis aside and strode angrily into the room going straight over to the couch to face Mrs. Challenger who had half risen with a white frightened look on her face.

"Now," said the landlady planting her feet wide apart and her hands on her ample hips, "I'd just have ya ta know that I'm not goin' ta stand fer ya snoopin' down inta my cellar, and wastin' my good kindlin' wood, and coal, and presumin' ta start up the fire till it's hot 'nuf to roast an ox. Yer lucky ya didn't set fire to the chimbley an' have the hull house ta pay fer in the bargain. I never see such turrible waste in my hull life an' I thought I'd die of the heat when I come back to my home. Yar no lady an' that's a fact, puttin' up yar fool kids to a spite trick like that when my back's turned. Yar codfish aristocracy, that's what ya are, an' I'll have the p'lice onta ya ef I ever ketch ya in a trick like that again. It's house breakin' I can hold ya fer, good and tight, darin' ta set fut in my cellar an' monkey 'ith my fire. An' all fer spite, jus' because I asked ya fer my rightful money accordin' ta the bargain."

"Stop!" shouted Bob in Mrs. Barkus large ear, "Don't you dare to talk like that ta my mother!"

Mrs. Barkus had stopped for breath and a fresh supply of words, but now she turned with blazes in her eyes and made a dive at Bob, bringing down her broad pudgy hand smartly where Bob's mouth had been but a second before. But Bob slid out neatly from under and faced her from the opposite side of the room, his best fighting grin on his impudent young face.

"Robert!" said Mrs. Challenger's distressed voice.

"Hush, Bob!" said Phyllis with a commanding hand upon his shoulder. "Listen, Mrs. Barkus. You needn't talk to my mother about that fire, nor to any of the rest of us. I was the one who made it. My mother has just got home, and she doesn't know anything about it. I understood that we were supposed to have heat when we rented the apartment, and the rooms had been so cold all day that my teeth were chattering. I knew Mother would be home pretty soon, and she was half sick any way when she went out, and I felt something must be done. So I went to your door to ask you to please give us more heat, and no one answered so I went down cellar to see if I could do anything myself, and I found the fire just going out. There was scarcely a spark left, and I did the best I could. You didn't want the fire to go entirely out, did you?"

Mrs. Barkus had faced around toward Phyllis like an old bull who had suddenly been deprived of a red flag, and was turning on a new victim. Red-eyed and angry she wagged her head at the frail young girl and roared.

"Want the fire ta go out? I certainly did. What else d'ya 'spose I wasted the hull day fer, takin' the baby ta my sister-in-law's what I don't scarcely speak ta most times, jest ta show ya ya couldn't beat me outta my money and expect heat while yer a doin' it? Ya impertinent huzzy ya! I'll teach ya ta meddle with my cellars an' my fires. An' I jest came in ta say that unless the money's paid now, right now, I'm goin' fer the p'lice. I got a nephew that's on the force, an' I ken get him right now by phone, an' I'll give ya jest five minutes ta fork over that money."

Mrs. Challenger had risen from the davenport and was holding on to the back to steady herself, and now she spoke. There was something in the clear distressed tones of her cultured voice that commanded attention even from the angry Barkus woman, and she whirled upon her and listened.

"Mrs. Barkus," the quiet voice said, "I told you last night that you should certainly be paid. I fully expected to have the money by this evening, but found it was impossible—" her voice wavered for an instant and trailed off weakly as if she had suddenly remembered something and was stunned by the thought. Then she rallied, and steadied herself by a fierce grip on the back of a chair.

"I certainly intend you shall be paid, and that very speedily, but I'm sorry to say that I haven't but ten cents in my purse to-night. Perhaps by to-morrow I shall be able to do something—" she gave a frightened helpless look around the room, and toward her girls who stood white and angry beside her, and tried to summon a faint smile, as she turned her sweet eyes back toward the furious landlady.

But Mrs. Barkus was not to be appeased.

"So ya think ya can put that over on me, with all the smell o' cookin' meat going through me house. Not on yer life ya can't. That's expensive meat that is, I can tell by the smell—"

She strode suddenly to the door of the kitchenette and peered in, to the table with its meager spread, and the glorious beefsteak steaming in the center.

"Yeah? That's jest what I thought. Best cut o' sirloin steak! Ain't we the swell crooks! Beatin' yar way in my house an' eatin' off the fat o'the land! Well, I'll jest carry that steak inta my own dinin' room and save myself gettin' any supper of my own. I'll allow fifty cents off on the kindlin' wood fer that!" and she made as if to sweep aside Melissa and make good her words.

But Bob suddenly planted himself in the doorway with his fists doubled.

"Not on yer life ya don't touch that steak. That's my steak! The butcher gave it ta me for goin' on an errand for him. My mother never spent a cent for it."

The angry woman was big enough and mad enough to make short work of Bob, but Phyllis suddenly stood in front of her and spoke quietly.

"Mrs. Barkus, my mother needs that steak. She hasn't had anything to eat all day but a cup of tea just now, and she must eat or she'll die. If there is anything among our things here that you will accept until we can pay you what we owe you, you can have it I'm sure. Can't she mother?"

"Of course!" said the strained voice of the mother.

"Well, alrighty! How about that gimcrack of a clock?" asked the landlady fixing gloating eyes on a lovely cuckoo clock, the only really valuable bit of furnishing in the whole sordid room. It was a clock that had been sent to Professor Challenger a short time before his illness by a former student in gratitude for all he had done for him, and had only escaped being in storage now with all their other household goods, because it had been forgotten till after the last load had gone to storage.

Mrs. Challenger did some swift thinking.

"Mrs. Barkus," she said trying to put strength into her voice, "that is a valuable clock that was given to my husband. I can raise money on that to-morrow and pay you what I owe you in case some money does not come in on the early mail. If you will just kindly withdraw and let us eat our dinner and get some rest I will undertake to see that you are paid by noon to-morrow."

A cunning look came into the woman's eyes.

"Not much ya won't! ya old crook ya!" she said, "I'll take the clock right now. Valuable, is it? We'll see. I'll take it ta a friend o'mine that keeps a junk shop an' see what it'll bring meself. I'm not waitin' any longer fer my money. Ya promised it this mornin' an' ya promised it this evenin' an' I've no reason ta believe ya'll pay ta-morra neither. I'll just take the clock now," and she walked over and began to reach up for the clock where it hung on the wall.

And suddenly, as if to protect itself, the little bird in the cunningly carved doorway, stepped out and said "Cuckoo! Cuckoo!" eight times right in her face.

The woman stepped back, startled, intrigued by the little bird. Indeed she had had a great desire to own that same bird ever since she had first heard its little song, and like a child, or a small dog, when something unusual happens, she was for the moment turned aside from her purpose to watch the cuckoo.

Nobody had noticed that Bob disappeared, but now suddenly there occurred a diversion, heavy footsteps on the doorstep, the quick opening and slamming of the front door, and a big figure in a white linen apron loomed in the doorway, though everybody was entirely too much occupied to notice.

Mrs. Challenger had just summoned her strength once more to speak.

"Mrs. Barkus, I couldn't let that clock go out of my possession without a receipt from you that you have it and are holding it until I have paid you my back rent," she was saying, trying to keep her voice from shaking. "You see my husband is very fond of that clock."

"Oh, is he?" mimicked Mrs. Barkus with a sneer. "Well, mebbe he'll be fond enough of it to pay me what he owes me and then some fer the damage his daughter done in my cellar this morning. I'm takin' this here clock right now. See?" And she reached up a strong hand and took firm hold of the clock.

But suddenly, a stronger hand reached out and grasped her wrist in such a vise-like grip that it became powerless.

The woman turned in fury and faced the big butcher from across the next corner. He lived over his store, and Bob, in his distress, had rushed for his friend, who did not delay to come at once.

"What you trying to do, Mrs. Barkus?" asked Butcher Brady looking as severe as his round good-natured face could. "That ain't your clock, is it?"

"You lemme alone!" snarled Mrs. Barkus trying her best to get her pudgy wrist away from the big grasp. "Don't ya dare ta lay a finger on me ur I'll have ya arrested fer salt and battry."

"Look here, Lady, I got a lot more on you than you ever could prove against me. I'm merely trying to protect the property of these people, and what's more there'll be a cop here in about five jerks of a lamb's tail, for I told my wife to call one. If you wantta get this good and straightened out be-fore he comes, alrighty. It won't take long. Just you drop your hand down at your side like a lady and tell me what this is all about."

"I don't have ta tell ya, ya impertinent meat chopper ya, but I don't mind ya nor a *po*liceman neither. I'm on my rights. These here folks owe me money, and they've prom-ised and promised to pay and they won't do it, and they're eatin' sirloin steaks, an' livin' on the fat o' the land, and me starvin' away an' givin' 'em house room—"

"You needn't go into particulars. How much rent do they owe you?"

"It's thirty-five dollars rent fer last month and fifteen fer the damage they done in the cellar this morning."

"Aw Gee!" murmured Bob loudly.

The butcher eyed Bob and swept a quick look around the room, his glance coming to rest on Phyllis' face.

"Damage? What damage?" he asked, and waited for her to speak.

"I made a fire," said Phyllis, "I chopped up two old boxes and put on ten shovels full of coal. Mrs. Barkus had gone away for the day and let the fire go out. My mother was com-ing home in the rain and I was afraid she would be sick."

"Doesn't your lease allow for heat?" asked the butcher keenly.

"Not heat like this!" snapped Mrs. Barkus.

"Yes," said Phyllis, "but we've hardly ever had it. It's never been really comfortable, and sometimes the register is per-fectly cold."

"I can't furnish heat when I don't get my pay," whined Mrs. Barkus.

"Well, if you're that bad off perhaps we better let you have the money to-night," said Brady suddenly digging down in his wide pocket and bringing out a fist full of bills. He counted out thirty-five.

"I'd sooner Mrs. Challenger should be owing me than

you," he said with a kindly look toward the lady, and he handed the money to the Barkus woman, who grabbed it greedily and began to count.

"But how about my damages?" she asked.

"Nothing doing!" said the butcher with a laugh. "It was up to you to furnish heat and when you went off and left the fire go out the young lady had a perfect right to look after the fire. I think you are fortunate she didn't sue you for damages instead. Look at that lady there, she looks sick enough to be in bed, and you making all this rumpus!"

Then, just as he spoke, Mrs. Challenger swayed, loosed her hold of the davenport, and slipped down again in a little limp heap on the floor.

The butcher sprang, picked her up and laid her down on the old davenport as gently as if she had been a baby.

"You girls get some water!" he said. "Bob, you go for Dr. Babcock. Barkus, you better get outta here in case she comes to. You've done enough damage for one night. You might have a case of manslaughter on yer hands if you keep this up long."

"If she goes and dies on me that'll be the last straw!" whimpered Barkus.

"Get out!" shouted the butcher. "There come them cops. Wantta go and let 'em in, ur shall I send 'em away?"

Mrs. Barkus hastily retreated to her own room and locked the door resoundingly. But the butcher went out in the hall and said in a good loud tone that would easily penetrate the thin partitions, as he swung open the front door:

"No, we don't need anybody just now. The trouble has passed for the time. But I'm right near by and these folks will phone me if they need any protection during the night, and I'll let ya know. So long. Sorry ta 've troubled ya. Hope there won't be any more nonsense ta-night."

Then he went back to the sorry little parlor and closed the door gently, lifting Mrs. Challenger into a more comfortable position, fanning her with a folded newspaper, and stepping out of sight when she showed signs of coming to again.

Bob brought the doctor almost at once. He scanned the white face with the closed eyes, he put a practiced finger on the slender wrist. He administered a restorative, and said what they all knew, that what she needed was food and rest and freedom from anxiety, and then he went away with the kindly admonition to call him if she felt any worse, no matter what time of night.

They were all alone together at last, with the door locked and the long neglected supper on the table. Melissa had rescued the beefsteak just after Mrs. Barkus advanced to take it over, and hidden it in the warming oven, so it was almost as fine as if they had eaten it right out of the broiling.

But when they brought a plate to their mother with the delicious smelling food upon it, she turned her head away and closed her eyes.

"I can't eat," she said, and to her horror Rosalie who was holding the plate, saw a great tear stealing out under her mother's lashes.

"But Mother, dear," she said, "the doctor said you must eat. Think how awful it would be if anything should happen to you! Suppose you were sick in the hospital too, like Father. What would we all do?"

"Oh, but my dear, there is so much trouble. I haven't told you yet."

"Never mind!" said Phyllis coming up briskly, "Whatever it is Mother, you're not going to tell us now, not till you've eaten. You will make us all sick you know, besides yourself. Now be a brave dear little mother and open your mouth. See this lovely bite of steak. And Mother, this is the best soaked bread I've ever made. It has lots of butter in it, and the onion is just right. And isn't it lovely that we can have supper at last? Did you ever taste such steak? Don't you mind that silly old Barkus woman. We'll get away from here sometime and never remember her again. She really doesn't amount to anything."

"Oh, but Phyllis, it is so humiliating. Your father would feel it so for us all."

"Well, let's just be thankful he can't know. We needn't ever tell him unless we want to, sometime when we are all happy and right again."

"Oh, but my dear, I'm afraid we'll never be happy and right again. I haven't told you all. Your father—!"

"Is Father worse? Tell me quick, Mother, it's better for us to know."

"No, he's no worse. He's better. But—the doctor says what he wants now is to go to the country and rest for a year. He mustn't have a care or worry. Absolute ease, absolute quiet. And it's all just as impossible as if he had said he must have heaven here on earth for a year."

Mrs. Challenger broke down and wept, and Phyllis, standing there with the nice fork full of beefsteak, just kept still for a minute and let her weep. Then she broke forth with a glad note in her voice.

"Why, that's lovely Mother. That's wonderful! Father well enough to leave the hospital and get out into the country somewhere. There's nothing to cry over in that. Come, let's be happy! Let's eat our nice supper. For Mumsie dear, we're all of us deadly hungry. Lissa and I haven't had a bite since crackers and tea this morning and you didn't even have the crackers."

"But how can we ever manage to give him what he needs, Phyllis?"

"Oh, there'll be a way, Mumsie dear. Let's forget it tonight and eat our supper."

"Yes, there'll be a way! There will truly, Mother!" said little Rosalie earnestly. "I prayed for an onion and a beefsteak and they both came! And this will come too!"

"You prayed for an onion!" exclaimed Melissa in horror, and then began to laugh.

"And a beefsteak!" added the little girl seriously. "Say, do let's go and eat it before it gets cold. I'm just awful hungry."

Something in her little girl's face made Mrs. Challenger rise above her weakness and go out to the table with her children.

They bolstered her up in her place with pillows, and gathered around excitedly, praising the steak, and hearing over and over again Bob's account of how he went ten miles with a basket to earn that beefsteak, and what a wonderful friend Butcher Brady was.

"But you don't mean you really prayed for a beefsteak," said Melissa suddenly remembering and turning toward her little sister. "Not honestly, and an *onion,* Rosalie."

"Sure I did," said the child somewhat abashed. "I asked Phyllie and she said it would be all right. Was there anything wrong about that Mother? He answered, anyway."

"Why, no dear, not wrong. I'm sure God understood that you needed something to eat, and that you were perfectly reverent about it. Melissa, dear, you ought not to laugh at your little sister."

"Well, but Mother, do you believe God is like that, knowing about what we need, and even onions and things. Do you really believe there *is* a God, Mother? Hardly anybody at college seemed to believe in God at all, or if they did it was just a great power or influence or something like that."

"Why, certainly I believe in God," said Mrs. Challenger. "I'm shocked at you Melissa. For pity's sake don't take up with all these common modern ideas. Of course there is a God. Your father would be shocked to hear you talk like that."

"Well, then, Mother, if you believe in God why are you so worried? Don't you think He will somehow make things better for us?" asked Phyllis softly.

"Well, yes, I suppose, eventually—I'm not sure—I don't know just what I believe. I really have been too much worried to think about it, Phyllis. When one is in such straits as we are it is no time to philosophize. But of course I believe in *God.*"

"How in the world did Mr. Brady happen to give you onions, Bob?" asked Melissa taking the last delicious bite of her beefsteak. "Of course it's wonderful to have them, but it's kind of queer he thought of them—when Rosy prayed for onions."

"Oh, he said of course we needed onions with beefsteak; said his wife always had 'em and he'd put 'em in," said Bob with his mouth full. "Say, pass me that butter, wontcha? I'm goin' ta get full for once."

"Hadn't you better save a little for breakfast?" suggested Phyllis.

"Nope! I'm goin' ta eat all I want. I got a fifty cent piece left and breakfast can go hang ta-night."

They all laughed at that and agreed with him.

"There's half a box of cereal left," said Phyllis, "I just found it. I thought it was all gone. If you get some milk that will make a nice breakfast."

"Aw, Gee! I'm goin' to get bacon and eggs!" said Bob taking a big bite of steak.

But every crumb of the supper was finished at last, and while Phyllis and Rosalie washed up the dishes and put the kitchenette in order for morning Melissa went to get her mother to bed.

It was after the lights were out and everybody had been still for a long time that Rosalie ventured:

"Mother, wouldn't it be nice if we all prayed for a home where Father could get well?"

The mother was still for a such a long time that they all, listening, thought she must be asleep, but then they heard her say in a low voice, deeply stirred.

"Yes, very nice, Rosalie, but—you better go to sleep now."

4

ONLY two letters came in the mail next morning, together with the usual collection of advertising or begging letters and pamphlets and magazines that still continued to pour down upon the once noted professor's family.

Rosalie and Bob had gone off to school, each with a couple of bacon sandwiches wrapped in paper for their lunch.

"We mustn't let them get hungry like that again!" sighed the mother as she sat down to look over the mail and throw most of it in the waste basket as usual. "We must do something—sell something perhaps. How about that chair? It's solid mahogany, and quite old. It ought to bring something. Could we get along without it? And somehow we must manage to pay back that kind Mr. Brady. It was wonderful of him to do what he did last night."

"Yes, and Mother, can't we get out of this house right away to-day? I feel as if I couldn't bear the sight of that Barkus woman ever again," this from Phyllis.

"I'm sure I don't know where we'd go, nor what we would move with if we did. Remember it costs money to move."

"But Mother, what about the bonds? Wasn't Father willing you should use them now? Surely things couldn't be much worse than they are at present."

"My dear, that's the trouble. There aren't any bonds."

"There aren't any bonds!" exclaimed both the girls in chorus. "But Mother, I remember when Father showed them to us, when we were little girls," added Phyllis.

"Yes, but it seems when Father was going to the hospital he thought there might be an emergency more than he knew at the time, and he took them and put them in the Mercer Loan and Trust Company, and that was the bank that closed its doors last week. They are there all right, in our own safety deposit box, and they belong to us, and eventually we can get them, but not now. The bank has closed its doors indefinitely, and nobody can get in even to their own boxes yet. It may be in a few days or a week or two things will be arranged. Of course it will for the bonds are ours. But that doesn't do us any good to-day. And, girls, there wasn't as much there as I thought there was. It seems Father invested all but two five-hundred dollar bonds in what he thought was going to bring in a bigger interest for us right now while we needed it. And the stock he bought has gone down, down, down, until it is worth practically nothing."

The girls were silent, trying to look life's sordid facts in the face. What a strange thing life was anyway! A week ago they were possessed of money enough to keep them from starving, and now—where was it? And yet they had not spent it. It had not been stolen. It was just gone into the infinite somewhere. What became of money you had and hadn't? How queer it was!

Mrs. Challenger looked at her letters:

"Oh, here is one from Stephen!" she exclaimed with a smile and a sigh. "Poor Steve! He doesn't know what we are going through!"

She began to read aloud.

DEAR MOTHER AND ALL:

I haven't much time to write this morning. I'm due over at the dining hall to sling hash in ten minutes. If it weren't for my need I wouldn't take time to write at all. And I'm awfully sorry to come to you at all for help with all the burdens you and Dad have while he is sick, but truly, Mud, I've *got* to have some more clothes. My pants are worn so thin I have to sit down when anybody very swell comes around, and I can't possibly graduate without a new suit.

I thought I could earn it myself, coaching football, but another guy got the job, and then I had to work pretty hard at my thesis nights when I got done work, and I've been so dead tired that I didn't try for anything else beyond what I'm already doing. But I thought, Mud, if you could just get one of those cheap blue serge suits they always have advertised at the department stores in the city, and have it sent up, you know I'm always a perfect thirty-eight, and anything will fit me. I'll pay it back to you and Dad the first week I get home. There'll be plenty of lawns to cut by that time out in the country and I can surely make twenty-five bucks in no time. I'll be glad if you'll send it as soon as possible, because, Mud, I truly haven't a thing but my old gray knickers that are fit to wear in company.

This will have to be all this time for I hear the bell ringing and I'm late already. Heaps of love to all,

Steve

Calamity sat upon every face as she finished reading. They looked at one another in dismay.

At last Phyllis spoke. Phyllis was always the practical one.

"What can we do, Mother? You can't charge anything any more, can you?"

"No, dear," said the Mother sadly struggling with the

tears. "There's an unpaid bill almost everywhere. You see I had to let them run, right away at first when Father was so sick. I had no time to think of anything else, and then came the crash of both banks where our money was, all the savings of the years, and our having to move, which took every cent and more— And then, this last bank closing that had our cash account. I don't see what we can do. Poor Steve! He's been so brave, and it must have taken a lot of nerve to humble his pride and work so hard doing sort of menial tasks. He's proud too, you know, and always kept himself looking so nice. I hadn't realized, but he hasn't had a new thing this year. If there was only something really valuable we could sell. Of course, that clock, but we never would know how to get its value, with Father sick. And besides Father would feel that it was almost criminal to let that go. It has a special value to him you know. And suppose that friend of his should come back? But then, we can't stop on that of course."

"But Mother, aren't there a lot of things in storage that could be sold?"

"I suppose there are some things," said the Mother thoughtfully, "but not much. We sold everything worth while you know when we broke up housekeeping. But even if there were, there's a big unpaid bill there too. I must see what I can do. Perhaps they will let me get a few things out, but the last time I spoke of it they objected to letting anything go till it was all paid. They sell them at auction themselves you know after a certain length of time."

"Oh!" said Phyllis sadly, "And I suppose there wouldn't be enough there, even if you sold everything, to cover all our needs anyway?"

"No, I suppose not," said Mother.

"Well, Mother, I don't see how you can believe in a God," said Melissa in the hard tone she had used the day before, "at least not in any God one would want to have."

"Oh, Melissa! How terrible! Don't speak like that child. Don't make things worse than they are."

Melissa laughed a hard little worldly laugh.

"Well, I don't see how that makes things any worse than they are. That's only looking facts in the face. It would be worse to my mind to believe in a God and have Him treat me the way He is, than not to believe in Him at all."

"Stop, Melissa! I can't listen to such things. Something even worse might come to us."

Melissa laughed again.

"How could there be anything worse?"

"There could be a lot worse!" said Phyllis indignantly, "you know there could. Look at us. We're all well, aren't we, but Father? And he's getting well fast. We ought to be all kinds of thankful for that."

"Well!" sneered Melissa. "Well enough to-day perhaps, but likely to starve to death before the week's out. How long does it take people to starve to death, anyway, Mother?"

"Don't, Melissa!" shuddered her mother.

"For pity's sake, Lissa, haven't you any sense? Can't you see that Mums has had all she can stand the last two days? Hurry up Mother and open your other letter. Let's forget about our troubles and try to find a way out of them."

"It's probably only a bill," said the mother dejectedly. "What's the use of opening it. Everybody we ever owed a cent to is coming down upon us to-day."

"Seems as if Steven might have managed without asking help when we're having such a hard time," mused Melissa sullenly.

"Remember we haven't told him a word about the bank closing, or the stocks going down till we're practically stripped of everything. It was enough that he should work his way through his last hard year of college without having to bear all that too," said Stephen's mother in defense.

"Well, I think it's high time he knew," said Melissa. "He'll be furious that we didn't tell him, if I know anything at all about Steve."

"Yes, I suppose he will. But it was your father's wish that

he shouldn't be told how bad things were at the beginning, and of course they're worse now. You know of course that when he is through this year he will have his diploma and be able to get a good position, and without his diploma it would be hard work to find anything."

"Yes," said Melissa remembering her experience with the library position and wilting into depression.

There was silence in the room again while the mother absently picked up the second letter, tore open the envelope and began to read. The two girls sat in troubled silence staring across the room, thinking their troubled thoughts. At last the silence was so long that they were seized with sudden new apprehension, and looking up both at once studied her face intent upon its letter. At last Phyllis could bear the suspense no longer.

"What is it, Mother? Some new trouble? A bill?"

"No, not a bill," sighed the mother, folding the letter up and putting it thoughtfully into her pocket.

"But what is it? Has something more terrible happened?"

"Oh, no, nothing happened at all. I guess it is nothing. Probably only some trifle. It's just a letter from some lawyers. I think perhaps somebody Father knows. I don't seem to remember the name, but it must be. Perhaps they have some word about our stocks, or it may be only some lawyer who has heard somehow that we had a deposit in the closed bank, and wants us to let their firm handle our claim. It might be something like that."

"But what is it? What do they want you to do?"

"Oh, they only want me to come in to their office and see them sometime soon."

"But you won't go, will you Mother? Isn't that what they call shyster lawyers, or something like that? I think I've heard Father speak of lawyers who are hanging around trying to get clients. Not real lawyers, only kind of frauds aren't they? Wouldn't Father tell you to keep away?"

"Oh, I don't know. I'll think about it. I'm not sure what I ought to do."

"But don't they say what they want to see you about?"

"Why, yes, they mention property, but I don't know what property they mean. I don't suppose it is anything of any moment. I really haven't time to bother with it this morning. I must look after getting some money together for us to live on. If Mr. Cass, that old friend of your father's, was at home I believe I would go to him and tell him all about our circumstances and ask his advice, only I know Father would hate so to have us tell anybody about it. Father is awfully proud and reticent you know. Still, when it comes to a place where we haven't enough to eat, I think he'd want us to do anything. Oh, I wish I dared ask him, but the doctor positively said he must not be bothered in any way. Of course that Mr. Cass has money himself, a lot of it, and was always very generous. He would probably lend us something, a hundred or so, at least until the bank would open and we could pay him back again. But Mr. Cass is in Europe this winter, so that's out of the question." She sighed deeply again and put her thin blue-veined hand up to her face.

"Mother," said Phyllis at last, looking down at her lap where she was pinching little folds of her apron into accordion pleats in an embarrassed way, "if you really believe in God, why couldn't you ask Him, the way Rosalie suggested?"

"Well, I could, of course. In fact, I did," said the Mother also embarrassedly.

"Well, go and ask Him again," said Phyllis. "Do it now! Lissa and I will go around this room and the kitchenette and make an inventory of all the things we think we might sell, and you go into the bedroom and ask God to do something about it."

"What a silly idea!" flamed out Melissa indignantly. "Don't make Mother ridiculous! I didn't know you were so superstitious. You certainly need a year at college!" and Melissa tossed her head in a superior way she had when her experience at college was mentioned.

"It's not superstition! It's good sense!" responded Phyllis good naturedly. "If there is a God and He wants us to pray I think we ought to try it. Come on, Liss. Get your pencil and begin work. There's that old chair, write that down first."

"Nobody would buy that!" scorned Melissa.

"You can't tell what folks would buy till you try them. I'm going out and get a second-hand man to come and give us his price. We'll put in everything we could actually do without, and see what it amounts to. There's one thing certain, what we sell we don't have to move, anyway, and outside of that cuckoo clock there isn't one thing in this room that I personally would weep for if it was gone. How about it? There's the sewing machine for the second item."

"It's old, and queer. Everybody has electric machines now."

"Not everybody. There's an old colored woman down that alley over there hasn't one. I shouldn't wonder if she'd give at least fifty cents for this one."

"Oh, fifty cents! What's that?" said Melissa contemptuously.

"It's something," said Phyllis. "Two of them make a whole dollar you know. Come get to work."

"But what would you sew with if it was gone?" queried Melissa thoughtfully.

"We still have a needle or two left," said Phyllis.

Mrs. Challenger lingered around a minute or two watching them, and then slipped shyly into her bedroom and shut the door. Later they thought they heard sounds of sobs, but half an hour later when she came out she wore a more peaceful look on her face, and smiled at them.

"I'm going out now, dears," she said, trying to make her voice sound cheerful. "I'll try to be back by lunch time. But if

I'm not, don't go without eating again. There's bacon enough isn't there?"

"Yes, lots of bacon yet," said Phyllis, "and a whole loaf of bread not touched. We'll lunch luxuriously. But don't you dare go without any lunch yourself. Here, I'll make a sandwich for you to take along in your bag. We still have half a roll of wax paper left, thank fortune. Yes, you've got to take it. Look how you came home last night, all in! Now, you'll be good and eat it, won't you Mother dear?"

"But where are you going?" asked Melissa, with troubled eyes. "You aren't going to the hospital again are you?"

"No, they wanted Father to have absolute quiet to-day after his examination yesterday. They promised him if he did just as he was told that he could come out and come 'home' they called it in a week or ten days now. Just think if he has to come to Slacker Street! It would set him all back again. He hasn't an idea what kind of place we are living in."

"Well, we're leaving here to-day," said Phyllis with determination. "Mother, have we your leave to sell some of this junk? And do you mind if we go out and find a room for to-night, even if it is only one room?"

"Sell whatever you think we can get along without," said the mother indifferently, "and find a room if you can. We can crowd in anywhere for a while till we can look around."

"I don't like the look in Mother's eyes," said Melissa after the mother was gone. "I believe she's gone to pawn her wedding ring."

"I'm afraid she has," said Phyllis looking out the window after her mother's slender figure.

"Well, we've got to do something, that's all," said Melissa. "Will you go out for that second-hand man or shall I?"

"You go," said Phyllis, "I'll stay here and get the things we want to sell all together so things won't get mixed up. You don't think we need this rug do you? It isn't a very grand one, nor very large, but it's oriental, or was once, and it ought to bring a little something. Go to that place on the corner of Tenth Street. They seem to look a little more respectable than the others."

But Mrs. Challenger had not gone to pawn her wedding ring yet. She was hurrying breathlessly down the street toward the main avenue and the business part of the town, and gripping closely in her hand the letter that had come to her that morning.

5

STEVEN Challenger sat on the edge of his iron bedstead in the top floor of his college dormitory, carefully darning a hole in his trousers. He had never had to do anything of the sort before, and he didn't know how to do it right he was sure, but he had to have the trousers, there wasn't anything else for him to wear, and before that objectionable hole had arrived in the trousers he had asked a girl to go with him to a college dance.

It was a terrible predicament to be in, and there seemed absolutely no way to get out of it. He simply couldn't tell the girl about it. She would wonder why he didn't wear another pair of trousers. He couldn't tell a girl he hadn't another pair of trousers, could he? He couldn't say that he had spilled soup on his second best ones when he was waiting on the table, and in cleaning them had worn a hole in the knee of one leg a great deal more noticeable than this one he was now mending in his very best ones. He couldn't ask her to go with another fellow, could he, when she was a girl he had been trying to get to go with him all winter, and he hadn't had a chance with her because Sam de Small had been rushing her? This was Stephen's one and only chance at Sylvia Saltaine.

Sylvia! He said her name over softly as he darned the coarse black thread in and out of the frayed dark blue serge that composed the hitherto seat of his best trousers.

Sylvia Saltaine. Her name glided along just like herself, all trailing chiffons, and soft fluttery scarfs, and pastel colors. Her garments always seemed to just drift about her as if they loved her. She was so feminine and lovely.

Her hair was lighter than most blond hair. It was almost startlingly gold, a sort of white gold. Was that what they called ash-blond? He wasn't sure. And her eyes were so very large and blue under those long curling dark lashes. Of course she did use too much mascara on her lashes sometimes, at least his mother might think so, but of course that was a minor matter, and it did set out her gold hair and very pink cheeks, and blue eyes. And her mouth!

But there was another point on which his mother might not quite agree with him. Her mouth was very red. Of course he had been brought up to think that really nice girls didn't do that, but he couldn't deny that on Sylvia it did make a wonderful combination. Oh, his mother couldn't help but see how lovely Sylvia was in spite of all these things.

Of course his sister Melissa was a pretty girl. He had always been proud of her looks. He was yet. He loved to take Melissa places, though she really was only a kid, a freshman at college, and he a senior. Yes, Melissa was a dear kid and pretty as a peach, and she never used lipstick. Mother wouldn't let her. But she was a different type, and perhaps even she, when she was older—Mother was apt to be a trifle victorian. It didn't do any harm to be that way. Sort of protected his kid sisters he supposed. But Sylvia was another type. Sylvia was—

Stephen left that sentence unfinished and gave his entire attention to his needle which had come unthreaded for the sixth time since he sat down to sew.

Gosh! Now he had stuck the blamed thing into his thumb! How did women manage to sew so much anyway? Well, he was doing his best, but somehow the hole looked all puckered around the edge. Would a good pressing take that out and make it seem all right, he wondered?

Steps sounded along the hall, long strides.

"Telegram!" a voice called. "Ho, everybody!"

Stephen's heart lost a beat. He dropped his sewing regardless of an unthreaded needle and went into the hall. Then his folks had come to time after all! They would have perhaps sent a new suit by airmail! Or no, they would likely be telegraphing money.

"Telegram for me?" he called out eagerly appearing in his doorway.

"Naw, not for you. Telegram for Ellicott Brender. Where is he?"

Stephen answered shortly that he did not know, and returned to his sewing, slamming his door sharply.

When he had retrieved his needle from under the bed where it had inexplicably slithered out of sight, and coaxed again the too heavy thread into its aperture, he began to reflect on life bitterly. Why did men in school with all the responsibilities of education and graduation on their shoulders, especially fellows that were so noble as to offer to work their way through their very most important last year, have to have things like this happen to them?

He began to think perplexing thoughts about his family. His letter had had plenty of time to reach Mother. Why hadn't she done something about it? It was not like Mother not to do something right off the bat, the minute she knew a need. Of course he had undertaken to care for himself this year, and that was all right, but the family would surely be glad to help him out to the extent of a new suit. They would want him to look decent. And he hadn't quite made it as bad in his letter as the state of his wardrobe really was. He was almost ashamed to let them know just how low he had let his stock of garments get.

Of course if he hadn't ordered the most expensive class

ring, the one with the real stone in it, he would have had plenty to get a new suit which would be good enough. But it hadn't seemed good economy to get just a cheap plated class ring with no stone in it. One had only one college graduating class ring in a lifetime, and it ought to be good. Sometime he might want to let a girl wear it, and he would be ashamed of just a common ring. Then of course he had got a new racket. He really couldn't do his best with the old one, and this was his last chance to make a record at the Spring tournament. Yes, and of course he had had to get a new raincoat on account of having left his old one on the train the time he went up with the football team in the fall.

Thus reasoning he drove his needle into his thumb again and flinging his trousers far into the corner he put his thumb into his mouth and danced around the room with the pain and the state of his nerves.

"Hang it all" he said, pulling his thumb out of his mouth and speaking aloud, "I b'lieve I'll call 'em up. I can charge the call and pay it at the end of the term, and then Mother can wire the money and get it here before the store down in the village closes at five o'clock. That suit down there would do. Of course, it's fifteen bucks more than she would pay in the city, but Cæsar! I've *gotta* have that suit tonight, no two ways about it."

So Stephen Challenger put his conscience in his pocket and went downstairs to the office.

"I want Long Distance, Buck," he said to the young man behind the desk, "and I want it charged to my account."

"O.K. with me," said Buck. "Take booth number two; I got a call ta N'Y'rk coming in on number one."

Stephen caught Phyllis just as she was going out to look up a cheap room somewhere. He had some trouble getting the call through because service had been discontinued the week before on account of a long overdue bill, but he persuaded the operator that his was an emergency call, and he would be personally responsible for that bill, and she put it through.

"Hello, Mater," he called joyously, "is that you?"

"Oh, Steve!" answered Phyllis. "Is that you?" There was a note of apprehension in her voice. "What's the matter?"

"I want to speak to Mother, Kid, call her quick!"

"She isn't here, Steve. She went out almost an hour ago, and I don't know when she'll be back. You'll have to tell me I guess."

Stephen considered. Phyllis was often apt to be too practical. Still, what else could he do?

"Did Mother get my letter?"

"Yes, just before she left."

"Oh." A dismal pause. "Then she's gone out to order me a suit I suppose."

"Oh, no she hasn't, Steve!"

"That's good," said the brother with relief in his voice, "because I'll have to get it here after all. I've got to use it to-night. It'll cost a little more but it can't be helped. Can you get hold of Mother in the next half hour and tell her to wire me fifty dollars before three o'clock? I simply must have it."

"She can't Steve, she hasn't got it." Phyllis' voice was full of distress.

"Well, but she can get it somewhere, surely. Tell her I *must* have it. I'll pay it back with interest as soon as the term is over. You're sure she hasn't gone to order the suit and charge it somewhere?"

"Yes, I'm sure, Stephen. We haven't any charge accounts anywhere any more. They won't let us charge anything because we can't pay our back bills. And Mother doesn't know anywhere to borrow a cent. We've been having an awful time. I think they ought to have let you know long ago, but Mother didn't want you bothered while you are studying so hard. But, Steve, dear, we haven't any money to send you. Not *any*."

"But listen, Kid," Steve's tone was a bit lofty and annoyed, "I'd pay it back in a few days, and I'm in a *hole*."

"So are we!" said Phyllis with a sob in her voice.

"But not like this, sister. Listen. I'm supposed to take a girl to a dance to-night, and my only good trousers have given out. I've tried to mend them but they look something terrible."

Phyllis was silent an instant trying to keep the sob out of her voice.

"No, not like that!" she burst forth bitterly. "We're not thinking of taking a girl to a dance, but—" she choked on the words, "Stephen Challenger, do you know that we almost got put out on the street last night because we couldn't pay last month's rent? Do you know that Lissa and I had nothing to eat yesterday all day long till eight o'clock at night, and mother nothing but a cup of weak tea and she fainted dead away twice after she got back from the hospital? Hasn't anybody told you that the bank where all Father's ready money was kept failed two months ago, and the bank where he kept a couple of bonds in a safety deposit box has closed its doors and we can't get them, and we're absolutely up against it? If it hadn't been for a kind butcher last night who gave Bob a beefsteak we'd have starved, or died of weakness; and if it hadn't been for that same butcher who paid our rent Mother and all of us would have been turned out on the street in the rain last night after a tirade of the most insulting language I ever heard a woman utter! Steve, I've just got back from selling everything we have that's out of storage, except our beds and a few necessities, to get money enough to feed us to-night. Now, do you understand why Mother can't get you a new suit or send you money?"

Phyllis had poured forth the truth in a torrent, and now she paused for breath, and the poor self-centered boy at the other end of the wire fairly gasped, for he loved his family.

"Gosh!" he said limply when she let him speak. "Gosh! No! I didn't know that. How was I to know? Nobody gave me even a hint! I think I oughtta been told. Gosh! I'll come right home t'night."

"Mercy, no, you won't! I don't know where we'd put you

if you did. We're moving just as soon as we can find a room, one room to hold us all. You stay where you are. At least you've got a bed and something to eat, which is more than we're likely to have. You stay and take your girl to a dance, and have a good time. Wear your old clothes! Wear patched trousers! Anything! Or wear your pajamas! But for pity's sake don't ask Mother for any money now! Oh, I'm sorry to talk so Steve, but—it's been—awful!"

"You poor Kid! Gosh, I'm sorry. Gosh, I've got to do something. How about Dad. Does he know?"

"No, he doesn't know, and don't you write to him about it either. He's better and the doctor says we can take him into the country to rest for a year in about ten days or two weeks. You don't know any fine country place that's going a begging, do you? That's about killed Mother, for she doesn't know where we can find a place for him. If only Uncle Timothy were alive now, or if all Father's friends hadn't gone to Europe for their sabbatic year, we might hope for something. But there, Steve, don't you worry. You just graduate and come home, and then everything will be all right. But Mother's main anxiety is for you not to be worried till your college course is over, and now I suppose she'll give me bally-hoo for telling you, only, Steve, I *had* to tell somebody or *bust*. But we're coming through, I can see we are. I just sold our old davenport for three seventy-five. Had to work hard to get the seventy-five instead of fifty. Now Bob'll have to sleep on a cot, but we've got enough to buy supper and breakfast tomorrow morning with some left over for lunch."

"Gosh, you poor Kid. I feel like a beast!"

"No, you're not, Brother, you're doing just what is right for you, only it did get under my skin for a minute to hear you talk about taking a girl to a dance when we were starving. But that's part of your life I suppose, and you go ahead and get all the fun you can, for I can see there's hard work ahead of you. Only for heaven's sake don't get engaged or anything."

"Of course not!" growled Stephen.

"Now hang up quick. You'll have an awful bill. Good-by, and don't you dare come back till your course is finished!" and Phyllis hung up for him, because she knew he would not.

Stephen Challenger came out of the Long Distance telephone booth and walked slowly, thoughtfully, up to his room. The things his sister had told him cut deep into his soul. He was not a naturally selfish person, though, being the oldest son, he had been badly spoiled. But now he was appalled.

Starving! A Challenger starving! It seemed incredible! Prunes, they had at college, and he hated them. Fish balls! Baked beans! Stewed tomatoes! A lot of cheap nourishing things that he disliked and made a terrible fuss over, together with the rest of his college mates, but they never starved. And there was always the pie shop down town to which even a "scholarship" man working his way by waiting on table, might resort at times. He had never known what it meant to starve even for one meal.

Mother! Starving! Melissa, delicate faced little Melissa, faint with hunger. Phyllis, and Rosalie and Bob! How awful! He dropped down on the edge of his bed in his room and dropped his elbows to his knees, his face in his hands and thought about it, and in that moment of unprecedented thought he almost grew up.

Then came the vision of Sylvia to interrupt, willowy Sylvia in her floating chiffons with her little red mouth pursed. He must do something about Sylvia. It was almost five o'clock. The store would be closed before he could possibly get there, even if he had any money, or any credit, which he had not. Besides, he had manliness enough not to be willing to go into debt to get a new suit to go to a dance when his family were penniless and hungry. He had lost all desire to take Sylvia to that dance. He only wanted now to find a good excuse to get out of it. Of course, she would never have anything to do with him again, but she probably wouldn't anyway. Sam de Small would be back next week, and he had her all dated up for the Commencement week anyway. Why waste any more time running after the moon? Nevertheless, he must retire from the field in a respectable way, and the best excuse he could possibly give was that he was starting home at once because there was trouble and his mother needed him. His father's illness gave plenty of excuse for a hazy explanation. There wouldn't be any trouble about that. But he must go at once and call off the dance. It was almost time for Sylvia to be getting dressed. He must hurry.

He cast about in his apartment for the most suitable clothes he owned to appear before her for the last time, for he knew in his soul that he was going home, that that was where he ought to have been all the time anyway, and that once there, of course he could do something to help out the fortunes of the family, in spite of what his sister had said.

He examined the bungled darn in the blue trousers and decided it would never get by without observation. At last he donned his old tweed knickers, and flannel shirt and hurried away. He would tell her he had no time to dress.

He looked up the address she had given him and started out with a heavy heart, trying to plan just what to do. His graduation was the least of all his troubles, he decided. He knew he had fairly good marks in all his studies, for being a Challenger studying came easily, and it was now so near to the end of the spring term, that he could probably get his examinations in by mail and get his diploma. The college would arrange that for him on Dad's account. Just now he was more concerned about standing up the girl he had tried all winter to get, than about his classical standing. But Gosh! Mother and the kids hungry! That was awful!

Stephen was surprised and somewhat crestfallen to find that his paragon of a girl lived in quite the lower part of the town, and in a messy little street with rows of common houses in intimate touch. It was half past five in the afternoon, and he found his lady standing on the unkempt front porch of her home in a very short dress of a former season's vintage, and an old sweater, calling silly nothings across two porches to the corner where a youth two or three years younger than himself and altogether tough-looking, was engaged in nailing up a broken window blind. Before she recognized Stephen, he noticed that she was using the same coquettish airs and graces with him that she employed with her college friends.

As he drew nearer he could hear what they were saying. The young lady seemed to be coaxing the boy to take her somewhere. At last he broke forth angrily:

"Aw, shut up, Syl. I've took you to a dance the last time I'm gonta. You didn't dance with me oncet the whole evenin' last Friday, just played around with Blackey. Oh, I know he's gotta big car an' all that, but *I tuk* ya, didn't I? Nothin' doin' any more, Syl. I'm cured. Go get some o' yer college cuties, and let real men alone."

Suddenly it came to Stephen that he would not have liked his mother and sisters to overhear this conversation. It did not give a good impression of Sylvia. His face flushed with annoyance. Who was this young animal that presumed to talk to Sylvia this way. Why didn't she resent it?

Far from resenting it, Sylvia was coaxing now.

"Aw, c'mon, Pat. I was jus' kiddin' ya."

Sylvia was using the same patois as her neighbor. Could it be that she had anything in common with such as he?

But suddenly Sylvia saw him and there was a quick change.

Sylvia looked down with deprecating grace, smoothed down her old red sweater, pulled it up around her chin piquantly, patted her hair, fluffing it out around her face, and pirouetted down the walk to meet him.

"Oh, Stevie, darling!" she exclaimed. "You haven't come already? It's not time to go? But no, of course not. You wouldn't be going like that to a dance. You just came down to find the way before dark, didn't you?"

Her tone, her very inflection, the way she pronounced her words, were all utterly different from the way she had talked to Pat, and Steve could see Pat glaring at him angrily from his porch railing where he had perched himself, hammer in hand, even as Steve had glared at him a moment before. It was all incomprehensible, only somehow Sylvia gave Steve no time to think about it. She was lifting her gorgeous blue eyes. Even without the mascara they were entrancing. She was dimpling into that bewitching smile. She was once more the girl he admired beyond all girls. He had forgotten her coarse intimate banter with this common youth.

"I've come to tell you I can't go to-night," he said sorrowfully. "I'm all kinds of sorry, you know that, for I've looked forward to it ever since you said you'd go. But you see I've just had a Long Distance from home, and they're having trouble down there. They need me and I've gotta beat it on the evening train."

The girl's little face hardened. Her glorious eyes narrowed with a feline glint behind her lashes, her mouth set into a thin little line of selfishness. He suddenly realized that her hair was uncombed and her fingernails were dirty. The setting sun flung out a revealing ray and showed a line of green tarnish on the white neck where a chain of imitation gold links had lain the night before, their marks not yet washed off.

"You're not goin' to stand me up, Steve Challenger! You don't mean to say you're going to stand me up? You're not that *yellow* kind!" She tilted her chin contemptuously. Stephen's face grew red with annoyance. He could not stand being called yellow.

"I'm not standing you up," he defended himself, "I came down to explain. I tell you my folks are in trouble. My dad's been sick a long time, and my mother needs me. Some things have come up. She needs me," he finished lamely, and then added, "I was sure you would excuse me. It certainly isn't my fault."

"Well, I *won't* excuse you," said the girl firmly, looking him straight in the eye. "When I give a date to a fella I'm used to having it appreciated, and I certainly shall expect you to keep your engagement. There's a midnight train you can take if you have to go to-night. But I should think since your dad's been sick so long he could wait a few hours longer. We're going to that dance to-night, *see?* You shouldn't have asked me if you didn't want to. I'm not going to have it said that any fella stood me up, especially any college fella," and she gave him such a look as made the shamed blood roll up into his nice, lean, kindly face.

He faced her for a moment and then said quietly:

"Very well, if you feel that way about it of course I'll stay, but I'll have to tell you the real reason why I can't go to the dance, even if I do stay. The suit I ordered from the city hasn't come, and I haven't anything else fit to wear. I had an accident and tore my second best suit."

Stephen had been brought up to tell the truth, but he couldn't somehow bring himself to say he had no money to buy a new one, and it was true in a way that he had ordered one from the city, he didn't have to say that he had found out later the order never went through. But it annoyed him that he was trying to explain himself to this girl. He wanted to stand crystal clear and self-respecting before her, that is, before his ideal of her.

But the girl's laugh rang out harshly, not at all the silver amusement that she used at college parties where he had seen her before.

"Oh, well, that's a good one. You know you can borrow a dress suit from any fella. My gracious! Can't you think up a better one that that?"

Now Stephen did not like to be laughed at. It angered him. He lifted his chin haughtily.

"I am not accustomed to borrow clothing," he said coldly. "Some fellows may like it but I don't. However, if you feel that way about it, I can rent a dress suit, of course. I guess Haney's is open yet."

"Oh, sure," laughed the girl. "Haney's is always open." Then she lifted her voice raucously and called across the neighboring porches, "Oh, I say, Pat, come over here and meet a fella that's too proud to borrow a dress suit."

"I'm too busy," glowered Pat, beginning to hammer with all his might.

"I'll call for you at eight-thirty," said Steve in a cold, hard voice. He felt as if he had suddenly committed himself to a life of crime.

"Allrighty," soothed Sylvia silkily, now she had got her own way with this handsome, reticent youth who had admired her so long without doing anything about it. "But mind you, bring a car for me. I don't like to walk in dancing slippers. Make it a snappy car please. Barney Blasius will lend you his. I'll call him up and tell him to."

Stephen whirled upon her.

"I don't care to borrow anybody's car," he said coldly. "If you don't want to walk—" But he got no further for Sylvia broke in:

"Oh, then *I'll* borrow it. He said he'd lend it to me any time, and he can't take me to-night. He's all tied up in a house-party at his old-maid aunt's. You can drive, can't you?"

"Yes, I can drive," said Stephen desperately. "But I don't want to drive Barney's car. It cost too much money.

"Oh, money, money, money!" taunted Sylvia prettily, "what's money among friends? I can drive myself if you don't want to."

"You needn't borrow Barney's car. I'll get a car," said Stephen desperately. "I know where there's a car I can hire."

"Well, we'll see," laughed Sylvia, waving her dirty little hand gracefully after him. "Hurry now, Mother's nice boy, or you'll be late."

He walked back toward the college with great heaviness upon him. Hire! Hire! Hire! He had not only arranged to stay over the evening when he knew he ought to go home and help his mother, but he had agreed to hire a dress suit, and an automobile, and he hadn't a cent with which to do it. He hadn't a cent with which to take a train home as far as that was concerned. He would have to hike it and trust to getting a lift now and then on the way. He would have to either borrow money from some of the fellows, or else charge these things to the college, and would they stand for it? He almost groaned as he walked along in the low light of the setting sun. When he reached his room he dropped wearily face down upon his bed like a tired, naughty, little boy and hid his face in the pillow. While he lay there a bit from an old nursery game began to jingle through his brain:

> *Heavy, heavy hangs over your head,*
> *What shall the owner do to redeem it?*

What was it that was hanging heavy over his head? His self respect? His good common sense that he had forfeited? Of course it didn't mean a thing but why did it have to keep ringing over and over again? And there was the clock striking! He must get up and get himself together. Somehow this evening must be gone through.

> *Heavy, heavy hangs over your head,*
> *What shall the owner do to redeem it?*

Forfeits. That was what the fool game had been called. What was he forfeiting by pleasing Sylvia this evening? Anything worth while? Anything he couldn't redeem?

And did he really want to please Sylvia any longer, any way? That was the question. But of course, this once, he had to. After to-night he would be sure, that was one thing certain. Yes, after to-night he would be *sure*.

6

PHYLLIS had just closed her furniture sale and seen the last of the things piled into a truck at the door when that telephone call came. After she had hung up the receiver she found herself trembling from head to foot, just why she wasn't sure. Partly because she had been very angry with her beloved brother, and had spoken much plainer to him about the family troubles than she knew her mother would have approved. Partly because of a hidden, underlying fear, that she had not named until now when she stood and faced it. It was that girl that was troubling her!

It was not just that Stephen was taking a girl to a college dance. Boys in college always did that she presumed. The Challenger family had been brought up with no conscientious scruples against the ordinary accepted amusements of the day. They had no opinions either for or against dancing. One was respectable of course in the way one did things, anything, and that was all. But what was there about the way Steve had said "a girl" that had made his sister feel uncomfortable about her? Of course the boys took the girls of the neighborhood to their parties. That was to be expected. And it was also to be expected that Steve would have a girl, a nice girl of course, some day. It was time he should. Why, this girl might not be any special girl at all, just a girl he had met, and invited. It might not mean a thing. Then why did she feel as if he had been reluctant to mention her, as if he were almost half ashamed about it?

No, that must be imagination after all, for when he had first mentioned her he had been quite insistent that she was of more importance than a lot of other things, important enough to make an expensive phone call in the middle of the day and demand money from an impecunious family.

Well, that of course was silly. She must get to work and put such thoughts out of her head. Perhaps she wouldn't mention the girl when she told Mother. It might worry her too. But no, that would not do. Mother would not understand why Steve had telephoned unless she explained how he had promised to take the girl, and therefore needed the money. Well, she must hurry. She would go out and get a few things for supper and get back before Rosalie came. The child must not find the house empty. She looked pale when she started off to school, and there was no use expecting Melissa so early. She had said she would stay out till she got a job, or got too hungry to walk any farther.

So Phyllis hurried over to the butcher shop. She wanted to thank Mr. Brady for his kindness again, and get a bit of meat for supper.

There was no one in the shop when Phyllis entered except the big kindly butcher himself and he came forward smiling.

"Everything going all right over there?" he asked anxiously. "I meant to run over this morning, but the shop kept pretty full all day till just now, and my errand boy was sick."

"It's been quiet as ten mice all the morning," said Phyllis. "I think you settled Mrs. Barkus for another month with your wonderful thirty-five dollars. My mother says she will never be able to repay you for all you did last night, though I hope she will soon be able to give you back the actual money you loaned us. My sister is trying hard to find a job to-day and, well, I think there will be a way pretty soon. I'm sure there will."

"Of course there will," said the kindly butcher, "I'm not worrying about my money. Your mother came in this morning a minute and I told her not to worry about paying that back. It was worth thirty-five dollars to me just to see that Barkus woman's face when I handed it out to her. That woman's a pain in the neck, she is. I was glad to get it back on her, the old crook! She's bullied many a poor tenant out of more money than they owed her. Don't you trust her out of your sight. She'll get that clock yet. Say, I was thinking, after your mommie left here this morning, are you folks figuring to stay there in that apartment?"

"Not a minute longer than we can help, Mr. Brady. Mother is out now looking for a room, just a tiny room even, where we can all squeeze in till things brighten up a little, and we've sold everything we just didn't have to have in order to live, so it can't take us long to move. I was hoping we could get out to-night, but unless Mother comes back pretty soon with some good news I'm afraid there isn't much chance, for all the places I went this morning were so high we couldn't possibly afford them."

"Well, now," said the butcher with a pleased look on his face, "this is what I was thinking. I've got a little two-story house down the next block vacant. The man just moved out last Friday. He got transferred to Pittsburgh and had to leave it in the middle of the month. I was wondering how it would be if you folks would just step in there for a little while till you could look around. It's all warm. I didn't let the fire go out yet for I was figuring to make a few repairs evenings there. And it wouldn't cost you a cent, for it's just lying there idle. I can't rent it till I make some changes, and I wasn't figuring to make them till the weather gets a little more steady. I want to change some of the pipes and it would mean digging outside some. So if you folks would come in, I'd be real glad. I could help you bring your things over in the truck. The man'll soon be back from the last delivery, and he'll give a hand to the heavy things. If you say so we'll just move you over nice and easy before night, and you won't know you are moving."

"Oh, Mr. Brady! How wonderful! It will seem just like heaven to get out of that house before another night."

"Well, I sort of thought you weren't so keen about staying there. Here's the key, suppose you just go down and look at the place and see if you like it before you decide. It ain't any grand house you know, just one of the row, but it's nice and clean, and it's got a dandy little gas range, and a crackerjack hot water heater. The misses, she had it all cleaned up slick when the other party moved out, and it ain't had time to even get dusty yet."

"We don't want a grand place, Mr. Brady," Phyllis assured him. "We just want a refuge. I don't believe it's even necessary for me to go and look, if you say it is all right."

"Well, you go look," insisted the owner, "and then I'll be better satisfied. And don't you be afraid to say if you don't think it will do. I shan't be at all hurt."

Rosalie came along from school as Phyllis came out of the shop with the key, and gladly skipped along with her, her face alight.

"Oh, Phyllis! Not a whole little house to ourselves! How wonderful! And we can move to-night?" she cried, "and will it do for Father to rest in too?"

"I'm afraid not, Rosy Posy. Father's got to be in the country, but this will do for a few days till we can find the right spot."

They came back from the house radiant, and the big butcher grinned his delight.

"I thought mebbe you'd like it. Need to wait till Mother gets back before we move, or do you wantta start right now? Dan's back with the truck," he said.

"We'll move at once!" said Phyllis joyously. "Mother will be so glad! and my sister too. I know she just hates the idea of coming back to that awful place again."

"How about the little feller, Bob? I reckon he'll be glad. He let on to me he didn't care fer that place. He was tellin' me this morning how your poppie had got ta go ta the country, and I says to myself that there house of mine would just be the place fer you to stay while you was lookin' round. Stay as long as you like. I ain't needin' ta rent it yet awhile, so ya needn't be in a hurry."

"I don't know how we can ever thank you, Mr. Brady," said Phyllis. "You've been so good to Bob too. I know he just adores you."

"He's a smart little kid, he is!" said the butcher. "There ain't no flies on him. Well, you run along and get your goods in line, an' my man'll be there in three jerks of a lamb's tail."

It was marvelous how quickly the now scanty furnishings of the apartment were transferred to the little brick house down in the next street, till nothing was left but the grimy little gas stove that belonged to the house, and the ugly iron sink which also belonged.

Mrs. Barkus seemed to be out again that afternoon, which Phyllis felt was fortunate. She did not want to have any further argument with her, though she rejoiced in the fact that genial Mr. Brady was there while the moving was going on to stand between them, if she should suddenly appear.

"Better let me say all there is to say," said Brady when she confided her fears to him. "We don't want her insultin' that lady mother of yours again like she did last night. When does your new month begin? Do you owe her anything more?"

"Well," said Phyllis, "The month began ten days ago, but of course it's not really due yet."

"We'll fix that up, too. You leave it to me," said Brady. "She's like to charge you for the whole month if she thought she could get away with it. Get out before she gets back if you can, and let the children watch in my shop for your mother and sister and steer them away. When she comes back, I'll run over and fix it all up so she can't make any trouble. If she comes while we're here you just keep still and let me tackle her. She knows I know good and plenty about her and she won't dare open her lips. I'll just tell her you're gettin' out because she didn't keep her contract and give you heat as she promised."

So Phyllis went to the new abode with a free mind and began to put things to rights, while Rosalie stayed at the shop to watch for the rest of the family and warn them not to go in.

There wasn't much "righting" to do it is true, for Brady, with fine instinct, had put a bed in each bed room, and placed the other belongings about as right as any stranger could.

So Phyllis opened up the leaves of the little table and spread a white cloth out of one of the bureau drawers. She discovered an ice box on the back porch, and meat and milk and butter already there with potatoes in a basket and several bundles from the grocery store.

"I just thought you might not have time to buy anything," apologized Bracy when she spoke to him about it later in the afternoon. "You see I wanted you to have it real pleasant this first night you spent in my house. I don't expect often to have such grand folks in my property, so I thought I had a right to help out a little," he ended with a beaming smile.

Mrs. Brady sent over an apple pie and a tin of hot biscuits just at dark, and the little round replica of Butcher Brady who brought them, said they were to call upon his mother for anything they needed, that she was right next door.

Melissa came soon after the pie, looking wan and discouraged, and attended by Bob and Rosalie, who were both so eager over the new order that they couldn't keep their tongues still.

Bob gave one radiant glance around and said, "Aw Gee! Ain't it great!" and then flew back to watch for his mother.

But Melissa looked around forlornly on the bare floors, and scant furniture, and said dejectedly:

"We're just on charity now, aren't we? I never thought any Challengers would come to that!" and dropped down into a chair and wept.

Phyllis paused in her tired, happy preparations in dismay:

"Well, now, Lissa!" she exclaimed. "I never thought a Challenger would take life that way. Sit up and cheer up. Barkus can't visit us to-night and that's at least one thing to be happy about. Charity nothing! Mr. Brady is having the time of his life making us comfortable. You ought to have seen his face when I said it was just heaven to be here. And gaze on that apple pie! Doesn't it just make your mouth water to see the juice ooze out so mellifluently? I guess that's the right word. I mean it seems like poetry and amber and a prayer all mixed up."

Melissa began to laugh hysterically, and Phyllis put down the butter plate on the table and went and hugged her.

"Sit up, Lissie, and drink this glass of milk. We have three whole quarts in the refrigerator, and you can have all you want. I'll just bet you didn't eat your lunch after all my care in fixing that sandwich for you."

"Yes, I did," giggled Melissa wearily, "I ate it on the bridge down by the park standing with my back to a bus that was unloading. We're just *tramps,* Phyl, just common tramps! Pretty soon I suppose we'll go from door to door and beg."

"Well, I hadn't thought of that, but of course we could, couldn't we? Still, there isn't any danger of that to-night. Do you know we have double chops for supper, great big juicy ones? And baked potatoes and sliced tomatoes on lettuce. It's a banquet, child! Why prate of begging? Be thankful and don't worry. It doesn't always stay dark. And, Lissa, I've a hunch there's Someone looking after us greater than Butcher Brady. *He's* only an under angel somehow. Melissa Challenger, did you know you had a little sister who is praying, and she seems to get what she prays for? Do you know that she was in the clothes closet last night praying for that onion and beefsteak when Bob came in with it? What do you think that was, anyway, Liss? Just thought-transference?"

"I'm sure I don't know what it was! Just happening I suppose! But you'll get that child's head turned if you let her go on like that. I think it's rather blasphemous myself—that is, if there is *anything* to it—talking about onions to a god! But for heaven's sake don't let's get some one in the family with a religious complex. They warned us a lot about that in college, at least one of my teachers talked a great deal about it. Said it was most unwise, it prevented openness of mind, and freedom of thought, and tended to narrowness and servitude to traditions. He said the only good of prayer at all was its reflex action on your own spirit, or something to that effect."

"For pity's sake, Lissa, where did you get all that high sounding blah? I thought you had too good sense to take up with such nonsense. You'll be saying yet that there isn't any such thing as sin in the world, and you *know* there is."

"I heard a very great preacher in New York say over the radio, the last time I was privileged to listen to a radio, that the greatest sin in the world was the sin against one's own personality!"

Melissa drew herself up languidly from the chair where she had dropped, and eyed her sister tragically.

"That's what makes life so utterly hopeless and impossible, Phyllis," she went on. "How can one help sinning constantly against one's own personality? It's perfectly impossible. I've been thinking a great deal about it to-day."

"Oh, fiddlesticks!" quoth Phyllis indignantly. "You make me tired! That sounds to me like selfishness spelled with a great big capital. Cut out that rot and get to work! *Forget* your personality! It isn't worth any more than anybody's else personality! Come and put the napkins around. Mother ought to be here any minute now. Let's make everybody have a good time. For my part I prefer Rosalie's view point to yours. Snap out of it, Liss, and get to work."

So Melissa took off her hat and coat, washed her hands and face and combed her hair, drank her milk and felt quite cheerful when the two children came joyously in with their mother, who looked wan and pale, but smiling.

They smothered her with hugs and kisses. Phyllis brought

a hot wet towel, washed her face softly and dried it with little gentle dabs, put her in a chair at the table and set a steaming cup of coffee before her.

"Mother's going to have something to eat before anybody asks any questions," she commanded, and they all set to and ate their delicious supper.

It was queer how the new surroundings pulled their thoughts away from their troubles.

"Why, there's a fireplace," said Mother, gazing about her, "and it looks as if it had been used recently, too."

"Yes," said Phyllis, "Mr. Brady said he had left some wood in that little closet so we could enjoy the open fire this evening. I haven't had time to lay it yet. I thought Bob might like to do it."

"Gee!" breathed Bob out of his glass of milk in which he had been taking deep draughts. "Sure I would!"

"What a wonderful man that butcher is!" said the mother with a great light in her eyes, "I must tell your father about him. It is enough to restore one's faith in human nature to meet a man like that."

"Did you see Father to-day, Mother?" asked Rosalie wistfully. "I wish I could see my father."

"You shall pretty soon, dear," said the mother, and then drew an anxious sigh, wondering if her words would really come true. "No, I didn't see him to-day. The nurses wanted him to rest after his examination yesterday."

"Where have you been all day, Mother?" the little girl persisted. "Have you hunted for apartments?"

"Some," said the mother noncommittally. "I've been making inquiries, and,—seeing some—real estate men."

"But where would we get the money, Muvver?" Rosalie's questions always went right on to the end of a subject if it had an end.

"Well, that's to be seen," said the mother again with a dreamy look in her eyes.

"Did you find anything yet, Mother?" went on Rosalie.

"Well, I'm not sure yet, dear. Not definitely. Not yet."

"But you heard of something that perhaps we could afford?" asked the little girl.

"Well, perhaps," said the mother. "I've got on track of a house in the country, but the owner is in Europe. The agent has cabled. Oh, I don't suppose we could possibly afford it, unless I can make some arrangements for a loan. I've been trying all the afternoon to get in touch with some of your father's old friends who might help, but they all seem to be out of town."

"Now, Rosalie, don't bother Mother any more. Can't you see she's dead tired?" protested Melissa.

"Yes, Rosy Posy, let's just enjoy our supper and our new house, for to-night and the next few days, and not worry about anything more. Let's just be glad we haven't any Barkus-woman to keep us from our nice supper."

Rosalie smiled.

"Awright!" she said and passed her plate for another potato.

After supper they put their mother in the one big chair that was left, and Bob built a lovely fire, while the three girls whisked the dishes away as fast as could be, and then they put out the light and sat around on the floor watching the flicker of the fire.

"Wouldn't this just be lovely if it were only in the country and Father could be here," said Rosalie; and the mother sighed again and put her hand on the child's head gently.

"Yes, it certainly would," she said. "But I'm very thankful for this little quiet house all to ourselves to-night."

By common consent they put away the cares and perplexities of their situation, and told only the pleasant or the funny things they had seen that day. Phyllis made them all laugh telling how she had made her second-hand man give her bigger prices for the things than he had at first offered, and she imitated his voice, and his plaintive surprise that she was not satisfied with the pittance he had suggested, until they were all filled with merriment.

Bob told about some boys at school who tied a girl's hat to a string and suspended it on a rod from a little transome above the teacher's desk, letting it down on his head right in the middle of the geography class. And Rosalie described how a girl forgot her piece in the recitations and went over and over it from the beginning, trying to remember it, till all the class were laughing. Even Melissa told about a little dog running away from a fine lady who had been walking with him on leash. She got up and imitated the lady's mincing step.

Only Mother did not tell anything that had happened to her that day. They all noticed it, but because she seemed cheerful and a little distraught, they did not speak of it. She was tired of course, they told themselves. It was nice not to have to think of puzzling questions. Just relax and enjoy the fire, and the good warm room.

Just before they went to bed Phyllis remembered Steve's phone call and told them about it. She made it quite commonplace, telling that he had promised to take "some one" to a dance, which was why he needed new clothes so badly. Somehow that seemed so much better than to say "a girl" in the tone Steve had used.

Mother understood, and a cloud of worry sat in her eyes for a moment during the talk, but as Phyllis went on to say that she had told him their circumstances, she relaxed again and commented:

"Poor boy! But I'm glad you told him. He wouldn't otherwise have understood why we couldn't help him in a crisis like that. I'm sorry he had to know before he was done, but it won't be long now before he can come home and understand it all."

They had a merry time getting to bed, finding the right sheets for each bed, finding their various night garments that Phyllis had had to stuff into any drawer that would hold them, finding their hair brushes, and locking up the new house for the night. After they were all settled in the three nice little upstairs bedrooms that opened out into the hall in a triangle and seemed so friendly and cozy, the cuckoo clock sang forth the hour of midnight, and they all cheered him. Good old cuckoo! He was theirs still and they were not starving either.

And so at last they settled to sleep. But no one had seen Rosalie in her little white night gown, kneeling in the darkness by her bed, before the others were ready, her curly head buried in her pillow, praying that God would give them a place where Father could rest and get well.

They were all nervously exhausted, and every one slept very late the next morning, so that when they woke they had to hurry to get some breakfast together and get the two children off to school.

It was just before they left for school that a boy came to the door with a telegram.

"Challenger live here?" he asked.

The mother's hand trembled as she opened the envelope. She thought at once of course of her husband, whose life had hung for so many months in the balance.

But the telegram was not from the hospital. It was signed by the dean of Steve's college. It said:

"Your son Stephen Challenger in hospital with broken leg and fractured skull, result of an automobile accident last night. He was driving a borrowed car. Nobody fatally injured. Challenger doing as well as could be expected."

7

THE family stood in absolute silence and watched their
mother read the telegram. They could tell by her face that it
was bad news. Her lips grew ashen. Phyllis was afraid she
was going to faint again, and put out her hand to steady her.

"Is it Father?" Melissa caught her breath in fear.

The mother shook her head and handed the telegram to
Phyllis.

"Read it," she said from a dry throat and dropped into the
nearest chair.

Phyllis read the telegram slowly, her young face harden-
ing. So, it was that girl again after all! How glad she was that
she had not mentioned the girl. Mother needn't bear that part
anyway.

There was an awful silence again while the family looked at
the future as at another blank wall shutting them in from all
that was right and good.

Then the mother spoke.

"How much money have you got, Phyllis?"

"Nineteen dollars and forty-three cents," said Phyllis deprecatingly. "It wouldn't be enough for carfare, would it? At
least not both ways."

"Somebody ought to go at once," said the mother in a pained voice, "but I don't see how we are to manage it."

"There is always the clock," said Phyllis thoughtfully, looking up at the exquisite carving of the little Gothic structure where the butler had hung it reverently on a hook and set it ticking again.

"No," said Mrs. Challenger, "we mustn't use that. I tried to ask your father about it, yesterday. I went down to the hospital after all, hoping to get to see him a minute and ask him about it. And they did let me in, just for fifteen minutes. Of course I didn't dare tell him all we are going through, nor that we needed money. He would have taken alarm at once. He doesn't know of course about the closing of the bank where our bonds are, and he thinks we have plenty to get along on with care. He said that so peacefully and thankfully yesterday that I just let him think it. But I told him we were trying to find a better apartment if we could, that the landlady wasn't pleasant, and in speaking of moving I brought in the clock, said it was rather hard to move, did he care to keep it or should I try to sell it? He spoke up right away and said most insistently, almost peremptorily, that we must not part with it on any account. It represented a great sacrifice on the part of the boy who gave it to him, and some day he might come to see us and would expect to find the clock. He said he would rather sell the coat off his back than part with that clock, that it represented not only great devotion, but a real victory in a life that had started on the downward track."

"Who was it, Mother, that gave it to him?" asked Melissa.

"Why, I can't remember his name. He was in college some years ago, and he only sent the clock last winter you know, from somewhere in Europe. I had no chance to question your father for the nurse came in and said he must not talk any more. But I could see it would disturb him greatly if we were to sell the clock."

"If he knew just how things were," began Melissa, "perhaps he would feel differently."

"No, Lissa, I wouldn't want to ask him. There must be some other way, and a mere clock couldn't make much difference one way or another," said the mother firmly.

"There'll be some other way," said Phyllis. "I've got an idea and I'm going out to try it out. If it materializes maybe I can rake in a few dollars by night. No, I'm not going to tell anything about it. Likely it won't come to anything and I can't stand being laughed at."

"But how are we going to find out about Steve?" asked Melissa, "something's got to be done, hasn't there?"

"I'm going out to a telephone station and get the dean or the hospital at once," said Mrs. Challenger. "It seems extravagant, but we've really got to know more before we can do anything, and anyway there's got to be some more money before anybody can go to Stephen. I think perhaps I might get in touch with our old college president in an emergency like this—" her voice trailed off vaguely. "I'll see what can be done about selling off the things in storage, too, and paying that debt."

"Couldn't we ask that nice butcher to lend us ten dollars more?" It was Melissa who ventured this.

"No, dear," vetoed the mother. "He has probably impoverished himself already with the things he has done for us. I couldn't think of asking. He would be embarrassed to say no, and he would feel he had to lend it if we asked, even if he couldn't spare it."

"I know," said Melissa, "I'll go and hunt up Mrs. Mowbray. She was always awfully fond of me when I used to go and play duets with Amelia. I'll ask her if she will lend us— how much would we need to go to Stephen? Twenty-five dollars? Fifty? Would that be enough? Well, I could tell her that Father was sick, and the bank had closed that had our safety deposit box with our bonds, and all our ready money was gone. She would understand—I'll go!" said Melissa watching her mother's face.

"Oh, my dear!" began her mother, "I do dislike to borrow

from strangers, even from rich people. Of course, we could pay her back as soon as the bank opens again, but—"

"She likely won't be at home," said Phyllis sorrowfully. "Those rich people never are. She'll be in Palm Beach, or the mountains or Europe or somewhere."

"Well, I mean to try anyway."

Then suddenly the young man of the house spoke. They had forgotten him in the general distress until now.

"Say, Mother, if that was a borrowed car will Steve havta pay for it?"

"Oh, Mercy! How could Steve pay for a car?" The mother turned white with dismay.

"He couldn't, but does he *havta*?"

"Oh, I don't know!" sighed the mother, and drooped down with her elbows on her knees and her head in her hands again.

"Oh, Bob, don't bother Mother with questions now. Don't you see she's got just all she can stand?" put in Phyllis.

"I ain't bothering her am I? I didn't smash up a borrowed car did I? But I guess I gotta get busy and do something about it, ain't I? I'm the only man left in the house now."

"You'd better get busy and go to school," said Phyllis suddenly looking at her watch. "Do you know it's twenty-five after?"

"Where's Rosalie?"

"Here I am," said Rosalie emerging from the dining-room door that went into the pantry, with a dewy look about her eyes and peace upon her brow; and somehow Phyllis knew what she had been doing, and wondered. Rosalie's family were keeping her pretty busy praying these days. Would it do any good, Phyllis wondered?

"Yes, you must hurry to school," said the mother rousing to the occasion. "There's no point in being late. You can't help out that way. Just do as well as you can, and don't worry dears."

"Don't you worry, Muth," said Bob diffidently, suddenly

flinging his arms about her neck and giving her a great bear-hug. Then abashed he rushed away, calling back to Rosalie to hurry.

With a sigh the mother donned her look of worry and got up.

"I'll go right away and telephone, and if some one has to go I guess it had better be Phyllis. I couldn't go without telling your Father about Steve and that might be serious, just now when he's in such a critical condition. The doctor said it might be fatal if he worried."

"Why shouldn't I go, Mother, I'm the oldest?" asked Melissa, thinking of the gay times and the glamour of a college town. She had always longed to visit Steve. She had hoped against hope that she might somehow get to his commencement.

"Well—" said the mother considering, "you might of course, but—Phyllis is always so practical—and you hate nursing you know."

"But he's in a hospital. He wouldn't need a nurse," protested Melissa.

"Well, we'll see, dear," evaded the mother, "I'm not sure anybody can go yet. It's all a question of money. Do you really think you would like to ask a small loan for a few days from Amelia's mother?"

"I certainly would," said Melissa, cheerfully, "I'll go right away. I'll have to polish my shoes first and clean that spot off my suit, but I can get started in fifteen minutes I guess."

"Well, I'm going out to try out an idea," said Phyllis, picking up her coat and hat which had been lying on a chair in the little hall. "I won't tell you what it is, but it will either work or it won't, and I'll likely be back inside an hour or two at most."

So they all went off, leaving Melissa dressing for a call on her fortunate friend's mother.

Melissa looked very pretty as she finally put the last touch to her hair, and pulled her small dark blue hat on. Of course her shoes and gloves were a bit shabby, but she couldn't help that, and they had once been the best of their kind.

She hunted out her best handkerchief, and put it into her hand bag, with the two dollars that had been doled from the family treasury as her share for carfare and necessity.

Just as she turned from a last survey of herself in the looking glass she heard a knock on the door.

She hurried down stairs and found a good-looking young man standing impatiently, looking up at the front windows and then trying to peer through the muslin curtain Phyllis had pinned up last night for protection.

As she swung the door open she caught a glimpse of a large shiny blue car much benickeled, standing in front of the house, with a lady of ample proportions in a handsome furred coat sitting inside. Melissa always knew what people wore. It was the first thing she usually noticed.

"Anybody by the name of Challenger live here?" demanded the good-looking young man; and then getting a glimpse of Melissa he stepped back and lifted his hat.

"I am Miss Challenger!" said Melissa, lifting her pretty patrician chin with composure. And then, suddenly aware of his quick glance of surprise into the empty little living room behind her, she explained, almost haughtily, "we don't live here. We're just staying here a few days while we look around for another apartment."

"Well, I'm glad I've found you," said the young man. "I had all kinds of a time and had almost given it up when I went into a butcher shop and found a man who said he knew you."

"Oh, yes," said Melissa, the color stealing up into her fair cheeks again. She hoped he wouldn't think the butcher was a relative or anything. "We—he—" and then realized that she did not have to explain to a stranger, and the stranger wasn't wanting an explanation.

"Well, my name's Hollister, Gene Hollister. Perhaps you've heard of my brother, Jack Hollister. I believe he's a classmate of your brother Steve, or a fraternity brother or something. But anyhow he went on the same joy-ride last night, and now he's in the same hospital with a busted rib, and a nasty cut around his eye. And he called me up this morning, and suggested some of Steve's folks might like to drive up with us to-day, so I came around to see. Tried to get you on the phone but couldn't get a response so we just drove around. Any of the family like to go? My mother's out in the car with me, and she says you're mighty welcome."

Melissa eyed the wonderful high-powered car, and the lady in the deep furs, and gasped. What an opportunity!

"Oh, how wonderful of you!" she exclaimed. "But—Mother's not here. I don't know what to say. She went out to telephone to the college about Steve. There isn't any wire in this funny little house. How soon do you start?"

"Why, we're on the way now. Sorry to hurry you but the Mater is all kinds of anxious of course to see the kid and make sure he isn't hurt seriously. How soon will your mother be back?"

"Oh, I don't know. She didn't know what to do about Steve when she left. She had to see Father first. He's in the hospital, getting well of a long illness. I don't know when she will be back. If she only were here—but you ought not to wait. She mightn't be back all the morning. I'm not sure she could get away from Father to go. And my sister isn't here either."

"Well, why don't you go yourself? It would be a nice ride and it's a cinch your brother would be glad enough to see you." He added this with an almost too admiring glance at Melissa.

Melissa was all in a flutter.

"Oh!" she said excitedly, "I don't know what Mother would think. I suppose I might, but—"

"Oh, your mother wouldn't care. She'd be glad you had the chance to go so soon. You say she wasn't sure she could get away to-day? She would surely be glad to have you go well chaperoned," and he waved his hand toward the stout woman in the furs. "The Mater would like company I know.

Come on, you can leave a note. Aren't you all ready to go? Run up and put your tooth brush in your bag and come on. We ought to be getting started." He glanced at his watch, and beamed persuasively upon her with his great black eyes so flattering. Melissa had never had eyes flatter her so.

"But—Mother intended my sister should go, in case she couldn't," Melissa said looking troubled.

"But your sister isn't here you say. Surely one sister is as good as another. Besides, we can't wait for somebody to come. Here, take my pen and this leaf from my notebook and write a line. Say you'll wire when you get there and you are in good hands, or shall I write it?"

"Oh, no thank you," said Melissa accepting the pencil and going over to the table to write. Then she hesitated again.

"What's the matter now, sister?" urged the young man, "we're wasting good traveling time, and your brother is probably having a pink fit this minute because some of his family haven't arrived. You aren't afraid to go with strangers are you?"

"Oh, no," laughed Melissa assuredly, "I know who you are. I've seen your picture in Steve's college album. You were football Captain last year, weren't you?"

"Sure thing!" beamed the handsome young giant. "Now, get a hustle on, sister."

"Well, I was just thinking," said Melissa anxiously, "I haven't very much money in the house, not enough to go on a journey. I don't know as I could go until Mother comes."

"Oh, forget it," laughed the young man. "I have all kinds of money with me. I can lend you all you want. Besides you won't need anything. You're going in the car."

"When," asked Melissa with sudden new anxiety, "are you coming back? I would have to tell Mother that. She would be anxious."

"Oh, we're coming back day after to-morrow, sure thing. The Mater has a bridge party at the house the next day so you see she couldn't stay any longer."

With fear and trembling Melissa ran upstairs and hunted out her mother's little overnight bag in which she carried things to the hospital for Father, flung her night things and her only other good dress into it excitedy, wondering all the while whether she was doing wrong. She wrote only a brief explanation:

> Dear Mother:
> The mother and brother of a classmate of Steve's are driving up to college and have asked me to go along. I thought this would help out a lot as it doesn't cost me anything. I'll phone or wire when I get there. We are coming back day after to-morrow. Hoping you will think I did the best thing. They were in a hurry so I had no time to decide, Lovingly,
>
> > Lissa

She carried the note down and laid it on the dining table where they would be sure to see it at once, then locked the house and went out with her heart in her mouth to that great shiny car, almost trembling visibly from the excitement of it all. She, Melissa Challenger, taking decisions like this into her own hands and going off in a great expensive car!

"I'll have to ask you to stop a minute at the butcher shop," she explained to the young man, as he took her shabby little bag from her and helped her down the steps so gallantly. "I'll have to leave the key with him and ask him to give a message to my mother about the order he will be sending up."

"Oh, sure! It won't take long will it?"

So Melissa rushed into the butcher shop and up to the pleasant faced butcher. He drew away from the customer he was serving and leaned over so that she would not have to talk loud. "Oh, Mr. Brady," she said sweetly, "May I trouble you to do one thing more for us? My brother was hurt last night in an accident—"

"Yes, the kid told me on his way to school," said the kindly voice gravely, "he said he didn't know whether your ma was going up or not."

"No, she wasn't sure she could. It costs a lot to travel and you know we are rather poor just now, but I've got a chance to go for nothing, and I'm going. The family of a classmate of my brother's are going up to visit him, and they asked me to go with them. Mother and the rest are all away, and I can't stop to explain, so I'm just leaving the key here. Would you mind watching for them and giving it to them? I've left a short note at the house, but I thought they might feel better about my going so suddenly if you told them you had seen me."

"H'm!" said Brady eyeing her anxiously, "you know this chap you're going with?"

"Well, not exactly know him, but I've seen his picture and Steve has of course spoken of his brother, the roommate."

Brady cast an appraising glance out of the door at the expensive car.

"That the chap that came here asking for you?" he asked.

"Why yes, I guess it is," granted Melissa. She was beginning to feel a trifle out of breath with the suddenness of it all.

"Got any money?" Brady seemed to search down to her very soul for the answer.

Melissa colored uncomfortably.

"Oh, I shan't need money," she said airily, "we're driving you know, and they are bringing me back day after to-morrow."

"How much you got?"

"Two dollars," said Melissa haughtily as if she had said two thousand.

"Well, here," said Brady pulling out a fat roll of bills from his pocket and peeling off a few, "there's fifty. Take that and pin it in your dress somewheres, and don't let anybody know you got it, understand? I can't let your mother's little girl run off alone this way with strangers and no money. Here's a piece of wax paper, wrap it up and pin it inside your dress. You go in back there by my desk and fix it up. Quick!"

"Oh, Mr. Brady!" said Melissa with very red cheeks, "I couldn't think of taking your money. Mother wouldn't like it at all. You've done altogether too much for us already."

"Nonsense! You're not taking it, you're only having it with you in case of emergency. You don't need to use it unless you have to. You give it back to me when you get home if you don't need it, but I'll feel safer and so will your mother if you have it along. And don't you let that chap know you got it, hear? He may be all right, but what he don't know won't hurt him, see?" From under the lapel of his coat he produced two safety pins. "Now run along back there and fix it up and I'll take a look at the car you're going in so I can tell your family about it."

Melissa somehow felt she had to obey, and she hurried back for she did not want to keep these kind strangers waiting.

Brady was stalking leisurely in from the door as she came out from the little alcove where the desk was, feeling much more confident, truly, with that bit of wax paper pinned safely inside her dress.

"Who's the dame?" he asked Melissa as she tried to thank him with her best smile.

"His mother."

"H'm! Well! You take care o'yerself!" he admonished, and then stood in the door and watched her with a troubled frown as the big car started away from the door.

Melissa felt a little like crying as she settled back on the soft cushions, and realized that she was really started on a journey in this wonderful car. She looked back at the big troubled butcher there in his doorway and waved a little white hand at him, and then took a deep breath to choke back those excited tears.

What would her mother say when she got home and read

that note? What would they all say? Would they think she had done right? Well, for once, she, Melissa Challenger, had taken things in her own hands and gone ahead without waiting for anybody!

8

MRS. Challenger started out to the corner drug store where there was a telephone booth. She shivered as she went down the badly paved street, stepping carefully because the bricks were so uneven.

The sunshine was bright and warmer than yesterday, but she felt cold to the bone, and sick at heart. The outside air seemed to strike a chill through her, and there was a frightened feeling at the pit of her stomach. It seemed to her that she could not drag her heavy heart through another day of anxiety and uncertainty. It was all right to say be thankful because John was getting better, was undoubtedly past the danger point now, unless some bad set-back came! But supposing there was no place to take him for that year of utter quiet and rest that the physician said was an absolute necessity to his regaining his normal health again?

And how were they even to live and provide the necessary food and clothes just to keep the breath of life in them and be barely decent? With all the money gone, absolutely *gone,* except that thousand that they couldn't get yet, how long would a thousand dollars last for six people who hadn't a job among them and couldn't get one? She had begun to realize that there *weren't* any jobs anywhere and perhaps were not going to be any for months, even years, if this depression kept on. Just what could they do? The poor house? Charity! She shuddered again and drew the collar of her shabby coat up closer. Had God forgotten the world? Was it as Melissa had so shockingly put it, ridiculous to expect a God to look after trifles of daily life? *Was* there a God as Melissa had asked?

It was perhaps the first time in her hitherto well regulated life that such a real doubt had ever entered her mind. She had been brought up to believe in God, of course, and go to church regularly whenever possible. She didn't know much about God or the Bible but she had always asserted that she believed in them. Now she was appalled by the sudden thoughts that assailed her. Why, what did her circumstances have to do with those facts of the ages? All respectable people believed in a God, and the Bible as a sacred book. Of course she believed in it. This was folly. This was the product of a tired, sick, discouraged mind. This had no bearing on her burdens. Another time she would carefully consider these questions and think out a way to reconcile the fact of trouble, with a loving God such as she had always been taught to believe her God was. But she had no time to consider such things now. She would go insane if she couldn't think that God somewhere, somehow, was the same as always. It was better just to blindly believe. It certainly did make one feel better to pray about things, even if nothing happened. Of course it was hard to believe a God could spare time to look after every one of His creatures' daily needs. Poor little Rosalie and her beefsteak and onions! Of course, that was just a coincidence. Yet she herself had been helped to get rest and some relief from her anxiety last night after she had prayed. Well, if there wasn't anything in prayer she didn't want to know it just now. There certainly wasn't anything else to depend on, anyway.

And now this trouble with Steve. That was what made her stomach feel so strange and empty, though she had made herself eat quite a good breakfast. Steve, her good eldest boy! Steve in trouble like this! It couldn't be that Steve had borrowed somebody's car and smashed it up. There must be some other explanation. Steve had always been such a sensible boy. Full of fun and mischief of course, but always careful of other people's things. And his father had always laid such stress on never borrowing things. It couldn't be possible!

She drew a heavy sigh as she stepped into the drug store and proceeded to study the telephone directory, sudden tears blurring her eyes as she thought of her bright handsome Steve laid low with a broken leg, and no telling how many other bruises and dangers, and she not there to help. Concussion! That might mean all sorts of things. It might be even worse than the telegram had stated. His very life might be in danger, and here she was shut up to telephoning instead of flying to him instantly!

It was with difficulty that she controlled her tears and set herself to find some one in that distant college town.

A person to person call to the dean who had wired her. That was the only thing that could satisfy her. She must talk with the one who had worded that message, with its half sneering insinuation of blame for Steve, "a borrowed automobile," telling a whole tragedy in a single phrase! She would make him understand that her son was responsible. That there need be no insinuations about what Steve had done. Steve's family would of course be responsible, and make good whatever loss—! Her thoughts stopped short, suddenly faced by the fact of the family's new poverty. They had never been rich of course; one didn't expect college professors to be wealthy, but they had been fairly well off, having saved early in their married life, and continued it throughout the years. And now grimly the appalling fact looked her in the face that the family could make nothing good now. Nothing! Not even a dollar's worth! She had not money enough even to go to her son's bedside!

It seemed hours before she finally got her call through and

was informed by the operator that the dean had gone to New York for three or four days, was there anybody else with whom she would talk?

The college president.

Another age of waiting, and then, the college president had gone south to give an address at some seat of learning.

Some other official? There was no one around at the time. When she frantically suggested the name of a professor Steve had mentioned in his letters she was told that it was impossible to locate him at this hour.

She tried pathetically to think of the names of some of Steve's associates, but only the nicknames would come to her bewildered mind.

When, in desperation, she said she would talk with the office clerk, she was merely told that they had no information concerning Mr. Stephen Challenger except that he was in the hospital in a nearby town where the accident had occurred. The clerk did not know the name of the hospital, but she would try to get it somewhere. If Mrs. Challenger would telephone again at twelve o'clock there might be somebody in the office who would know more about it.

Heartsick the mother hung up the receiver and leaned her head down with a soft moan on the box under the instrument.

The druggist, passing the booth, hesitated and finally tapped on the glass door and asked if there was anything he could do for her, was she ill, or in trouble?

Mrs. Challenger lifted her white face, and tried to answer. She did not know what to say. She didn't feel like telling him that she was at her wit's end and had just been asking God to somehow help her out and show her what to do.

"Oh, I just don't know what to do next!" she said desperately. "My son has been hurt and I can't seem to get anybody. I don't even know what hospital he's in, and nobody seems to know!"

The druggist asked a few keen questions and then called up

information. In a few minutes he summoned the frantic mother to a conversation with the hospital authorities.

But, there were more delays. Accurate information from Stephen's room had to be awaited, and when it came it was most indefinite.

Yes, young Challenger was there. Yes, he had a broken leg, and some other injuries, not very likely to be fatal, but the house doctor had not made his rounds yet. The nurse said he was doing as well as could be expected. Was there a telephone in his room? Would he be able to talk to her for a moment? More delay. Then a decided answer. No, he was not able to talk. He was under opiates and must not be disturbed. A message? Yes, she could leave a message, but she saw from the tone of the impatient nurse who was conducting the conversation, that it was a long doubt as to when it would be delivered.

"Tell him I'm coming as soon as I can arrange to get away from his father who is sick," she said desperately.

"All right!" answered the nurse indifferently, "I'll make a note of that and have them tell him when he is able."

"You will keep me informed of his condition?" The mother's voice was almost a sob.

"Oh yes." The nurse took the address and the Brady telephone number, and then it was over and the receiver hung up. A blank wall of trouble seemed to surround the poor woman as she turned away, tried to thank the druggist for his kindness, and stumbled out into the chilly sunshine again. What should she do now? She had spent three dollars and fifty-five cents of her much needed money and found out scarcely anything that she did not already know.

Out on the street again she paused bewildered. What should she do next? Her inclination was to go back to the house and crawl into her bed. She felt as if she had received a death blow, and her legs would no longer bear her on her way. She turned and walked slowly, very slowly, in the uptown direction, wondering what was the matter with her senses. They seemed benumbed. Perhaps she was going to have a stroke of apoplexy, or paralysis. How did those things begin? And what would her poor children do then? Her husband in one hospital, her boy in another far away! Rosalie her baby, and brave little Bob not long since in the baby class! The two dear girls who needed her so much!

The thought stung her into keenness again. She must do something. There must be some way to get money, borrow it somewhere. She was so utterly ignorant about banking and such things. She had always been so guarded, first by her father, long since gone, and then by her wonderful husband! But it was not right. Every woman ought to understand a little business.

As she paced along she forced herself to think of all the business men they knew who had money, or who could at least tell her what to do. She resolved to humble her pride, her husband's pride too she knew it would be, for he shrank so from telling any one of his private affairs. But this was an emergency. He would surely approve.

There were a few names. She counted them over, Garwood, Warrington, Haverfield, Stowe, and Prevost. They knew her husband well, but were men socially so aloof, so high, so cold and haughty of manner, that it had not been a subject of consideration to turn to them. Now in her utter despair she resolved to humble pride and go to them.

With trembling limbs she walked to the business office of Garwood and Sons, and after an unconscionable wait was informed that Mr. Garwood was out of town for a week or more.

She hurried away in relief from Garwood and Sons, so glad that she did not know the "sons" nor they her. Dr. Warrington was the next in her mind's list, a surgeon of renown. Dr. Warrington had always a pleasant smile on his face, the few times she had met him, usually at some faculty affair where he occasionally lent his presence, or on some great occasion where notables were present.

Breathlessly she entered the elevator in the great building where he had his office, and ascended. But a frightened appeal to the severe person in shell-rimmed glasses who guarded him, brought utter refusal. Dr. Warrington was performing a major operation, and was occupied every minute until three o'clock when he had to take a train for Chicago to speak at the Medical Association. Mrs. Challenger was conscious of the recurring relief when she found she did not have to ask the learned doctor for charity. He would undoubtedly have given it, freely, smilingly, of course, but—how could she ever have got over asking him, an almost utter stranger? Perhaps such pride was wrong, but surely she was doing her best in spite of it.

As she dragged her weary feet back to the elevator, she found herself saying over and over "Oh, God! What shall I do? Oh, God, I'm doing my best! In spite of failure I'm doing my best. I surely am not to be blamed, am I? I can't help it that I hate this, but I'm doing it!"

Thus she justified herself to God so that perhaps He would see the injustice of her position and somehow turn the luck for the Challengers, who had always been so respectable and right living. They didn't really deserve such treatment. That was the undercurrent of her reasoning, "I'm doing my best, God. Why do things go against me all the time?"

She was not surprised when she was told that the noted lawyer Haverfield was in court pleading a murder case, and it might be days before she could have an interview; and when they asked her if she would like an appointment for next week with him, she only sighed hopelessly and said it didn't matter. She had a feeling that if something didn't happen before next week they wouldn't be alive to need help.

Mr. Stowe was the president of a bank and by the time she reached the bank it was three o'clock and banking hours were over. She was firmly and smilingly refused admittance. The doorkeeper, on seeing her discouraged face, reluctantly admitted that Mr. Stowe was sometimes to be found at his club after banking hours, and the discouraged woman dragged herself wearily to the great Mercantile Club building, where, after a wait of fifteen minutes, Mr. Stowe who was playing a game of billiards with some friends and enjoying a series of expensive cocktails between shots, sent up word that he was in an important conference just now but if she would come to his private office in the bank at eleven-thirty the next day he would be pleased to grant her an interview.

Mrs. Challenger, with a feeling of unexpected deliverance, arose and started toward the great revolving outer door, but as she passed the Grill Room door a sudden breath of delicious hot food was wafted to her, that made her faint and dizzy. She wavered and would have fallen had not a hand been reached out to catch her and steady her to a chair.

There was instant solicitation. Two porters rushed to her assistance, two or three gentlemen lifted their hats respectfully with offers of help as she came slowly back to a weary consciousness, lifting bewildered blue eyes that had almost the same sweetness in them that her three daughters wore in theirs, quivering a little smile of apology with her delicate cameo lips.

"I was just a little faint, thank you," she trembled out the words and tried to rise, "I was so hurried I did not take time for lunch," she tried to explain.

A waiter came hurrying with a cup of hot tea and a little wine glass of something stronger. She refused the liquor but took the tea gratefully, a faint color coming into her pretty cheeks as she drank it, and a slight lift of her chin as she handed the waiter a bit of silver. Then, though they would have detained her, she slipped away like a faint patrician shadow, trying to concentrate her mind on the one more call she had to make. One more and then she would be done, she told herself, half forgetting the reason for these calls in the distaste of making them.

Mr. Prevost was the head buyer in a great department store and she was fairly trembling with weariness when after taking various elevators, and traveling acres of aisles and departments, she at last arrived at his mahogany-front office, and made her simple request to see him.

She was led to an inner office, after declining to tell her errand to the underling set to guard him, and found a severe young woman like a perpetual icicle seated at a plate glass desk top.

"Mr. Prevost is in Europe on a buying trip," explained the icicle. "I am taking his place. What can I do for you?"

"Oh!" said Mrs. Challenger meekly. Then, with relief, "Oh! Nothing thank you. Mr. Prevost is a friend. My business was with him personally. I am sorry to have troubled you."

Then she walked out of the office with true Challenger dignity. It seemed to her that the burdens of the nations had been lifted from her shoulders. She had not had to ask loans or charity from any high-and-mighty acquaintance. She had faithfully been to every one and been prevented from doing the thing that was so against her pride.

It was not until she was seated in the bus that would take her to the hospital that it suddenly came over her that her real plight was even worse than in the morning. True, she had not had to humiliate herself, but her husband was still needing a quiet place in the country, her son was still lying very ill far away and she unable to go to him for lack of money and the entire family were not only in debt to a butcher, but on the verge of starvation.

She was glad that there were no other passengers except an old woman with bundles who appeared to be asleep, for she could not keep the tears back, and had to continually wipe them away.

The tea which she had at the club had only given her brief stimulation, and now she realized that she should have stopped long enough in the city to get something to eat before going on to see her husband. But it was too late. She dared not waste another fare by going back. She would have to bear up somehow. Perhaps she would feel all right if she took a good drink of ice water at the fountain in the hallway at the hospital.

Mr. Challenger was sitting up when she got there. He smiled lovingly, and there was a light in his eyes as he greeted her.

"I began to think you were not coming," he said, as she stooped to receive his lover-like kiss. "You are tired! Mary! I shouldn't let you come to see me so often. It must be a long, long pilgrimage for you."

"It's not so far," said Mary Challenger lovingly, and then remembered that her husband was reckoning from Glencove, the suburban home where he had left them when he was first taken sick. He was still in ignorance that they had moved when the first crash came three months before.

"You've not eaten your lunch!" said the wife, her eyes lighting on the untouched tray. "Why, you've not eaten a thing! How is it they left the tray so long?"

The sick man smiled.

"I asked them to leave it a little while," he said, "I was drowsy, but I must have slept a long time. I just woke up a few minutes ago. My regular nurse is off duty this afternoon, and the substitute doesn't bother to come in unless I call her. You see I thought perhaps you would come early enough to have lunch with me if I waited a little. They always send twice as much as I can possibly eat. But it will be all cold now, and I suppose you had your lunch hours ago."

"Why, no," said Mary Challenger smiling, "I didn't take time for anything but a cup of tea. I had—some business—to attend to downtown, that's what made me—so late! What fun it will be to have a meal together again. What have you got? Chicken? That's just as good cold anyway, and there's a whole breast! How good they are to you! And John, the potatoes aren't stone cold yet. Here, let me fix you so that you can reach the tray."

She roused herself to be bright and smiling, and tried to

make herself eat with a zest so that he should not suspect how utterly weary and heartsick she was. His eyes watched her lovingly, as he ate bits of chicken, and the roll that she spread for him, and drank his milk obediently.

Mary was no longer hungry. She had gone too long and was too nervously exhausted to want to eat, but knowing she would be ill if she did not, and realizing that here was a real meal which would not cost her a cent of the precious few dollars she carried she forced herself to eat, slowly, smilingly, trying to forget her troubles.

"And what do you hear from Steve?" asked the father when he had finished the last bite of the snow pudding that had been his half of the dessert.

Stephen's mother dropped her handkerchief and stooped quickly to pick it up, trying to hide the distress in face and voice, and steady her trembling lips to answer him.

"Why, he seemed cheerful—and busy—the last time he wrote!" she managed to say, and then with the new skill she had been acquiring in changing the subject she asked guilelessly, "What's your idea about what he shall do after he graduates? By the way, your youngest son says he doesn't think *he* shall go to college at all. He says it seems a waste of time to him. He wants to get to earning money. He says he is going to be a millionaire!"

They laughed together pleasantly over that, and if there was a bit of artificiality in Mary's laugh the invalid did not notice it.

So they talked until it began to get dark, and suddenly Mary Challenger remembered that night had come upon her, and she had as yet no way to get to her boy who was in trouble. She was no nearer a decision about what to do than when the telegram first came. She had an inexpressible longing to lay her head down on the shoulder that until this last six months had always been so strong to shelter her from all sorts of trouble, and just have her husband take the decisions from her, and tell her what to do. Yet she knew that she must not.

That if he knew all that was weighing upon her at this moment it might be fatal to him. The doctor had warned her most effectually not to startle or alarm him in any way until his heart was in a conditon to bear it.

So she summoned a smile as best she could, glanced at her watch, and got up in a hurry.

"Why, it is almost dark," she said brightly, "and I must hurry along. There are some things I must get on the way for dinner."

And so, hurrying, lest she break into a forlorn sob, she left him with a smile, that almost turned to tears as she went out the door. When she reached home she found Phyllis was still absent.

Rosalie was sitting in a forlorn little heap in the big chair looking out of the window watching for her, tears on her cheeks, her eyes wide with frightened imaginings. She had read the note that Melissa left, and her young heart was beating excitedly as the dark came down, but in her hand she clutched a fifty cent piece that she had earned by caring for a baby next door to Brady's while its mother went to a funeral.

She rushed to her mother with a sob, and clutched her close and then in the same breath began to tell her about the fifty cent piece.

"Look, Mother, a whole half dollar! I earned it myself! I prayed that I might have a chance and I did. Wasn't that wonderful?"

The mother smothered a worry, wondering if it was quite right to let the child pray constantly for small material trifles, and then remembered that she herself was praying for larger ones. The fifty cents was as much needed in the household as the larger sum she needed. She sank down in a chair, too weary to question it, or think it out, only wishing that she knew whether God really cared. Well, she had done her best, anyway, gone to all five of those terrible men and not been able to find one. Surely God would realize.

But her thoughts were suddenly interrupted by Rosalie, handing her Melissa's note.

"Look, Mother, what Lissa's done. Are you pleased that she did it? Or were you going to send Phyllie the way you said this morning?"

The mother roused suddenly and read the note, and the terrors and disappointments of the day suddenly fell into oblivion beside this new order of things. Melissa gone to her brother! Melissa, taking things in her own hands! She somehow felt an instant alarm that would not have been present had it been Phyllis who had gone. Phyllis was so sober and dependable, and Melissa was so very pretty and impulsive.

White and anxious the mother read the note over again, and her fearful heart saw all the possibilities for worry that it contained. Where was Phyllis? Why hadn't she come? It was very dark now, and a glance about the room showed no preparations for dinner. How very strange. It was not like Phyllis who was always so solicitous for her mother's comfort.

"How did you get in Rosalie?" she suddenly asked.

"Why the Butcher-Brady man unlocked the door for me. He said he knew my sisters were away and you had gone, and he thought I might not like to come into the house alone. So he came over and started the fire, and lit the lights, and said he'd be back before long if he didn't see some of the folks coming."

"How kind he is," murmured the distracted woman.

"There he is now," said Rosalie running to the door to let him in.

The butcher loomed in the doorway with a hot dish covered with a napkin in his hands.

"The missis sent this meat pie over. She thought ya might not have time fer much cooking ta-night, and being as one of the girls is away we thought it might come in handy."

"Oh, how kind you are!" said Mrs. Challenger rising. "You really mustn't put us under so much obligation. I don't know that we shall ever be able to repay it on this earth."

"That's all right, ma'am," said Brady with a big grin, "We're just doin' it because we like ya, the missis and me, so don't spoil our pleasure. I was comin' over anyway, seein' as I promised the little lady this mornin' that I'd give ya her message. She left the key with me, and wanted I should tell ya she was all right. She seemed afraid you might not find her note. I hope it didn't worry ya any."

Mrs. Challenger's face clouded over anxiously again:

"But I am worried, Mr. Brady," she said, "I don't know these people she went with at all. I don't think Melissa did."

"I ast her did she know the chap, an' she said she knew *who* he was, she'd heard her brother talk about him in some of their sports, and she'd seen his picture. I went out and sized up the guy. He didn't look much, but it was a swell outfit. He had an old dame in the back seat, his mother, your girl said it was. She was all dolled up in furs, and they had a peach of a car. Ef I'd only dared, though, I'd a made her wait till you got back. But I guess you needn't worry. They oughta be gettin' there about now. She'll likely phone won't she?"

"Oh, I don't know!" said the distracted mother. "She's never been away from home alone, except to college, and then her father took her there, and she came back with friends."

"Oh, she knows her way about," said the butcher confidently, "she'll make out."

"But she hadn't but two dollars with her," said the mother, wild at a new thought.

"No, you're mistaken about that," said the big man looking sheepish, "I ast her did she have money enough and she said yes, she had two dollars and wouldn't need any more because they was bringing her back day after ta-morrow. But I couldn't see a nice pretty little girl like that goin' off without money in case of an emergency, so I just loaned her enough ta make her safe. Oh, you needn't worry. She didn't wanta take it. She said her mother wouldn't like it and all that, but I made her, see, I told her she didn't have ta spend it unless she got in a tight place and she could bring it all back with her again, and no harm done if there didn't come a need of it, so at last I got her ta take it. I give her two safety pins and made her go back by my desk and pin it tight inside her dress, so you don't need ta worry a mite. She'll be all right."

"How very good you are, Mr. Brady!" said the mother with her eyes full of tears, "I can't ever, ever thank you enough."

"Aw, that's nothin'," grinned the big pleased man, "I kep' a thinkin', 'spose she was my child, an' you had a chancet ta help her out a bit! There, now you just set down an' eat yer supper while it's hot. Where's Bob? Ain't he come home yet?"

"He's coming now," announced Rosalie who had her face anxiously plastered against the window; and just then with a stamp and a bang of the door the boy entered.

"What's the matter, Robert?" asked his mother aghast. For Robert had a great pad of antiseptic gauze over one eye held on by neat cross bars of adhesive tape.

"Aw, nothin' much! I just had a fight with a feller at school. He got fresh about my little sister, and I let him see where ta get off. He's got a worse eye 'n I have all righty!"

"Robert! My child! Fighting! Who put that bandage on your eye? Have you been to the doctor?"

"Aw, Ma, don't get fussy!" said Bob drawing away from her anxious grasp, "It's awright! It was right in front of the hospital it happened, and some guy took us in there. It's only a little bruise. It don't hurt much. The house doctor said it would be all right in a few days. Anyhow, I couldn't let that kid get fresh about my little sister, could I?"

"Who was it, Robert?" asked Rosalie her eyes wide with unspeakable things.

"Aw, just that Flip Whiting. You don't needta worry, Rosie. I beat him up all right, ef he *is* bigger'n I am."

Mrs. Challenger moaned, but the big butcher grinned.

"Good boy!" he said with a clap on Bob's shoulder. "You'll do. You c'n take care o' your fambly all right. Your mom's got good right ta be proud of ya. But where's yer other sister? Miss Phyllis? I seen her go down the street this morning just afore Miss Melissa come ta leave me the key. Ain't she come back yet?"

"Oh, no!" said the mother rising with a new anxiety in her eyes. "I wonder what can have happened to Phyllis? She's always so thoughtful not to worry me."

"Where'd she go?" asked Brady.

"She said she was going to hunt a job. She didn't want to tell us what she had in mind till she would see if it came to anything. It didn't worry me because she's always so dependable, and she knows the city well. But—oh, it seems as if everything, just *every*thing was happening to us now."

"There! There! Now don'tcha worry!" coaxed Brady. "She'll turn up all right. She's maybe got a job and hadta wait er something. She'll come in soon. It ain't late. You folks just get yer supper on and begin to eat. She'll come walkin' in before ya know it, and ef she don't come pretty soon I'll get busy and find her. Don'tcha worry!"

"Oh," said Mrs. Challenger with a bit of a hysterical laugh, "You'll think we are more trouble than a whole orphan asylum!"

"No trouble at all. All my pleasure," he said gallantly, and waved aside her thanks, hurrying away with assurance that he would be back later to make sure Miss Phyllis had arrived safely.

The children were instantly eager as soon as the door closed:

"Gee! That meat pie smells good!" said Bob, "We don't havta wait for Phyl to come to eat, do we? I'm starved, I am."

"Why, no, I guess not," said the mother casting an anxious eye toward the darkening window. "She ought to be here pretty soon, but we can keep her share warm of course. No, go ahead and let's have supper. Oh, dear, I wish she would come. There seems to be so many things to worry about."

"Don't worry, Mother dear," said Rosalie earnestly, "it will all come right. I'm just sure it will."

"I wish I had your faith!" said the mother bitterly, turning to take her things off.

Rosalie flew around setting the table, putting on butter and milk and bread, and warming up the coffee that was left from breakfast, and presently they sat down.

Mrs. Challenger put some of the delicious food on her plate, and sat before it, for the sake of the children, but ate very little. Her eyes were constantly turning toward the window, and she started at every sound from the street. There really were so many things to worry about that she did not know which to concentrate upon. Father, Steve, the borrowed automobile, Melissa, Phyllis and Bob's eye. She cast a glance, too, at Rosalie. Her delicate baby exposed to the coarseness of the common horde of children. The public school in that peculiar quarter of the city filled with children from the lower walks of life was no place for their cherished daughter to go. If her father knew it he would be frantic. But, what could she do about it? If only Phyllis would come! Where *could* Phyllis be?

But nine o'clock came, and then half past and no Phyllis! Quarter of ten! She had not come!

At ten minutes after ten Brady looked in to see if she had arrived, and went away with cheerful encouragement upon his lips, but an anxious look in his eyes.

9

MELISSA had not been a half hour on the way before she discovered that most emphatically her mother would never have selected the Hollister family to chaperon her on her journey.

Mrs. Hollister and her massive furs were spread out on the back seat of the car, occupying it most fully, and she made no move to shove over and make room for Melissa as her son introduced her. The young man put her into the car beside himself, and even through traffic it became apparent that his mind was far more on carrying on a conversation with her than on guiding his car.

They had several hair-breadth escapes from smashing into cars, and once a traffic cop stopped the car and administered some angry words, but the young man only laughed in his face and tossed him a bill as he drove on.

Out of traffic at last, speeding along the highway, no other car could possibly pass them, and they spun past everything in their path at a rate of speed that made even Melissa who loved thrills catch her breath many times. She realized keenly that if her mother could see her she would be really alarmed.

But as the day passed on and she grew better acquainted with Gene Hollister, she became more and more uneasy. For one thing, though he was driving like mad most of the time, he persisted every now and then in throwing one arm across the back of the seat and snuggling her up to him intimately.

The first time he did it she was frightened and mortified. What would his mother think of him—of her—allowing such a thing? She drew away instantly, though trying to do it so casually that it would appear that she had not really done it at all. She did not want him to know that she recognized what he had done. Her cheeks blazed and her heart beat with frightened throbs. Probably he would think she wasn't at all sophisticated, but she could not help it. She had been brought up to regard such intimacies as unpardonable, and the handsome rowdy seemed suddenly coarse and rude to her, yet she did not want to make him angry. He was of course doing her a favor, which made it awkward in the extreme. And probably he thought nothing of hugging a girl, any girl, and would laugh at her for a poor prude if she protested.

She tried to get a glimpse of his mother's face in the little mirror up over the windshield, and discovered it bland, and satisfied, and sound asleep, which made her still more uncomfortable. She found it most disturbing to feel herself practically alone with a possessive stranger in this headlong flight through space. It was exciting of course, rather wonderful when one stopped to think about it, and remember yesterday, that she, Melissa Challenger, should be riding away in this expensive car, and having the undivided attention of a young man who probably counted his fortune by the millions. It would be something to tell about when she got home At the same time she owned frankly to herself that she would be really glad when the experience was over, for she had a feeling that she didn't know what he might do next.

He was telling her that if she just had a touch of lipstick on her lips her mouth would be pretty enough to kiss, when a sudden lurch of the car as he swerved to pass a great moving van, shook the placid chaperone out of her nap, and brought her into the picture again.

With a feeling that she had had a couple of narrow escapes, Melissa slid over to the extreme far side of the seat, and half turned around to call Mrs. Hollister's attention to a dim purple mountain in the distance. Just in time she was, for the plump eyelids were beginning to blink again, and the whole bulky mountain of flesh was about to nod back into unconsciousness as Melissa's fresh voice called her to attention.

She sat up with an effort and viewed the purple mirage indifferently.

"Very pretty! Very pretty, my dear. But say, Genie, darling, isn't it almost time we had a little refreshment of some sort? I feel almost as if I should be drowsy. A little drink would wake us up."

"Sure thing!" agreed Eugene, "just as quick as I see a likely place where they'll have something real."

Melissa was not alarmed at these words, being far too ignorant of the ways of the world and the road to take anything special out of such a suggestion. In fact she welcomed the idea. She was healthily hungry, for the oatmeal and milk and bacon and toast of the morning had become a forgotten dream in the excitements of the last two hours.

But when they drew up at a doubtful-looking roadside pavilion on the edge of a woods, and were seated at one of the rustic tables, she discovered that it was not to eat, but to drink that they had stopped their journey, and not water they were supposed to drink, not even soda water. The names of liquors that had until now been, to Melissa, merely names, were bandied about familiarly in the Hollister attempt to get something which they considered really worth drinking. They seemed utterly amazed and not a little disgusted with her that she ordered only a glass of milk, and would not be entreated to taste any of the liquors offered. They were having pretzels with their drinks, so Melissa took a hot dog sandwich and satisfied her hunger.

Mamma Hollister, after a brief bit of chatterpatter after lunch, during which she smilingly let a great many family cats out of their respective bags, and aired several family skeletons merrily, including her son Gene's recent divorce suit, settled off into another nap.

Melissa, feeling that she was a little lost sheep strayed off willfully into an unknown world, set herself to talk to this man of the world on topics that would be safe and help her keep her distance and her self-respect. She tried scenery, and, discovering that he had been abroad several times began to ply him with questions about Swiss scenery, the Alps, Italy, and France, but he veered at once to questionable stories of Parisian night clubs, and girls he had known abroad. She tried the subject of books, and he gave her a five minute account of a story that she had heard of only because it had been banned. Then he slipped into talk about the Movies, and Stars he had known, told anecdotes that made her feel as if she had been caught in the flow of a sewer, laughed heartily at his own rotten jokes, and ragged her about her own solemnity. He asked her if she had no sense of humor, and she tried to change the subject again back to the safety of college life, relating some of her own experiences which she had always counted most thrilling, escapades of such comparative innocence that he stared at her as if she had been a child of three masquerading as a woman. Then he went on to tell some of his own flagrant college stories, and her eyes grew wide with dismay, remembering that this college of which he was talking was the very one in which her brother had spent four years. Had Steve been through things like this? Did he know that such things went on? Oh, this couldn't all be true! Surely this man must be just talking to astonish her!

She sat back silent, displeased, wondering what to do to bring the conversation back to a sane normal place. Her head ached, her face was burning with shame and her eyes were heavy with weariness and excitement.

"Why so silent, darling? Not sore are you?" he said suddenly, his bold black eyes staring close into hers to the utter disre-
gard of the wheel he was managing.

Melissa drew a deep breath and tried to smile with dignity.
She was still trying to make it appear that she had not heard
some of his ribald jokes, had not understood, trying to pleasantly ignore them. A compromising policy that made her
most uncomfortable, yet she reasoned that there was nothing
else she could do so long as she had to finish out the ride with
him, and furthermore must return with him after two days.
She couldn't spend the butcher's money for her poor mother
to repay. She simply must get back again with these people,
therefore she must not anger this young man.

She tried to wear an air of sophistication, to pretend that she
was not bothered with the outrageous things he said. She
knew that young people to-day, many of them, called such
talk "frankness" and dubbed any one who objected to it "victorian." Well, she had sometimes argued with her mother that
she was far too particular, but now she began to change her
mind. Her soul revolted at the things that were being said to
her in this off-hand way, as if it were quite a common way to
speak. Yet all the time she had a dread back in her mind that
this young man saw she was unsophisticated and was trying
to see just how much she would stand for. She was divided
between a desire to have him understand that she was no
prude, and a great wish to strike his handsome filthy lips.

She reflected that if it had been Phyllis in her place she
would have probably told the young man long ago just where
she stood and that he could not speak so to her and have her
remain in the car with him. Phyllis would have flashed angry
eyes at him when he tried to put his arm around her. Phyllis
would even have got out and walked if it came to that. And
suddenly she understood why her mother would have sent
Phyllis instead of herself.

Melissa had always thought that she herself was far better

able to cope with people who were what she called "fresh" than Phyllis. She had always argued that to ignore evil was a better way of handling it than to be so frankly offensive against it. Yet now suddenly Melissa felt that she had failed utterly to create the impression she so much desired, and she began to wonder if after all she were right in her method.

They stopped for dinner at a grand hotel, and the Hollisters kindly insisted that Melissa was to be their guest. She felt small and unhappy and choked as she tried to eat. And once again she had to refuse the various drinks they offered, choosing only coffee. They laughed at her good-naturedly. Mrs. Hollister patted her hand as if she had been a child and called her very abstemious, which somehow managed to sound like contempt, and Melissa's discomfort grew. She was thankful to learn that the college town to which they were traveling was only fifty or sixty miles further on; thankful again when they went out to the car and found it dark that Mrs. Hollister asked her to sit in the back seat with her so she could talk with her a little while.

The conversation during that last fifty miles was general, mixed with a good deal of laughter about nothing Melissa felt. She sat back tired and worried, and wondered why she felt like crying. Here she was on her very first long automobile trip in a grand car, saving the family money by going without expense to look after her brother, and yet she somehow felt that every step she went she was displeasing them all and making more trouble for herself. It was just that she was tired and excited. That must be the explanation, for of course she had done perfectly right to come. There would have been no other sensible way to look at it. She *had* to come.

So she braced herself, sat up, and tried to laugh and be good company, talking of things about which she knew nothing, just talking to make talk. It seemed a nightmare that would never end, and her weariness was growing almost sickening now. Late in the afternoon young Hollister charged her with being silent and she had pled that she was sleepy. He had at once tried to make her lay her head on his shoulder and take a nap, and since then she had scarcely dared to wink, lest the offer would be repeated. She felt as if she were fighting a force she did not understand, and it frightened her.

She had always in a quiet way rather chaffed at the conventionalities with which her family had surrounded her, but now to her amazement she found that she resented any breaking down of the barriers. She wondered with a weary sigh what it all meant. Was she somehow spiritually hampered by her upbringing, so that even if she had the chance she could not unbend and do as the world was doing?

But she was altogether too tired to think it out, and was more glad than she dared to own when she saw the lights of the college town at last coming into view.

Those buildings to the right were the dormitories, they told her, and beyond were the fraternity houses. Off to the left were the college buildings, the auditorium, the observatory, the library and the gymnasium.

Suddenly she forgot her fears and thrilled to the thought that she was actually here, seeing Steve's college. The other things fell away, she forgot that her brother was lying in bed with a broken leg and a questionable record, forgot that her journey had been strenuous, and her companions terrifying at times, and that she had to go back again quite soon with them. Forgot even that she was not sure her family would be pleased that she had come at all. She just looked with delight on the twinkling lights that beckoned to her from every charmed window.

"And which is the hospital?" she asked suddenly, recalling with a pang her strange unpleasant reason for being there at all.

"Blamed if I know," responded Gene indifferently. "Seems to me they said something about its being changed. It used to be in the basement of the science building, just behind the dining halls, when I was here, but it might be in that new dorm over there. It won't take long to find out. We'll step into the office and see."

But when they reached the office they were told that the accident cases were in a nearby village at the new hospital that had just been built. They were taken there when the accident happened, and it had been impossible to move them. Besides, they had more facilities for caring for serious cases.

Melissa's heart sank. Then Steve's was considered a serious case. She turned pale and felt in a real panic. She turned for explanation and comfort to young Hollister but he seemed as gay as a bird with no idea of anxiety. But then he might perhaps have more information about his brother. They likely had talked over Long Distance before they started, and were not alarmed. He turned to go back to the car.

"Come on Darling," he addressed her flippantly, "I'll run you over there."

"But," said Melissa hesitating, "hadn't I better ask where I am to stay to-night?"

"Oh, there'll be a hotel in the village somewhere," he answered carelessly. "They wouldn't know anything about it here."

"A hotel!" said Melissa in dismay, "But I thought—, why—wouldn't they expect me to stay here? That's the way families of students always did at my college in case of the sickness of a student."

"Stay *here?* Holy Mackerel, Kid!" said Hollister facing rudely about and staring at her, "What do you think this institution is? A day nursery? No, Darling, this is a university! Any one that visits here looks out for himself. They certainly would howl you down in a hurry if you were to suggest such a thing."

A wave of deep color swept over Melissa's tired, pretty face, and troubled dignity sat upon her as she still hesitated.

"But, oughtn't I to go first to see the president? Or the dean? He was the one who telegraphed to Mother. Wouldn't he think it strange that I did not come straight to him? Won't he be wondering that he has not heard from my brother's people?"

"They're both out of town to-night," snapped the desk clerk shortly, but Gene Hollister laughed immoderately:

"The President! The Dean? Sweet Mamma! How do you get that way, Kid? Don't you know there are thousands of students here? Do you suppose the president and the dean run around feeding them every two hours and taking their temperature? Come along, Kid. I'll show you the ropes. We can go over to the hospital and get wise to conditions, and then we'll find a hotel and get dinner and have a large evening, see a picture, have a dance or something. Come on! The Mater will be sound asleep again and that would be too bad!"

So in a new dismay Melissa followed him out to the car. He seemed to think he had brought her along to have some kind of celebration, or picnic. What should she do? And a hotel? She must not stay in a hotel. She could never pay for even the cheapest room without using Mr. Brady's money, and she simply must not do that. That was only for an emergency which she fondly hoped would never arise. As for having these Hollisters pay her board, that was not to be thought of even if she had to sit up all night in some railroad station.

The hospital was a big pretentious building, and Melissa felt overawed as she entered, but when she went to the desk for information she was appalled to find that while Jack Hollister was established in a private room, one of the best in the place, her own brother was in the ward! A Challenger lying ill among the poorest of the poor! That hit the Challenger pride hard. She felt indignation that some one in the college had not cared for him better than that. Poor Steve! He knew the family were hard up and he had likely told them to put him there. Her eyes filled with tears, and she turned away to hide them. But when she turned back to the desk and the starched, white-capped person who presided there, she found that the Hollisters had gone gayly off to see Jack and left her to her own fate. And her fate was that it was after hours to visit the ward and she would have to wait until to-morrow!

She stood aghast, the tears really coming now, and rolling down her white tired cheeks.

"But I must see my brother at once!" she said. "I've traveled all day to get here, and my mother will be frightened to death if I don't telephone her at once how he is."

The nurse eyed her thoughtfully, asked where she lived, ran over a bunch of record cards, consulted with a ward nurse who was passing, and who studied Melissa indifferently, and finally relented.

"You could go to the door and look in," she said. "Your brother is right next to the door and you could see him, but he won't know you. He's under opiates. It wouldn't do you much good, but you can look in on him if you like."

Melissa who had never been in a hospital but once or twice before, and then to take flowers to a girl friend who had had her tonsils out, walked the awesome halls with her heart beating wildly. The whiteness, and cleanliness, the odors of disinfectant, the far cry of a baby, the utter stillness in the dim recesses, made her feel as if she were walking among tombs.

Steve unconscious! He must be a great deal worse hurt than they had feared. She held the little overnight bag as if it weighed a ton, and her feet seemed loaded with lead. She could hardly keep up with the nurse who led the way.

At last she stood in the doorway looking into a room with rows of beds against the wall. She was aware of a battery of eyes watching her, aware of sheeted screens drawn about certain beds, an air of terrible earnestness everywhere. Instantly aware, too, of one screened bed on the left where three relatives of a sick man stood weeping about him. She knew without being told that the man must be dying. And her brother was here among all this! Steve! Her merry-hearted brother, with his gay smile and his strong body! How could he survive in a place of death like this?

Then she saw him in the narrow white bed on the right of

the door, his obstreperous brown curls swathed in bandages, plaster on one cheek, his strong lithe arms flung out helplessly on the coverlet, restlessly picking at the edge of the sheet. A frame was at the foot of the bed to hold the covers from the broken leg, a weight hanging from the foot of the bed to pull the leg straight. Stephen with his merry lips muttering strange words, crying out, from a face so bruised and bandaged that only the muttering lips and the cleft in the fine Challenger chin were recognizable. Stephen, moving his head from side to side in that strange monotonous way, with closed eyes, the motion of a lion or a leopard caged in the zoo padding back and forth in his cell! She stood and watched him, the tears flowing down her face.

Suddenly as she stood there, he cried out:

"Don't Sylvia! Don't touch that wheel! Can't you see we're on the edge of the cliff?" Then he flung his arms wildly out and half raised himself from the bed, falling back again with a moan.

The ward nurse sprang to hold him down and called to another nurse:

"This man will have to be strapped down. We can't have him thrashing around like that! He's probably slipped that bone out of place again. You better send for the house doctor to look him over. Where is the head nurse? She'll have to look after this."

Melissa stood there, shrinking against the wall out of the way as the doctor arrived and they began to work over Stephen, who tried to resist them. Poor Steve! Wild at their interference! He was all too evidently living over again the accident, and Melissa, watching, was getting illuminating side lights on what had happened. Steve! In a mess like that! Whisky flasks and the kind of girls that would be spoken to as her brother was speaking now! Steve, mixed up with people like that!

Her experiences of the day had somewhat prepared her to understand more than she would otherwise have done.

In the midst of this a nurse from another ward touched her on the arm and told her that Mrs. Hollister had sent word that they were going to the hotel now and she must come right away.

Melissa gasped and shook her head.

"Please tell her that I cannot come now. Tell her I must attend to telephoning my people. I will come to the hotel later if I find it possible," she said, with a quick relief that she had an excuse to get away from the Hollisters for a while at least. She had no desire for the "large evening" which had been suggested by Gene Hollister.

No one noticed her nor sent her away. She drew back in the corner almost out of sight behind the screen, but kept a fearsome watch on her brother. Oh, how was she going to tell her mother all about this? What had Steve to do with that Sylvia person, a girl who drank? "Sylvia, you're silly-drunk!" he cried out once. Had Steve been drinking too? Was that the cause of the accident?

She shuddered in her corner behind the screen.

But no, Steve's voice rang out again:

"I'm the only one in this outfit that isn't stewed! No, don't pass me that flask! I wouldn't touch a drop of the vile stuff. Jack, sit down! Don't you see the car is tipping! There she goes!—" and then a moan that was heart-rending.

They had finished strapping Steve to the bed. The doctor had administered some medicine, and only one nurse was left, straightening the bed clothes and putting everything in white order again. The nurse that had brought Melissa down the hall had gone. She was apparently forgotten. Standing on the other side of the screen, just at the head of her brother's bed, her back against the wall she wept silently, and watched him till he quieted down.

Across the aisle on the other side of the hall door the group around the dying bed turned suddenly away weeping, as the nurse drew a sheet up over the head of the bed, and hastily pushed the screen around the foot to make a better shelter.

The friends were drifting sorrowfully out into the hall now. The ward was very quiet. The patient just behind Melissa had his eyes closed. She gave a swift survey of the room, and saw they had averted their faces, those other patients who had to lie, sick and miserable, and know what was going on about them. Oh, what a terrible place was a hospital, thought Melissa, mopping her eyes with her wet handkerchief.

Steve had quieted down now, only a moan as he turned his head from side to side in that perpetual monotonous motion. A moan every time he faced the wall, keeping perfect rhythm with his turning. Melissa almost groaned aloud, and wished she had not come. What good was she doing here? How could she tell her mother how bad things were?

Then the head nurse came by and discovered her.

"Oh, my dear!" she said in her calm, matronly voice, "you can't stay here! Whoever let you come in?"

Melissa tried to stop her tears and steady her voice to answer.

"Isn't there some place I can sit down a little while?" she managed to ask between her sobs.

"Why, certainly, there is the visitors' room, down at the end of the corridor. You can sit there as long as you like. The doors of the hospital are usually closed to visitors at ten-thirty except in cases where patients are in a very critical condition and the friends have to stay all night. But you could go in there and sit for awhile till you feel like going home. Who are you? Is this patient a relative of yours? You're not the girl that was with him in the accident are you?" and Melissa caught an edge of contempt in her voice.

"Oh, no indeed!" said Melissa indignantly. "He's my brother! I don't know who was with him when he was hurt. I don't know anything about it. Would you mind telling me? I can't seem to find anybody who knows."

The head nurse led her out, down the hall to the reception room, but she could give her very little information. He had been brought in last night about half past two o'clock. It had been a wild drinking party she surmised because the other young man who was in the party had been dead drunk.

"Not *my brother?*" Melissa gasped out with a terrible question in her voice. "He *never* drinks!"

"Perhaps not," said the head nurse dryly as if she didn't believe that any young man did not drink nowadays, "but at least he was not under the influence of it. I understand there were two girls in the car and one of them jumped out just as the car went over the embankment. The other girl wasn't injured seriously, just some minor bruises and her people took her home this afternoon. Your brother got the worst of it for he was driving. They say he might have jumped and saved himself perhaps but he wouldn't leave his wheel. The other young man jumped, and being drunk of course fell limp and wasn't so badly hurt. Now, here is the room, and you can rest a little while, but if I were you I would go home pretty soon. It's getting late you know, and you can't do anybody any good by staying here. Your brother wouldn't know you were here. He may be several days like this."

"Oh," gasped Melissa forlornly, and then suddenly remembering her mother, "but I must telephone Mother. Is there a Long Distance phone in the building?"

The nurse gave her directions how to find it.

"Could you—just tell me—what I ought to tell Mother about Steve?" she asked like a little frightened child. "She will be terribly worried. She couldn't come herself because Father has been very ill and they don't dare tell him about it, and he would miss Mother and want to know why she had gone."

"Oh!" said the nurse looking her over swiftly, with that quick comprehension of nurses who are used to looking into other people's tragedies every day. "Well, you don't need to go into particulars then. Just tell her that he is doing as well as could be expected. He's holding his own so far of course, but it's hard to tell anything so soon. There's a concussion and a fractured leg, and plenty of bruises. He's got a lot to contend with, but so far there's no indication of internal injuries. Of course it's early yet to tell about that!"

Melissa's heart sank lower and lower.

"Will he be—out of this—this—this delirium by morning?" she asked shyly. She knew so pitifully little about illness.

"Probably not," said the nurse in a matter-of-fact tone. "It may last some days. Of course, he might develop fever and it might get worse. But I wouldn't worry—"

There was a sudden peremptory call for the head nurse and she vanished, leaving Melissa alone in a room with only one other occupant, a sad-faced woman sitting huddled in a willow rocker, sniffing and wiping her eyes occasionally.

"My girl's got a crisis comin' t'night!" she explained to Melissa who stood uncertainly, waiting to see if the head nurse would return. She wanted to ask her a few more questions before she telephoned her mother.

"Oh!" said Melissa a lump suddenly rising in her throat. Trouble, trouble, trouble! Every one was in trouble, everywhere! And they thought there was a God!

But the woman was eager to unburden herself. She had sat for a full half hour with no casual stranger in whom to confide. She was like a thing bottled up ready to burst.

"She's been a-layin' there in that bed fer nine days an' ain't knowed me," she went on, the tears readily accompanying her speech, "an' her with a little six month old baby what won't eat her food and cries day an' night! An' me past my seventies! I don't know how I'm agonta manage ef she's took. Iva was a good girl ef I do say so as raised her, even ef she was allus off ta the movies nights an' me ta tend the baby. But they say there's only just a chancet in a lifetime she'll come through."

"I'm sorry," said Melissa trying to turn away from more pain. She felt she had all of her own she could bear.

"She ain't ben lucky nohow," went on the garrulous voice meditatively. "When she was little I had all kindsa trouble with her. She come outta th' measles, only ta git whooping cough, an' the chicken-pox a month later, an' then she got runned over an' hed a broke rib an' a sprained fut, an' when she got jest so she cud he'p me a little she took ta goin' with this good-fer-nothin' Clip Fox, an' finally married him, an' after the baby was born he up an' died. Not to say he was any good ta her ef he'd lived. She hadta keep her job herself, ur she'd a starved. He never earned a cent an' when he did he kep' it hisself. He—"

"Excuse me!" said Melissa feeling that if she listened to another word she would either laugh or scream, "I've got to go and telephone. It's very important."

"Oh, that's all right," said the woman, "I'll tell ya the rest when ya come back. I'm gonta set up all night. They don't know how it'll turn, y'know."

"Oh, do they allow you to stay here all night?"

"How could they he'p it?" cackled the woman mirthlessly. "They couldn't put ya out in the street when yer only daughter was dyin', could they?"

Melissa shivered and hurried off down the hall resolved to try and find some other refuge than the guest-reception room if possible.

She did not venture toward the elevator. She had a feeling that she would rather get about herself. The elevator man would perhaps expect a tip, and she must not let a single cent go unnecessarily. So she stole down the stairs, floor after floor, three floors, to the office desk. But there was no one at the desk. Everything seemed to be shut up for the night.

Further search and inquiry developed a telephone booth, and after frantically trying to get connection with the house of Brady the head of which happened to be off hunting her sister Phyllis while the rest of his family attended the movies, Melissa finally resorted to a telegram.

"Arrived safely. Stephen sleeping. Can tell you more of his condition in morning. Don't worry. Melissa."

It seemed an unsatisfactory telegram when it was finished, but it had taken all her wits to compose it, and she was really relieved not to have to talk with her mother to-night, for it was certain she could tell nothing good about her brother from what she had so far seen, and her mother would be sure to worm it all out of her. Melissa was not good at hiding things, especially if she was troubled about them. Phyllis could keep things to herself if she thought it would do harm to tell them.

As she turned away from the telephone booth at last she was suddenly aware that she was overpoweringly hungry. She looked around for some one to tell her where to find a restaurant, but the elevator boy had gone off duty.

A glance outside showed wide lawns in every direction, with distant houses lighted, showing it was a residential section. She felt too tired to walk far and it would not do to get lost and perhaps not be allowed back in the hospital again. But what should she do? There did not seem to be a taxi in sight. She thought there were always plenty of taxis in the vicinity of hospitals. Well, she would have to go back upstairs and ask.

On the third floor she encountered a pleasant looking nurse carrying a glass of milk.

"Could you tell me where I can find a restaurant? I haven't had any supper, and I'm getting rather hungry," she asked wistfully.

The nurse paused and eyed her.

"A restaurant? There isn't such a thing nearer than down in the village and I doubt if it would be open at this hour. The hotel of course, but that's a long distance too. Are you here for the night?"

"Why, yes. I thought I'd sit in the waiting room, if nobody objected. I got here so late and I don't know where to find a lodging I could afford. If I just could get a cracker or two, or even a drink of water, I could go out early and get breakfast."

"There's plenty of ice water in the cooler around at the end of that corridor to the right, but you ought to have something else. How about this glass of milk? I saved it for my patient to take if she wanted it but she's gone to sleep and won't need it.

You can have it if you like. And—why I can get you some crackers. Just come down this way. You needn't say anything about it. We're not supposed to do this of course, but I can't see any harm. Nobody will care. Come."

Melissa followed her to a clean bare room like a kitchen; long bare tables, a great icebox, and a gas stove and sink. The nurse produced a box of crackers, and Melissa drank the milk and ate and felt refreshed.

"Sorry I can't give you a room to rest in," said the nurse reappearing for a moment just as Melissa finished her repast, "but that's against rules. But I brought you a pillow, and there's no one in the waiting room on this floor now. You can turn out the light and lie down on the couch for a while. Did you say you had some one on this floor sick?"

"Why no," said Melissa flushing guiltily, "My brother is up on the next floor, but I was walking up and met you. Perhaps I don't belong here. Should I go up to the next floor waiting room?"

"Oh, no, that's all right. Just go in here. This one is empty, and you might find a lot of gabbing people up there." Melissa remembering the queer old woman, thankfully walked into the darkness of the empty room and curled down on a humpy davenport with her pillow.

She thought she was tired enough to fall asleep at once, but instead she had to live over again the whole awful day. Those dreadful Hollisters! The terrible hour in the ward watching poor Steve! Even the poor old babbling woman and her erring daughter. What a troublous world it was. How it needed a God or some one to help. But it was out of the question to believe in a God in a world like this one.

She fell asleep at last wondering, fearfully, what the morrow would bring forth.

IT was nearly midnight when Phyllis walked in on her anxious mother, with Butcher Brady just behind her, his genial face in a broad grin.

"I told ya I'd find her all right," he said, wagging his head and beaming. "I just hadta drive up one street and down another a coupla times and there she was right on the sidewalk walking along as fast as she could."

"Walking!" said Mrs. Challenger lifting a white face, from which the anxiety had not yet faded. "Oh, Phyllis, my child! How frightened I have been! And what were you walking for at this time of night? Didn't you have money for carfare? I told you to be sure—"

"Yes, Mother," lilted Phyllis, "I had it, but I came on a bus from away up town, and it stopped only three blocks from here. I thought it was better to walk than hang around waiting for a car. There wasn't one in sight."

"But where have you been? *All day!* Phyllis how *could* you stay so long without sending any word?"

"I couldn't help it, Mother dear," said Phyllis, taking off her hat and sitting down wearily, "I tried to get Mr. Brady at eight o'clock to let him know I would be late, but they didn't answer. He says they were all out. Why, you see, Mother, I got some work to do, and the man said he would give me ten dollars if I would get it done to-night. It was thousands of circulars that had to be addressed and stamped and sealed and mailed, and I *just* got them all done. Is there anything to eat, Mother? I'm hungry as a bear. I didn't dare stop to get any dinner, I was afraid I wouldn't get done, and it was getting so late."

"Oh, my dear!" gasped her mother brushing away the quick tears. But Rosalie had already hurried into the kitchen and was back in a minute with a covered plate containing a nice warm dinner that she had set in the warming oven for her sister, and a glass of cold milk from the refrigerator.

Phyllis sat down and began to eat, while the others hovered near watching her, eager with questions. Even Butcher Brady lingered by the door wistfully, eager as the rest.

"But how did you get work, Phyllis?" asked the mother, "Was it one of our friends who gave it—?"

"No, Mother," said Phyllis setting down her glass of milk, "It was just a man, a stranger. His name is Lucius Brown, Incorporated. You see, I had a plan when I left this morning. I had decided to take a street and just go into every place of business and ask for the proprietor, and ask if there was any-thing at all he needed done, even if it was only for a day."

"What an idea, child!"

"Well, there wasn't apparently any use in trying for a regu-lar job. I'd answered all the advertisements I found, and asked all the people I knew that would have any likelihood of need-ing a helper. I started away up town because I had seen a no-tice in a window on that street, and I thought perhaps they still wanted some one, but I found it was filled, of course."

"Poor child!" murmured Mrs. Challenger.

"So then I started going into every place, up one side of the block," went on Phyllis spreading the bread that Rosalie brought her. "There was a baker and confectioner, a drug store, a wholesale toy place, a news agency, a second hand place, a cheap restaurant—"

"Oh, Phyllis. *Not* a place like that!"

"Sure, Mother, I'd take anything that wasn't actually low down. Well, and then I came to this place. A kind of a stationer's, with dusty pencils and erasers in the window. I almost didn't go in, it seemed such a kind of a dusty useless little place. But I'd vowed to try every place on the block so I went.

"There was a customer in there and a young man waiting on him to fountain pens. I asked for the proprietor and he nodded toward the back of the store. Mr. Brown was at the telephone talking so I went back and stood in front of the desk waiting.

"I could see he was worried, and very impatient with the people on the wire, and he looked at me as if he would bite me. I almost turned and ran. But just then he turned to me and snapped:

"'What do *you* want? Can't you see I'm busy?'

"'I'll wait,' I said.

"'What do you *want?*' he snapped again just like a dog barking.

"It didn't seem worth while but I said my little speech just to have it over with: 'I've come in to see if you've got anything at all I could do for you to-day. I've got to earn some money and I'll work by the day.'

"He grunted and looked me up and down.

"'Can you write?' he asked and shoved a desk pen and pad at me.

"'Of course,' I said.

"'Well, write down your name and address.'

"'So I wrote it.

"'That'll do,' he snapped, 'When can you go to work?'

"'Now,' I said.

"'Will you last out the day?'

"'I certainly will,' I said.

"'Who are you?' he asked looking me through as if his eyes were gimlets. 'Did you ever work before?'

"I said I was the daughter of a university professor and had done a lot of his secretarial work, and he was sick and I had to earn some money right away. I said I would like to be paid by the day if possible.

"He slammed up the receiver and said: 'All right. I'll give you ten dollars if you'll get every one of those circulars addressed and stamped and sealed and in the mail before midnight to-night. I was trying to get the agency for a stenographer, but they are so slow I can't wait.'

"There was an awful stack of them and I hadn't an idea how long it would take to do it but I said I'd do my best, and I went right to work. Of course I was a little slow at first, but I'd write addresses till my hand ached and then I would fold and put in envelopes awhile, and so I managed, but I just got the last one finished about half an hour ago."

"Didn't you have any lunch, Sister?" asked Rosalie aghast.

"Yes," said Phyllis, "I had two sandwiches in my hand bag, and I ran down to the corner and got an apple to eat with them. That was all the time I could spare. I was afraid I wouldn't get them done."

"And did he pay you, Sister?"

"Yes. Here's the ten dollar bill. He came in at half past ten and gave it to me. He said I was a first rate worker, and if I didn't have anything else by that time I might come back Monday. He might have more work for me."

"Ten whole dollars in a day!" said Rosalie with shining eyes, "that's great, Phyllie dear!"

"She's some business woman!" said Brady beaming on her. "Well, I guess I better be getting along or my missis will be wondering what's got me. Goodnight. I hope ye hear good news of yer son in the morning."

Mrs. Challenger looked up, suddenly anxious again.

"Oh, but isn't it strange that we haven't had word from Melissa yet? How many miles did you say it was?"

"Oh, she likely wouldn't get there till near midnight," hazarded the butcher cheerily, and mebbe the telegraph offices were all shut up.

They discussed Melissa and her journey after Brady had left, and Phyllis tried to cheer her mother.

"I don't see why you're so anxious, Mother," she said as she finished the last bite of her supper. "Melissa has good sense. What would you have her do? Turn down a perfectly good chance to go to Steve when it didn't cost her a cent? You know you would have had her go if you had had it to decide. You said yourself you couldn't get away without telling Father all about it and that wouldn't be so good. These people must be nice kind people to stop and suggest taking her. Having a son in that college of course they're sort of nice people I suppose."

"Oh, I suppose so," sighed Mrs. Challenger. "But there are so many automobile accidents these days."

"Well, don't think about that. Nothing will likely happen to Lissa. Think how many people go in automobiles every day and don't ever get hurt. It's just because you are not used to having one. Why you know if we had one you wouldn't think anything of it. Lissa and I would both likely be driving everywhere."

"Well, it's all a terribly anxious time," murmured the weary mother. "You going off to work till midnight in a store with two strange men, and Lissa going miles away with strangers in a strange car. How do we know that she hasn't been kidnaped?"

Phyllis laughed.

"My eye! What would they kidnap Lissa for? They never do that unless there's money somewhere. No, not even when the girl is as pretty as Lissa. Cheer up, Mumsy! You don't make matters any better by worrying over an accident that may never happen. As for me, my boss has grizzly gray hair and an old wife, and the salesman in the dusty front of the store has a girl without any chin. She runs in from the ten cent store around the corner where she works, to see him at noon. Now, come, let's get to bed. To-morrow's on the way."

"Gee!" said Bob, out of the darkness of his bedroom, after they thought he was asleep, "Gee, Phyl, you're great. Ten bucks in one day! Some sister, I'll say!"

The next morning was very hard for Mrs. Challenger. There was nothing she could do about their situation, no one she could think of further to go and see. Her soul shrank in horror from going again to those five men whom she had failed to meet yesterday. It was all foolishness anyway. They were not intimate friends. Why should they be responsible for mere acquaintances? There was nothing else she could do. She was shut up to prayer. If God couldn't do something they would all have to go to the poorhouse. They couldn't expect Phyllis to earn ten dollars every day.

She could not settle to anything, even her desolate kind of prayer, until she heard from Melissa. She walked the floor from window to door and back again watching for a telegram or for the butcher's boy to summon her to the telephone. And finally when Melissa's message did come it brought her no comfort, only anxiety longer drawn out.

Phyllis had departed to seek for another day's work, promising, however, not to stay all day without sending some kind of word. Mrs. Challenger did not intend to go to the hospital. She had told her husband that she had some things to do that would keep her at home to-day, thinking it possible that she might have to go to Stephen after all, and wanting to pave the way for a brief absence if it became necessary.

The telegram came about ten o'clock. The boy had been wandering around the city hunting for the right place, because Melissa had made a mistake in the street number. That was another thing to be anxious about. Suppose Melissa sent another message, perhaps it too would be delayed. And so the morning passed in anxious waiting. Once she saw a newsboy pass and summoned him, spending a precious two cents for a paper, and carefully studying the suburban "For Rent" advertisements, then sighing to think that even if she could find a reasonably cheap place in the outskirts of the city where would the money come from to pay the rent, move their piti-fully few belongings, and get their other things out of stor-age? Even ten dollars a day now and then wouldn't do all that.

The morning passed in anxiety with no further message from Melissa. The mother dared not go out of the house for a moment lest one would come while she was gone and she would miss it. She tried to understand why Melissa should be so silent. Surely she would understand how anxious they were. She conjured all sorts of reasons why no news had come. She could no longer worry lest her eldest daughter was kidnaped, for her first message had allayed that trouble. But as the hours dragged by, she grew fairly frantic.

She had done a little cooking early with a view to being ready for a possible visit to Steve, but there was very little else in the bare little house that she could do beyond making the beds and sweeping and dusting a little.

At last she went to her room, locked the door and knelt down, with a feeling that now she must have it out with God somehow. If He had it in his power to set the life of the Chal-lengers into smoother grooves and there was anything He was waiting for her to do—for them to do—it was time it was made clear. She was going to make a business of praying. It was the last thing left her. True she came to it with little faith. She had an inward conviction that her prayers were about as worthless as if she were to write her requests on a piece of paper and go and lay them on some wealthy indiffer-ent man's front door steps.

However, she went into her room and not being willing to have Bob or Rosalie or Phyllis perhaps come home unexpect-edly and find her praying in the daytime, she locked her door. Praying at night was of course customary, in the dark by one's bedside, but praying in the daytime was out of the regu-lar order of things, making almost too much of prayer, put-ting one's self in a class with fanatics. Mary Challenger did not analyze her feeling. She merely locked the door, and knelt down. Then she tried to think of some new and convincing argument to put up before the throne in behalf of her suffering family.

It was strange how her mind wandered. "Oh, God—" she said, and that was as far as she would get in her petition. "Oh, God—" and her mind would wander off, trying to think of something more that she herself could do. Of course it wouldn't be right to trouble a God with what one could do for one's self. Perhaps she might pray that God would help her to think of some one to go to who would help her out of her difficulty. And her fertile brain would begin at the beginning of all their long list of friends of the years who might possibly do something if they knew the situation. But that was just the crux of the matter. She and Father didn't want their friends to know their desperate situation. They didn't want to be objects of charity. Oh, if there was just some one, a near relative, loving, kind, with plenty of money! She wouldn't mind humbling herself to ask such a one. Surely,— there must be something she could do—!

So her mind wandered from the throne; so she puzzled over her perplexities.

She had not really prayed yet, although she had knelt beside her bed for a long time, when she heard a knock at the door. The telegram at last! Perhaps this was part of the answer to her prayer, she thought as she hurried down the stairs.

Her hand trembled as she opened her purse to pay the messenger boy. It trembled so that she could scarcely sign for the telegram, and she tore it jaggedly across when she opened it she was so agitated.

She read it and then looked blankly at it. What more did it tell than she already knew? How could she possibly know what to do from this? How could Melissa be so incoherent, so unsatisfactory! If it had only been Phyllis now she would have put the situation clearly. It was a day letter. It read:

Stephen still under opiates. Leg had to be reset. Doctor says no immediate danger. Not necessary for you to come yet. He will need you more later when recovering. Expect me to-morrow afternoon about three.

It had been a triumph of careful thought, that telegram, wrought out with painstaking mathematical precision during lucid intervals in that awful night curled up on the short willow couch in the visitor's room of the hospital. How not to say the things that would worry her mother. How to tell some of the truth and not let her mother understand that she could not herself find out the whole truth about Steve's condition, these were some of her problems, and to an unaccustomed mind they presented a mountain of difficulty. Melissa was one who had always been sheltered and had questions decided for her. Phyllis had not been that way. She had been much with her father, helping him in his work, and had learned to make quick decisions. Phyllis would have worded that telegram in a trice, and made it both soothing and true. But it was a load off of Melissa's mind when it was sent off.

It became however a load on her mother's mind when it was received. Stephen her eldest born lying under opiates, unable to know any one, and she not beside him to watch! It made her heart writhe to think of it. And then, why, there hadn't been any answer to her prayer after all. Everything was just a blank wall as it had been all along. She had asked— Why! What *had* she asked? Had she really asked anything at all?

A look of determination went over her face. She would carry this thing through. She would go back again to her knees and really pray, not just let her mind wander.

So back she went and locked her door.

"Oh, God," she prayed, "Thou seest that we are in terrible trouble." She spread her telegram out on the bed and wept bitter tears upon it. "My boy! My boy! Oh, save my boy and help him to get well. Give us back our money, and make us find a nice home in the country where John can get well."

She paused for lack of definite material and then went on: "I'm going out now to see Mr. Mandell. I've just thought of him. He owes John a thousand dollars, and if he knew how we needed it he might pay it now. He could go out and borrow it. I know John didn't want to press him, but please make it right for me to go to him, and please make him give it to me to-day. I'm going out to look at that suburban house that was advertised too. Won't you please bless my efforts, and make things come right. It's all I know to do."

After a few earnest tears she rose from her knees and made herself ready.

She walked away with a brisk step. She had decided on a plan and asked God's blessing upon it. Things ought to be different now if prayers were of avail at any time.

She decided that yesterday's action was a failure because she had not followed up anything after one discouragement. When, therefore she arrived at J. P. Mandell's house and found it closed with a sign for sale on the door, she did not give up. She went to the next door neighbor and found that Mr. Mandell had moved. The neighbor did not know the exact address, but there was the postman, he might be able to tell. Mrs. Challenger tried the postman, and received directions to a far suburb of the city, a rather common, cheap suburb she had always considered it, but perhaps Mr. Mandell did not have her standards of things. So she took a slow trolley line and eventually arrived at the suburb, only to find that Mr. Mandell had been taken very ill with fever, and only a few moments before her arrival had been taken in an ambulance to the hospital. The kindly neighbor, who was caring for the children while Mrs. Mandell accompanied her husband to the hospital, confided in the stranger that Mr. Mandell had lost everything in the bank crash last week, and they all thought that was the cause of his sudden illness.

"Ain't it awful?" finished the confiding neighbor, and Mrs. Challenger with sudden smarting tears owned that it was awful indeed, and beat a hasty retreat, a lump of dismay in her throat, and bewilderment in her eyes. Had God then failed her again? She had started out so confidently, after having asked His blessing. What more could she have done? Surely He had promised, hadn't He, to answer prayers? How could He expect her to have faith in Him if He treated her like that! Not that she put these thoughts into words, even to herself, but they ran in an undertone in her mind, and kept her stirred up.

It was after three o'clock when she reached home, having eaten nothing except the cracker she had carried with her in her hand bag.

She stopped at Brady's to find out if he had seen anything of Melissa. She had not meant to be so late coming home. She wanted to be sure to be there when Melissa arrived. But Brady said he had kept a watch out for her and that she had not arrived.

He handed her a small package as she left.

"Take that home with ya," he said. "It's just a bit of veal cutlet I had left on me hands. You might as well have it as save it over till to-morrow."

"Oh, Mr. Brady!" protested Mary Challenger. "You mustn't! You really mustn't! I'll take this only on condition that you keep account of what we've had and it shall be all paid, every cent, as soon as we get our money."

"That's all right, Mrs. Challenger! Anything you like. Sure! Only don't worry about paying till you are easy in money."

She hurried to the house, but there was no sign of Melissa. Bob of course was on his paper route by this time, and Rosalie was to care for that baby again for two hours, so she wouldn't be home. Phyllis? Perhaps she had found another bit of work.

Mrs. Challenger sighed as she took off her things, and prepared to set the table and get things ready for dinner. The children would all be hungry and Melissa would be here presently.

But as she worked the tears kept coming continually. She felt she had a real grievance against God. Why should He choose them, the Challengers, for all this to happen to? They had always been good church-going, well-behaved people, God-fearing, moral. How could He have any better people than they were? The children were well brought up, not like the modern girls and boys of to-day. Really, it didn't seem fair. They deserved better treatment. Perhaps after all there wasn't any God. Perhaps it was even as Melissa had suggested, and her college professors believed. It began to look that way. What real ground had they ever had anyway to believe in a God who cared for individuals and noticed trifles, other than that their forefathers had trusted in Him?

These thoughts ran wildly around in her mind until she was in a feverish state of irritation.

Phyllis came at half past six, having earned three dollars for her day, waiting on the table at a little tea room where one of the waitresses had been suddenly taken sick.

"Oh, Phyllis!" her mother reproached.

Rosalie and Bob came in together, Bob hungry and noisy, Rosalie shining and sweet, displaying another fifty cents for the family coffer.

But where was Melissa?

At seven o'clock they sat down to dinner. They simply could not wait any longer for Melissa. Perhaps she would come before they were through.

"And anyhow, Mother," Phyllis reminded, "you can't tell but you might have to start right back on the next train after she gets here. You ought to be ready to go. You'll have to eat something, and we're all half starved."

So they sat down. But Mary Challenger could hardly make herself swallow a mouthful of the delicious food. She was by this time a victim of her own tormented mind.

Things were bad enough, but if one couldn't feel that there was a God comfortably up in His heaven, and all would eventually be right with the world, what was the use of trying to go on living any longer?

The evening wore on and still Melissa did not come.

Brady came in to inquire about the son, and hearing that his sister had not yet arrived, looked serious and asked what time it was. He tried to bluff it off by saying they likely had a flat tire; tried to joke a little, and then went off again, saying they must remember to call him if they needed any help, but they needn't worry, the young man had his "mom" with him, and Miss Melissa would be all right even if they did have to stay somewhere overnight.

By this time Mary Challenger was in despair. She went with white face and set lips to her room and locked the door again. The children could hear her crying.

Rosalie crept softly into the closet and knelt down. Phyllis went into the kitchen and looked out into the dark back alley, and by and by, Bob came out and got a drink at the sink. Then he fussed with the electric light turning it off and on, and eyeing his sister's back. At last he said:

"Aw, gee! Why'n't we all pray? Rosy got a beefsteak, why couldn't we get something too?"

Phyllis was silent for a moment, still looking out of the window, then she said in a serious voice:

"I'm not so sure that we have any right to ask for things. We've never paid any attention to God before. It doesn't seem reasonable. We have no real claim—that is—does it seem quite fair? We don't even go to church nowadays. I haven't had anything fit to wear to church in a long time."

"Gee! I go ta Boy Scouts when I get home from school in time, an' that's in the basement of a church!" mused Bob.

Phyllis eyed him thoughtfully.

"Somehow that doesn't seem to me to count," she said at last. "You go just for your own fun don't you? You don't go to worship God, or thank Him, or anything, do you?"

"We have God in our opening exercises sometimes. There's usually a prayer, ur the Lord's prayer, anyhow."

"But that's not *you* paying any attention to God, is it? You're usually thinking about other things, aren't you?"

"I s'pose so," admitted Bob, reluctantly. "Gee! Whaddaya have ta do anyway? Dya havta *work* fer the things ya pray for? What's the use o' prayin' for them then? Don't He *give* ya things?"

"Well, I don't know much about God," said Phyllis thoughtfully. "Yes, I suppose He gives things—if He answers at all—that's not what I mean. Take it as if He was a man. Take Mr. Brady for instance. Suppose you'd been too busy to go that errand for him. Suppose you'd wanted to play ball instead. Suppose you never went near him, and didn't smile back when he said good morning. Suppose you'd just simply paid no attention to his kindness at all. You wouldn't feel just like going and asking him for a hundred dollars, would you?"

Bob stood thoughtfully grinding his heel into a crack of the kitchen floor.

"No, I 'spose not," he reluctantly admitted at last, "But say, if Mother was awful sick, and going ta die ef I couldn't get a hundred dollars to bring the right doctor to her, you bet I'd go ask him anyhow. I'd tell him I was awful sore at myself fer the way I'd treated him, an' I oughtta be kicked all around the place, an' I wouldn't ever act that way again. I'd tell him I'd be his errand boy, and to just whatever he wanted done. I'd tell him I knew I hadn't any right to ask him a favor, the way I'd treated him, but wouldn't he just help me out fer Mother's sake, 'cause he was the only one I knew ta go ta."

Phyllis looked at him thoughtfully.

"That's what I mean," she said. "You understand. You might try that, if you mean it, it wouldn't do any good just to *say* it if you didn't mean it, because if He's a God He would know you were faking."

"Oh, sure!" said Bob dropping his eyes in embarrassment. "But you couldn't exactly ask God 'for Mother's sake' could you, Bob? Mother hasn't paid much attention to God either. At least I never heard her say much about it."

Bob looked at her aghast, then his face suddenly brightened.

"Say, what's that ya say after baby-prayers? 'Fer Jesus' sake.' Wouldn't that be all right?"

"Why, yes, I suppose it would," said Phyllis slowly. "Most prayers do end something like that. But there you are again. We've never paid any attention to Jesus either, except just sing a few hymns with His name in them."

"Aw, Gee! Ain't He supposed ta love everybody? Didn't He die fer the whole world? He wouldn't be like that, would He?"

"He died for the world," reasoned Phyllis, "but it's not supposed to count unless you do something about it. You've got to *accept* it, or *some*thing. I don't know just what it is."

"I know," said Bob with a swagger, "I went to Bible School last summer for a whole week when I was up in the country with Mick. It's John three sixteen."

"John three sixteen! What on earth do you mean, Bob Challenger?"

"Ho! Don'tcha know what John three sixteen is? It's 'God so loved the world that He gave His only begotten Son, that whosoever believeth on Him, should not perish, but have everlasting life.' Yer just supposed ta *b'lieve* an' then yer *in* somehow. They explained it all out."

"But, do you believe? Are you sure you do it in the way they mean?"

"Sure, I b'lieve. Whaddaya think I am? A heathen? There ain't any special *way* ta do it. Ya just take it at what it says."

"*What* do you believe?" asked his sister wonderingly.

"Why, I b'lieve God's Son died on the cross ta pay fer my sin. Ain't that what it says? I know I haven't been doin' much about it lately, but I gave my name at that Bible School that I wanted ta, and b'lieve me I'm a gonta hereafter. I guess that gives me my right, don't it? An' gee whiz! I'm gonta pray fer my mother whether you do ur not! I'm gonta pray fer a home an' money enough ta live on, an' fer Lissa ta come home safe, and fer Steve ta get well, an' fer dad ta come back, an' a lotta other things. *Good night!* What's the use lettin' things go like this when we gotta Heavenly Father?"

Bob suddenly stamped out of the kitchen and up to his room, thumped around noisily for a minute or two, then Phyllis, still standing by the window where he had left her, heard his door shut, and all was very still. Was Bob Challenger having audience with the King of Heaven? Who could tell?

On her knees in the room next to her little son's, knelt Mary Challenger, weeping her heart out now, sobbing incoherent sentences into the ear of the Almighty.

"I've reached the end . . . !" she told God, "I've done my best, and it didn't do any good! . . . I'm utterly helpless! If you can't help we'll have to die! We'll *all* have to die! We're helpless! Utterly helpless! Ruined! Undone! My boy Steve! Oh, don't let him die! My precious little Lissa! Don't let anything awful have happened to her. O, God! I've sinned! I haven't taught her to believe in you. I thought I had, but I hadn't. She said awful things about you I know, but forgive her, Lord. Don't punish her for it. It was my fault. O God, forgive me! I am a sinner! O God, my poor husband! My poor children! We have lost everything! We have no home! There is no chance for John ever to get well unless you do something for us! O, God, I am at the end of myself! *I give up!* Please do something! I must trust everything to you. If you don't help we perish! O God! Hear my cry! Out of the depths of despair I cry!"

And between every cry, she listened, listened, for the sound of a car that did not come. Melissa, dear, pretty, proud little scatter-brained Melissa, out somewhere alone in the dark and the night with strangers!

MELISSA awoke from her night on the hard wicker couch in the hospital reception room, stiff and sore. Though she had her coat on she was chilled to the bone. Her dress was crumpled, her hair was tumbled about her face, and she felt sticky and dirty.

She awoke to the smell of antiseptics, to the sound of the ambulance gong, to the sight of a stretcher being borne through the hall to the operating room, and a glimpse of a wan frightened face.

She sat up quickly and gazed about her half dazed. Then a nurse hurrying along the hall aroused her to a sense of her whereabouts.

She put her hands up to her hair and tried to locate her hair pins. While she was doing it a handsome young interne put his head in at the door and smiled familiarly at her.

"Hello, Kid! It's morning, didn't you know it? Been there all night? Rocky bed you had. Cheer up, this is another day!"

She resented the tone of familiarity, but somehow his voice did cheer her as he went on his way. After all she had nothing to be so haughty about. Here she was sleeping like a young bum in a public waiting room. Why should he think she was any better than anybody else? Well, perhaps, she wasn't. She had never had such a thought before, she a Challenger, "that pretty Challenger girl" people called her sometimes. But here she was dragging the proud Challenger name down to the common walks of life, her brother in a hospital ward, and she sitting up all night out in the open as it were.

She went to the wash room and bathed her face, combed her hair and smoothed out her crumpled garments. Then she slipped up to the next floor, and tried to get a glimpse of Steve. But there was a screen close around Steve's bed and groans were coming from behind it. She could see the white skirts of the nurse now and then, and her rubber-soled feet beneath the screen, but she could not see her brother. She hovered anxiously near the door till the head nurse came and shooed her severely away, the day head nurse, not the one she had seen last night. She tried to find out something but was only told that the doctor had not made his rounds yet, and no information was available. After she had gone and Melissa was walking slowly toward the waiting room again she met another nurse who smiled and volunteered to find out for her what kind of a night her brother has passed. But she came back a few minutes later with the news that he had been very delirious all night, and his condition was little different from yesterday.

With a heavy heart Melissa decided to go out and hunt something to eat.

The brisk air of the morning brought a faint color to her cheeks, but she found that her limbs were trembling under her. She had never spent a wakeful night like last night in her life, and she did not know what to make of herself, she felt so wretched.

It was a long walk down to the village, almost a mile, Melissa judged, perhaps more. She found a little restaurant and ate a frugal breakfast of toast and coffee. She dared not spend much. It frightened her to see how fast her two dollars were fading away, and she must telegraph this morning as soon as she could see the doctor.

She went into a grocery store and purchased a box of crackers, two oranges and a small piece of cheese. These, she calculated, ought to get her through the day, with economy, so that she would not have to come down to the village again. She wanted to keep within her two dollars if possible.

The day stretched ahead of her as a long weary way full of anxiety. Oh, what should she do about Steve? Perhaps she should tell her mother to come at once in spite of what the nurse said about waiting till he would know her. What if Steve should die and no one there but herself!

She thought of the forlorn little bed yesterday, with the dying man, and the group of weeping relatives. Would she be standing so, alone and weeping, by Steve before the day passed? She shuddered. She was afraid of death. It had never touched her before, save through a schoolmate to whose funeral the class had gone in a body. She had wanted to stay away, but was ashamed. She had shrunk behind the others, persistently avoiding a glimpse of the casket, telling her mates that she wanted to remember Frances as she was when she was alive. She had never looked upon a dead face. It would be terrible to look at a dead face of one she loved. Her own brother! Poor Steve! And they hadn't been able to send him the clothes he needed to go to a dance! Such fantastic things went through her mind.

The front entrance of the hospital was full of people when she got back. Visitors' hours had started. She shrank back and hated to pass people as she crossed the crowded corridor to the stairs. Every seat was full and some people were standing. They stared at her sadly, every one with a tragedy upstairs somewhere. She hated it all that she should be classed with these worried, sorrowful people. There was a little sick baby with its head and shoulders strapped in a cast, wailing pitifully, waiting for the baby clinic. Sorrow, sorrow, sorrow! Everywhere trouble. It really wasn't at all the pleasant world she had always thought. How could people stand it to have sorrow and sickness and death always walking about among them? Why hadn't some scientist invented something that would stop death, stop trouble? They couldn't do it, that was it. Why! Scientists weren't any more infallible than religionists. She had never realized that before. Ever since her year at college she had come to feel that scientists were the highest word in everything. They dared to fling down God and the Bible, yet they couldn't stop death, nor all sickness, nor sorrow. They couldn't do a thing about sorrow. They could only tell you to have a good time while life lasted, but how could you when those you loved were in pain, were perhaps going to die?

Of course, some might tell you not to love anybody, just look out for yourself, develop your own personality, see how great you could become, and all that sort of bunk; but that didn't get you anywhere either. Might as well be a Bolshevist and be done with it.

Wearily she climbed the stairs.

And now she found that she could get a glimpse of Stephen behind his screen. It was visitors' hours and they would allow her to peek at him through just a small aperture.

There he lay swathed in his bandages, turning his head incessantly as yesterday, moaning and crying out. Muttering words she could not understand, with an occasional lucid word about the car, or a call to Sylvia. How could she tell her mother about that Sylvia?

She ventured to ask one of the nurses if they knew Sylvia, but they shook their heads. Later in the day one nodded. Yes, she knew who she was. A 'college widow' some of the girls called her. Melissa wondered just what that meant. She could see it was a term of opprobrium. She wondered if perhaps she ought to hunt her up and question her, be able to tell the family about her. Then she shrank from that, and decided against it.

Once, wandering about the hospital halls because she just could not sit still any longer, she came into the private hall, and passing a door saw Mrs. Hollister in a loud purple, variegated, knit dress, sitting placidly in a big chair beside a bed in which lay a slimmer edition of Gene Hollister, only with a more conceited tilt to his nose than the older brother boasted.

She averted her gaze at once, hoping to escape notice and passed quickly on down the hall, but Mrs. Hollister had seen her, and came paddling out after her.

"Miss Challenger!" she called. "Do come back and see my poor boy a little while. Jack's fairly frantic with having to lie still so long. He wants to see you."

She tried to excuse herself on the ground that she must hurry down and try to waylay the doctor, but Mrs. Hollister assured her that she would get hold of no doctor at this hour, and insistently drew her back.

Melissa could think of only one thing as she entered the room, and that was that the nurse had said that Jack Hollister had been dead drunk when he was brought into the hospital. She lifted her big blue eyes seriously to his face, and had to own that he was strikingly good looking. A clear pallor over a face that knew its own best points, dark hair that curled engagingly, great blue eyes that dared any impudence and got away with it.

He held out a slim graceful hand and grasped her unwilling one, then looked her impertinently in the eyes.

"Say, the Challengers are all good-lookers, aren't they?" he said. "Isn't she a peach, Mater? Why didn't you think to bring her up here before? What's your name? Melissa? Say! That's an odd one. I'll call you Meliss, how's that? I want a name all my own, see? Got any boy friend back home that calls you Meliss? Sit down on the edge of the bed, Baby-girl, and hold my hand a while. I feel better already. Say, what was the matter with Steve Challenger? He never told us what a little beaut his sister was! Sit down, Treasure. We'll have a great old time. You certainly are a pippin! Don't be afraid. Sit down!"

But Melissa, wide-eyed, shrank far away from the bed, her color high, her heart beating angrily. This was the same kind of thing that the older brother did, only a shade worse. How could she get out of here without angering the family? For she must go home with them to-morrow. How she dreaded it!

"I really can't stay," she said in a frightened little voice. "My brother is worse, I think, this morning. I must go right back. You will excuse me please if I hurry!"

But Mother Hollister had bulked herself in the doorway, and an exit was not an easy matter to negotiate, unless she simply thrust her aside.

"Oh, Steve'll be all right," said the young man gayly. "He's tough. He'll pull through. Steve's one of our great athletes. You don't kill him in a hurry. I asked the doc this morning about him. He said he was holding his own all right. You don't need to hold his hand, Treasure. He'll pull through. Anyhow he doesn't know anybody. The nurse told me so. He's only getting his for being such a fool as to stick by an old machine instead of getting out as I did while the getting was good. That machine's insured, and there won't be any trouble about that. Barney's glad it happened. He says his dad'll come across now with a new one, and that was what he wanted. He's been lending it to everybody in the hope of getting it crippled. His dad is kind of close you know, but he'll have to come across now. The only trouble is we're afraid of Steve. He's so darned honest he'll maybe blab that he was driving it, and make a mess with the insurance company. Barney is pulling all ways to get the thing through while Steve's delirious so they can't get his testimony."

Melissa stood spellbound listening, afraid to ask questions, afraid to stay, afraid to go.

"Aw, come on and sit down by me just a little while, Meliss," pleaded the young man with the caressing tone that got so many girls. "Meliss, Meliss, give me a kiss! There, I've made some poetry out of your name. Come over here and let's try it. Oh, don't mind the Mater, she's used to petting. Come on and kiss me Meliss—"

But Melissa had fled, her cheeks flaming, her frightened heart beating wildly. What kind of a terrible family was this anyway? And *must* she go home with them to-morrow? How was she ever to face that mother again? But of course she would have to. She would keep carefully out of sight till it came time to leave, and she would manage to sit with the mother, and then she would explain how sick her brother was, and apologize for hurrying away.

The day held no respite for Melissa.

The doctor, when she at last got audience with him, had very little encouragement to give. He said that her brother was very ill indeed, that he had a great deal to contend with. He could not tell yet how serious the concussion would be. He looked her steadily, gravely in the eyes, with a kind of pity for her worn young face, but no time to talk about it. He agreed with the nurse, after he had heard the story, that there was no need to bring her mother away from her sick husband immediately, perhaps in a day or two, and then he looked at his watch, and hurried off to an appointment of life and death, somewhere else.

Melissa had a feeling when he left that she should run right quickly home and send her mother back with all dispatch, yet there in her way stood the lack of money. What a barrier the lack of money could be! She must go home to-morrow with those awful Hollisters just to keep from spending Mr. Brady's money. It crackled in her breast and seemed a shield from many an alarm, but yet she must not spend it unless she had to, and at present she did not have to.

She went down to the second floor visitors' room and ate her crackers and cheese in a sheltered corner where she could not be seen from the hall. She scuttled here and there out of sight like a white little lost soul all the afternoon, only hovering now and again near the door where her brother lay, tossing his head and going over and over the same monotonous murmur. She felt that she would never again be able to forget the awfulness of that unearthly chant.

The nurses grew accustomed to her standing like a little shadow near the door. They ceased to shoo her off. They even smiled a hurried pity as they passed, and one of them called her into the diet kitchen and gave her a tray.

"There, eat that," she said in a whisper, "and don't say anything to anybody. The woman it was meant for had to be hurried down to the operating room. She won't be able to eat it. But it was all ordered so nobody is any worse off, and you look as if you need it."

Melissa smiled her wan thanks, and slipped into the diet kitchen. But she had little appetite to eat the delicious soup, the nice brown chop and baked potato, the delicate custard that were on the inviting tray. It seemed as if her heart would always be hearing now the echo of that awful monotone in her brother's voice that sounded so lost and despairing.

The day wore away, and the night came at last, with still no change in Stephen's condition.

When she caught a glimpse of Gene Hollister coming to hunt her, Melissa slid out on the fire escape and stood in the shadow for a long time. She wanted no "large evenings." All she asked was to be let alone until time to go home. Later she got a panic lest perhaps he had been summoning her to start at once, but when she ventured out into the hall again the head nurse beckoned her and said a gentleman had left a message for her. She must be at the front entrance to-morrow morning at half past ten ready to go if she wanted to drive back home with him.

Melissa caught her breath with relief. But, half past ten! That was two hours later than he had said at first. That would bring them home later. But surely Mother would understand that one couldn't always be sure just how long it would take to drive anywhere.

The kind nurse on the second floor got her a pillow again that night and gave her a comforting little smile.

"You know it always seems a lot worse than it sometimes is when a man gets out of his head. Some people get delirious pretty easy. I was asking the nurse up there about your brother. Challenger, you said the name was, didn't you? Well, I remembered it because it was such an unusual name. And she said there wasn't anything to be alarmed about yet. He would likely be this way for several days yet. If I was you I would get a good sleep to-night and not worry. You're going home to-morrow, aren't you? Well, just rest up. Tell you what I'll do. I'll be up on that floor a couple of times during the night to get milk for my patients because our ice box has got something the matter with it and won't work. I'll just look in on him, and if there's any change at all I'll come down and let you know."

Melissa thanked her with a wan smile and lay down with a feeling that somebody else had taken a little corner of the burden from her heavy heart.

She awoke late for it was a cloudy morning, with a drizzly rain beginning. She felt very shabby to go on a journey in the dress and coat she had slept in, but she had no other choice. And just a little before ten o'clock she stole to the door of the men's ward and told the nurse that she was leaving. Couldn't she come in for just a minute and stand beside her brother?

The nurse let her come in behind the screen and she laid a trembling, cool hand on his hot one. It was the nearest to a caress she could give him, for forehead and cheeks were pretty well swathed in bandages. But he flung it off roughly.

"You let me alone!" he said hoarsely. "Can't you see I've got to drive this car? If you touch my hand again while it's on this wheel I'll have to stop and tie you up. And I can do it too, don't you forget it, you little silly fool! For heaven's sake, can this mush!"

Melissa drew away with a little catch of a sob in her throat, and the nurse drew her out into the hall compassionately. "Don't you feel bad about that," she said. "He thinks you're some one else. His mind's on that accident, you can see. He felt responsible for that car. If those insurance people want evidence that he was perfectly sober when the accident occurred I think I can give it. I've heard enough to know pretty well how it all happened."

"Oh," said Melissa gratefully, "would you? If there is any trouble would you tell them about it? He isn't a boy who drinks, I'm sure. He never did."

"No, he isn't. If he had been he wouldn't be getting along as well as he is. His fever doesn't run any higher, that's one good thing. And he looks as if he had a pretty good constitution. But I can tell you one thing, he doesn't think much of that girl that was with him, if you can believe what he says. She must be a coward. I wonder why she hasn't been to see him. They say she wasn't hurt at all. She jumped out and ran away while the car almost stopped just before it went over the cliff. Nice girl to run away. Sylvia! I guess that must be her name. Do you know her?"

The nurse eyed Melissa's delicate face and noted the mounting, sensitive flush with curious glance.

But Melissa only shook her head, and then, summoning her self-control she thanked the nurse.

"I wonder if you would mind sending me a postal to-morrow and the next day, till Mother can get here?" she asked wistfully. "You see Father is sick too, and Mother couldn't get away without telling him yet, and we dare not, he's been so sick."

"Isn't that a shame!" said the nurse. "Sure, I'll send you a postal every night till he's better. I'll send one this evening when I go off duty."

Melissa wrote down the address and gave her the last quarter in her purse. She wouldn't be needing it now that she was going home, of course.

"I wish I had more to give you," she said deprecatingly. "It won't pay anything but the postage, but I'll be wonderfully grateful."

"That's all right," smiled the nurse, "I like you. I like your brother too. He's a good sport. He'll pull through. Don't you worry."

Melissa was greatly comforted, yet she went away realizing that every one who knew her brother's case felt that he was in a very serious condition, and that it was not at all certain that he was going to get well.

Down in the front hall Melissa waited. She was there at quarter past ten to make sure she did not keep them waiting. She sat next a blind man, with two cripples across the hall from her, and watched a crying baby being walked up and down by a frantic mother.

Melissa watched the clock until half past ten. Then she went and stood in the doorway where she could watch both hall and street, but nowhere could she see the big shiny car that had brought her to this place.

At eleven o'clock she began to think she had somehow missed them. Perhaps they had said half past nine and the nurse had given the message wrong. Oh, she ought to have gone right up there to that horrible Jack's room and found out for herself just what time they were going. If only she hadn't been so afraid of an unpleasant experience again! And now it was even later than they had said they were going to start, and that would make it later at the other end.

Finally, she went to the desk and asked the telephone girl to call up Jack Hollister's room and see if his brother and mother had gone yet, and word came back that they had not, but would be downstairs in a little while. She was just to sit there and wait.

When it got to be half past one, Melissa ate the last two crackers left from her cracker box, ate them surreptitiously, breaking off little bits of pieces and slipping them into her mouth without seeming to be eating. The patients had nearly all of them gone at last, and even the visitors waiting to see some doctor, or ask about a friend, had gone to get lunch. Melissa thought she never had been so tired in her life. Here she had been sitting for three hours doing nothing but wait! And how she longed to slip upstairs and see if there was any change yet in her brother, only she dared not lest she miss the Hollisters.

It was nearly three o'clock when she saw through the open door a car drive up to the curb, and there at last was Gene Hollister.

He was all alone. Doubtless he was going up after his mother and she might take the chance and run up again just for a last look at Steve. But no, he walked in exactly as if she had been keeping him waiting.

"Ready?" he asked carelessly. "Well, c'mon!"

She followed him out to the car, and was relieved that he put her in the back seat, thinking now she would be safe with his mother, but to her astonishment he got into the front seat himself and slammed the door shut, starting his engine at once.

"Why, where is your mother?" she asked in alarm. "You haven't forgotten her, have you? Or is she at the hotel?"

"No, the Mater decided not to go back to-day. She phoned and put off her bridge party till next week. Jack put up such a fight at her leaving him alone that she had to stay. I'm taking some other people back with us for the ride. They're great company. You'll like them all right."

Melissa gasped and sat back trying to think what to do? Would they be all men, these friends of his? Mother wouldn't approve at all of her driving late at night with a lot of men and no woman. Dared she say anything about it? Would it look as if she were being very rude when they were taking her all the way for nothing, and had been kind enough to offer? Perhaps she had better wait and see when they stopped to pick up the other people. If they were all men she might say that if they didn't mind she would get out and go back and stay another day since his mother was staying also. Only, what should she do about money? She would certainly have to call up and ask her mother. Oh, she must somehow stick this thing through. But if she once got home she would never go away on her own hook again without advice from some one.

They turned down a mean little street with rows of cheap houses and Melissa looked anxiously out.

Gene stopped the car at an untidy house and knocked at the door. Melissa was relieved to see a girl come out with her hat on, and a suit case in her hand. So there was to be another girl. Well that wasn't so bad. Perhaps the girl was the only one. There did not seem to be any other person coming out.

Hollister put the other girl in the front seat with himself, waving an informal introduction:

"Meet Miss Challenger, Miss Saltaine!" and took his place beside her.

12

THE girl gave Melissa one quick startled stare and then turned to her escort.

"Challenger, d'ya say? Gosh, Gene, is that what you're handing out as an inducement? What's the little old idea, anyhow? Tryin' ta put one over on me?"

"Nothing of the kind, girlie," said the genial Gene, starting up his car with a jerk. "Just taking Miss Challenger back home. I brought her down you know. She's been down to see her brother. Got any objections? If you have speak them now or forever after, etc."

Melissa did not quite know what it was all about, only that there was a hostile attitude in the girl. She supposed that probably she was disappointed at not having the ride alone with Hollister. She very likely didn't want to feel that a stranger was watching her.

But it presently developed that the young woman on the front seat had no objections to being watched. She regarded the girl in the back seat as so much nothing. She snuggled herself up to the driver affectionately, looked into his eyes, lighted a cigarette for him, and one for herself, and taking off her hat with a care-free motion settled her golden head firmly on Hollister's shoulder.

After Melissa got over her surprise and embarrassment at such actions she was rather glad to be thus utterly left out of the picture. At least it left her free to rest and enjoy the scenery, if there was any capacity to enjoy anything left in her weary troubled soul.

She studied the new girl with curiosity. She had never met a girl quite like this one. She was startlingly, unnaturally beautiful, with a complexion so brilliant, and so brazenly artificial that it seemed to Melissa, who had been brought up in an extremely conservative atmosphere, absolutely a caricature of a human face. And yet she had to own it was lovely, in a flashy way. She was as lovely as the most perfect doll one could think of. Just pretty flesh, but nothing in the expression but vanity. A selfish cupid's bow of a mouth, gold hair that curled, whether naturally or artificially, in a most engaging and arresting manner, fluffed out like a dandelion, waving around in the breeze like golden tulle, brushing the face of the young man upon whom she reclined, tossing itself into bright little billows and wavelets. It really was fascinating to watch, and Melissa watched it, unaware that the owner of the hair was all the time watching her in the little mirror up in front.

Melissa, lovely as a drooping flower in the back seat, had no idea that her own face, off its guard because she thought herself unseen, was mirroring forth as water the thoughts that were in her heart; and when the girl in the front seat looked into the little mirror, she saw a pity for herself mingled with contempt in the eyes of the girl in the back seat that galled her to the soul.

Suddenly she raised her head and deliberately turning round blew a long brath of smoke straight at Melissa.

"For cat's sake, what are you staring at?" she snapped out at Melissa.

Melissa summoned a faint little smile, trying to answer pleasantly.

"I was looking at your hair and thinking how beautiful it is," she said quietly.

"Oh, blah! I don't believe you!" said the other girl. "Turn your little sissy gaze on the landscape. I don't choose to be looked at and admired by you, nor any of your doggone fool family. I'm done with 'em once and fer all. Get me?"

For answer Melissa raised her Challenger chin just the least little bit and looked steadily into the other girl's insolent eyes, a grave sweet disconcerting look that only angered her the more. And then Melissa was aware of another pair of amused eyes watching her in that fatal little mirror that she had not noticed until now.

"Oh, for Pete's sake, Sylvia, cut it! This isn't a battlefield. I brought you girls along to have a good time together. Be a good sport and forget what bothers you! Let's get together on a little friendliness."

"Not me!" said Sylvia shrugging her shoulders. "You never told me you were bringing along a fancy peacock for company, or I'd have gone with somebody else, to-day."

"Oh, shut up, Sylvia," said Hollister crossly. "You don't need to be a cat!"

"Well, why doesn't she smoke, if she wantsta be one of us?" demanded the golden beauty with a sneer. "Here, take mine and I'll light another," she said taking her half-smoked cigarette out of her bedizened mouth and handing it to Melissa.

"Thank you, no," said Melissa haughtily withdrawing her gaze from the girl, and sitting back in the seat. Then she turned to Hollister and spoke with as much dignity as she could summon:

"Mr. Hollister, I'll be grateful if you will just put me down in the next village you come to. I feel that I'm intruding and it would be better for me to go home by train."

As she spoke she remembered that this must be the emergency of which Brady had been fearful. She felt that she must get away from these dreadful people at once.

Hollister's answer was to step on the gas and send the car flying on the faster.

There was a stubborn look on his face, albeit veiled by a half grin as he spoke:

"You cut it out too! This is a party, not a sparring match. Just hold on a little while longer and the fun will begin. Here's where we stop for a friend of mine! You'll get rid of your grouch when you have a little attention of your own." And suddenly he dashed into a deeply wooded road, that was barely a trail, presently arriving at a little cabin in the wilderness.

A young man in city attire, looking strangely out of place, stood on the crude porch awaiting them. Beside him on the wooden platform lay a case of bottles.

As the car drew up before the house, the young man stooped and lifted this case, swinging it into the tonneau, springing in, and throwing his overcoat over the case. The car started almost instantly again with such a lurch that it threw the stranger over into Melissa's lap. In horror she tried to move over, reaching out to unfasten the door. Obviously this would be her place to get out if she could manage it, but it was too late. The car was tearing along at a fearful rate of speed now. Straight through the woods they were going, crashing into little saplings and laying them low, grazing a rock on one side with a fearful grinding and scraping of metal, rocking over a log across the path. There absolutely was no possibility of getting out now.

Melissa sat back white and frightened, holding to the side of the car. The young stranger whom they called "Hen," presumably Henry, sprawled all over the back seat, and took no pains to keep to his own side of the car.

"Better shy outta this road," he muttered to Hollister, as he lurched back into place again after a fearful jouncing. "They warned me there were state cops around here. Better cross the creek ahead there and get outta the state."

His utterance was thick, and Melissa began to be terribly frightened. Before she had felt only distaste, now it was something that unnerved her.

"That's all right," said Hollister carelessly, "we're just going to sit by in the trees here a few minutes and have a little drink. All hands'll feel better after that. So, Sylvia?"

He drew up the car sharply, and was about to stop his engine, when in the sudden lull there came the sound of a motor cycle in the distance, followed by a shot, sharp and terrifying.

Melissa cringed, and thought of screaming for help, but the car lurched forward again so suddenly that it threw her to her knees, and she had all she could do to get herself back in the seat before her companion on the back seat fell on top of her.

"Whad' I tell ya?" said Henry thickly.

Then all at once Melissa knew that he had turned his attention to her. He was looking her straight in the face with a pair of bleared eyes that could scarcely focus, and the realization came to her that he was drunk. Melissa was not used to seeing people in that state. She never remembered to have been so near to a drunken person in her life before. The idea almost paralyzed her.

"Hello, beautiful!" he said, bringing his unpleasant face with its loathsome breath nearer to her own. "Hello, Beautiful! Where'd they dig you up from? Kiss me, Beautiful!" and he brought his fulsome red lips close to hers with that sickening breath of alcohol pouring into her nostrils.

As his lips touched hers, Melissa screamed, not just an ordinary scream, it was a shriek that echoed piercingly through the woods, and almost at once they heard another shot, and the rumble of the motor cycle nearer by.

Hollister turned in his seat with a scowl that transformed him into something like a demon.

"You shut up, you little devil, do you hear?" he growled at Melissa. "If you make another sound I'll gag and bind you, understand? Now, that'll be about all we'll hear from anybody just now. They're onto us. I don't reckon you wantta get dragged into court, do you? Yes, you, Melissa Challenger. That's where we'll all land if you give us any more of your mouth right now. This is a mess! Shut up till we get out of it."

A road suddenly appeared to the left and Hollister almost upset the car turning into it. They tore along at such a rate of speed that Melissa felt that every moment would be the last, and all she could do was to close her eyes, grip her hands together, and try to keep from bumping all over the car.

Henry, meantime, was growing sleepy, and when at last they turned into a reasonably smooth road, and went skimming through space in a quieter manner, he suddenly toppled over sideways with his head on Melissa's shoulder and declared he was going to sleep.

Melissa tried to slip out from under his weight, but found to her horror that he only slid down more firmly whenever she stirred. All she could do was to turn her face as far away from his as possible, and hide her hands down in the cushion next to the side of the car. But the heavy unpleasant head continued to rest inertly upon her unwilling shoulder.

The sky was darkening now. There seemed to be a storm coming up. The horror of the way grew worse every minute. The girl Sylvia—was this the same Sylvia who had attended her brother on his fateful ride two nights ago?—reached back under the overcoat and took a bottle from the case. She drank from it, and passed it to Hollister who took a long pull before he gave it back. Were the terrors of the way to be made still more alarming by a drunken driver? What would her mother think now if she could see her riding along at this pace with a drunken man's head upon her shoulder! And another drunken man driving? What did God mean by letting this awful thing happen to her?

Suddenly it came to her that He hadn't let it happen. She had walked straight into it with her eyes open. She knew in her heart that her mother would not have approved of her going, knew it when she started, and just wanted to go for the experience of going by herself in a great car like that with rich people.

Poor little trembling Melissa, hating herself and her surroundings, weary and hungry and frightened to the last degree. "O, God," she began to say over and over again in her heart. "O, God! Help me. Help me! Help! Help! Help!"

The night began to come down and the clouds grew thicker. The man who slept on her shoulder grew heavier, as he sank deeper in sleep. She tried to shake him off again, but all to no purpose. She thought of appealing to Hollister to help her, but the two on the front seat were drinking heavily now, and she dared not draw their atteniton to herself. She began to think of herself as a coward too. She dared not speak nor stir lest she make her plight even worse. She had read awful stories of things like this happening, but it had never seemed possible that they could happen to her.

The storm was gathering force now. Lightning trickled through a cloud and cut it in a bright half straight ahead of them above a mountain. Thunder rolled in majesty all around them. Melissa never had been fond of thunder storms. She liked to be under shelter when they were going on. But now she thought how happy and safe she would feel if she could just get out there alone in the fast coming darkness. Wind and rain and lightning, but nothing as terrifying as the hostile drunken company inside this luxurious car. She never would want to ride in a fine car again. She was cured forever.

Darkness had really come at last and hidden some of the perils of the way except when a sudden flash lit up the world for miles around. The two on the front seat began to talk about eating.

"We'll find a good road house and have dinner and a little dance!" said Hollister genially and tipsily, turning around to rouse Henry. "Say, Hen! Oh, I say Henry Brille, wake up! We're going to stop at the Holly Whistle road house and whoop it up. Sit up! We're almost there!"

Melissa crouched fearfully in her corner and wondered what she should do, wondered what new horror would appear when this man woke up.

He stretched and turned. Oh, if she could only get away from under his head so that he would not know he had been sleeping on her shoulder. It seemed as if she never could bear herself again if he knew that she had had to sit there and bear it ignominiously.

She writhed away from him and slid to the floor of the car as he lurched down the full width of the seat, and there she crouched until he finally roused to Hollister's call, and straightened up, rubbing his eyes.

To her great relief he did not seem to realize what had been going on at all. He sat back relaxed in his corner, and Melissa slid silently back into her place as far from him as the seat would allow. He had for the moment forgotten her.

They were turning into a long lane now, with great stone pillars at either side bearing balls of electric light. The spirits of her three companions roused to song, and they drove up the hill, around the lighted curving way, with a boisterous round of what they seemed to think was music. They also handed another bottle around, and Henry tried to put it to her lips in turn. Melissa took it in the dark and put it on the floor, holding it with her foot. She was afraid to protest lest they might hold her and pour some down her throat.

And now they were stopping in front of a long low house that looked like a farm house built over. Its porches were rimmed with garish red and yellow electric light bulbs, and its windows and doors were well darkened. She could hear Hollister telling Sylvia about a raid that had been made here once when he was present, and how he escaped without being caught. She shrank back into her corner and wondered what she could do? Would there be any chance to get away? They had come through a village a few miles back. Oh, if she could but get back there. She would rather walk every step of the way home than ride another mile in this awful car with these terrible people.

Trembling so that she could scarcely walk she obeyed their command to get out.

"Come on, Beautiful!" said Henry, drawing her reluctant hand within his arm, and guiding her uncertainly toward the steps. "We'll show you a good time!"

It was dark close by the steps. One had to go slowly and look down to make sure where to walk. There were people coming out as they came up. It became necessary to go single file to pass each other. Suddenly Melissa jerked her arm out of the clasp that held it and slipped behind her escort, just as two men and a woman came noisily down the steps brushing past her.

Instantly she darted into the hemlocks that grew close to the steps, slid behind them in the dark and held her breath. Oh, if she could only manage to evade them.

Henry had gone up two steps without her. Now she could hear him pawing around in the dark trying to find her, grabbing the arm of a stranger who was coming out. There were angry words, and Henry turned and went down two steps again, calling "Beautiful! Beautiful! Where are you?"

Fear lent courage to Melissa, and strength to her numb feet. She made a quick plunge into the blackness behind where she stood, not knowing if it were brush or brier, or a heap of stones. But it proved to be only shrubs that gave way before her touch, and like a rabbit in the grass she passed along the end of the house, touching it lightly with her finger tips as she went, to keep her direction, for it was very dark. She could not see at all, until she came to the corner, at the back, near to the kitchen. There was light here from an open window and she could hear the clatter of dishes, the clink of bottles among the ice.

On she plunged recklessly, holding herself tense, stepping as lightly as she could in this unknown darkness. She rounded the corner, and came on a latticed porch. There were people inside, waiters, dishing ice cream, carrying trays of bottles. She must not draw their attention. She must not get into the line of the light.

She was glad that she had had presence of mind to grasp her little overnight bag when she knew she would have to get out of the car. She did not care so much for the bag or the things in it, as to have gotten it away from the car. The thought of having that terrible Sylvia handling over her few simple things with a sneer seemed like a pinprick to her thoughts as she went more slowly, step by step, cautiously, lest some of those waiters should hear her. There was a big dog, too, chained by the back door. He had risen now and his hair seemed to be bristling on his supple neck. His eyes glared toward her like baleful lamps. Ah! She must skirt that garden patch. It would not do to get that dog to barking.

And now she could hear Henry calling louder:

"Beautiful! I say! Where are you?"

There was a stirring as of pursuing feet toward the front of the house, and Melissa made another wild plunge off behind a shadowing building, an old chicken house perhaps. She slid around behind it till she found a fence through which she crept into a field, and then hearing voices behind her she started to run, and fell headlong down a little hill in the deep grass!

She dared not rise but lay there in the darkness, with the wet cool grass against her face, and the tears slipping hot and big down her cheeks.

She heard them come out somewhere over there by the building and call her, and she lay perfectly still with closed eyes, scarcely breathing for a long long time, till they seemed to give up and go back again. She could hear their voices dying away in the distance, and then a far door closed, and there was only dim chatter of jazz by an orchestra, clink of glasses, and the voices of servants.

A long time afterwards, for she was afraid some one was still lurking out there watching for a movement, she cautiously stirred, and little by little crept painfully down that hill, across the field, and by a wide skirting reached the road.

She could not be sure, but she thought that it was the same road by which they had just come to the house. Now, if she could follow it and hide in the foliage whenever a car came down that way, she might sometime in the course of the night, find that village again through which they had passed, and perhaps find a railroad train. Certainly she was justified now in using Mr. Brady's money, for no more alarming emergency could possibly be conjured than that she was now in.

But oh, it was dark, and she was tired, deadly tired. She would have been glad just to drop down in her tracks and die, she was so troubled and weary. And the hot tears were coursing down her face in a continuous salt tide till her lips smarted and her eyes were fairly blinded.

At last she reached the main road. She was sure it was the road from which they had turned a few minutes ago. She stumbled down the embankment and hurried breathlessly along. The thunder roared ominously. Another storm was coming up. The lightning shivered out in blinding sheets and showed the way ahead, a long road with no turning. She felt so alone and terrified. The rain was coming down now in large detached drops. There would be a downpour in a minute and she would be drenched. If she could only get to a shelter somewhere!

She cast a wild look about in the darkness, and then another blinding flash of lightning showed the great hulk of an old barn looming at the roadside not many rods away.

She began to run with all her might and clambered up the bank just as the rain came like an avalanche. Groping breathlessly she found an open doorway and crept fearfully inside, as much afraid of what might be lurking there as of what she was leaving behind.

Just inside the old stone walls she hid, and tried to penetrate the darkness, till another flash revealed somewhat the dusty, empty interior. The barn was evidently unused now. An old farm wagon with a broken wheel, a plow with a rusty share were the only occupants of the place besides herself.

Somewhat reassured she slipped farther back out of the rain and sank upon the bare floor. Her trembling limbs would scarcely bear her up to stand, and she must not waste her strength. She would need it all to get back to that village and find a railroad. How glad and thankful she was now that Brady had insisted upon her taking that money.

An automobile shot by in the road, and set her trembling again just as she was getting her nerves a little steady. What if those two drunken fools should take it into their heads to chase after her? Hollister, even with his brains stupid with drink, might think he had a responsibility for her. Oh, she ought to get on, yet no one could make any headway in a storm like this, and she would be soaked to the skin if she tried to make time now.

She drooped against the old wall and closed her eyes, listening to the rain till she almost fell asleep. But in a little while it stopped, and another car going by startled her awake again. Its headlights played within the doorway, and her heart came into her throat. Had they come for her?

Alert, now, she listened till the car was out of sight, then stole forth, her hand up to feel for rain. No, it was not raining now. She must get on. Of course, if it started again she would have to keep on for it was not likely she would find another empty barn wide open to receive her.

Her feet were heavy and wet. Her clothes were a little wet too, and her head was heavy with sleep. But she plodded on, as fast as she could make herself go.

Once a car came behind her, its headlights brightening the path she trod, and she scuttled into the shadows at the roadside, fearful lest it was the Hollister car. They must know she would be somewhere along the road. They could easily have found her if they tried, had they not been drunk. But this constant fear of pursuit made her going doubly hard, for she had to be ready to spring at an instant's notice into the ditch or whatever shelter she could find. However, there were not many cars going at that hour.

She tried to calculate what time it was. It seemed ages since she left the hospital. But her watch had stopped and it was too dark to see it anyway.

It seemed to her that she had walked three times as far as they must have come from that village before some scattering houses began to make it look like the outskirts of a village, and gave her new hope.

She plodded on down a long main street of small houses, all asleep in the dark. The storm had gone now to other places, with only a distant rumble of thunder now and then, and an occasional lighting of the sky in vivid sheets from afar. But this light showed her the sleeping town and guided her steps to the sidewalk from the road and down through the little huddle of stores to the railroad station.

Being city bred Melissa had hoped for an open station where she might sit and wait for the next train going her way. She tried the door of the dark little brick building that stood beside the tracks with dismay. It was closed till morning. Of course. She should have known that. And there would not be trains stopping either. How hopeless everything was! She sank down upon the bare platform for there were no benches in sight and she was too tired to try to hunt a better seat. There did not seem to be any lights in the village either except the street lamps at long intervals. There was nowhere she could go, nothing she could do but wait. She was alone in a dark world that was asleep.

Before her the track stretched in endless miles, lighted now and then by the more and more distant storm. A woods menaced darkly behind the station. The boards where she sat were wet, and already the dampness was striking through her garments. Her feet were wet and cold. She shivered as she curled them under her and leaned her head against the wall of the station. Suddenly she put her face down into her hands and cried, shaking from head to foot with great sobs such as she had not known since she was a little child and fell down a long flight of stairs. They wrenched out from the depths of her being, every little nerve in her tired body crying out for redress. She ached from head to foot, and her head ached so that she could scarcely hold it up.

Then to her lips unbidden came that cry of the lost soul that has reached its limit:

"Oh God!" she cried, "won't you help me? If you are a God you can! I know I haven't believed in you, but if you'll just help me now, I'll know you are a real God, and I'll believe in you always! O, I will, truly."

Having registered this vow, made as it were her bargain with God, her sobs gradually grew less. She seemed to have cried it out, all the misery that was in her soul. She had given in against her pride and prejudice and put the matter into God's hands. There simply was nothing else that she could do.

Then because she was too tired to hold up any longer, she put her little overnight bag down upon the wet board platform, laid her head upon it for a pillow, and sank into a deep sleep. •

About two hours later, just as a faint gray began to appear off toward the eastern horizon, there came quiet steps down a side street, paused a moment on the platform, then came softly toward her till a dark form stood over her, stooping a little, and looking down upon her.

Still Melissa slept on.

13

QUITE early in the morning, Phyllis, who had slept very little all night, and had occasionally in the intervals of rest, kept her promise to her young brother about praying, stole forth from the house before anybody was awake.

She hurried to a near-by drug store where she knew there was a telephone booth, her mouth set firmly, her smooth brow knit in anxiety. She had with her enough of her precious ten dollar bill to pay for several Long Distance telephone calls if necessary, and also Melissa's two telegrams.

She did not try for the president or the dean of the college in that distant town to which Melissa had gone. She knew it was too early in the morning to get either gentleman. She went straight for the hospital authorities, and after much delay was informed about her brother being in a near-by village hospital. A little more insistence, and she was connected with the right hospital at last. She asked if they knew where her sister, Miss Challenger was, and could she speak with her, and after more delay there came word that Miss Challenger left for home yesterday about half past ten in the morning.

Fear clutched at Phyllis' throat. Half past ten in the morning! That ought to have brought her home by dark at the most. Phyllis had asked discreet questions of Brady last night and knew the time it took a good driver to get to the city from the college. More fear! One accident in a family quickly begets the fear of another. What had happened to Melissa, and how would Mother take it? Mother was just about all in now. It didn't take brains to see that. Phyllis had been aghast at her mother's sobs last night. She had never heard her sweet little mother give way and cry aloud before. Tears there had been, many quiet sad tears when worries came; when Rosalie had had the scarlet fever; when Bob had the mastoid operation; but no such soul-shaking sobs. Mother had reached the limit and something must be done.

Phyllis came out of the telephone booth white with anxiety wondering whether to let her mother know or to keep still about it. Only Rosalie was up when Phyllis got back, and she made the excuse of having gone out to get more butter for breakfast.

"Phyllis, you're worried," said the child looking at her keenly.

"Oh, a little," said Phyllis evasively.

"But you needn't be," said Rosalie. "You know if God is going to take care of us we can't do any good by worrying."

"How can you help worrying?" said Phyllis with a tired hopeless look in her eyes.

"You *can*," said Rosalie, "if you just keep trusting Him. Phyllis, there are three dandelions open in the back yard. And it's only March, just think! One is between the bricks in the walk by the ash can, one is by the fence where the sun shines brightest, that is the big one, and the other is just poking its head out from under a board. Do you think, Phyllis, that it would be nice for me to pick them for the breakfast table, or should I leave them to make the yard bright?"

"Oh, I'd pick them," said Phyllis trying to speak brightly. "There are always plenty of dandelions, aren't there?"

"Not this time of year, Phyllie! And not when people are

poor and don't have flowers on their tables. I think dandelions are pretty."

"You poor little precious!" said her sister stooping to kiss her and hide the desire for tears. "You've never been much in the country, have you? When I was a little girl we lived in the suburbs and had a lovely garden of flowers and vegetables. I remember I had a bed of forgetmenots, and Melissa had mignonette in hers."

"What's mignonette?"

"Oh, a kind of fuzzy little knob of a flower that looks like fringed gingham and has a heavenly smell."

They were suddenly interrupted by the sharp turning of a key in their mother's door, and her footsteps coming down the stairs. Both girls stopped their conversation and turned anxious eyes to the stairs as she came down.

Mary Challenger's face was white and drawn, her eyes full of her night of agonizing prayer.

"I thought I heard the postman come!" she exclaimed.

"Oh, I'll see!" said Rosalie running to the front door., "Yes, here's a letter."

"Oh!" said the mother with a gleam of hope in her eyes. "From Melissa, is it? Perhaps she felt it better to stay over another day, and she likely thought we'd get the letter in time to save anxiety. She wanted to save money of course."

But the little girl shook her head as she handed out the letter.

"No, Mother dear," she said, "it's not her writing. It's typewritten. I think it's from those same people that the other letter came from the night Mrs. Barkus acted so dreadfully."

"Oh!" said Mary Challenger tossing the letter on the table and coming slowly down the stairs, the cloud settling down again upon her wan face.

"What was it, Mother?" asked the little girl picking up the letter and examining the name in the upper left hand corner.

"Was it anything interesting? You went to see them and you

never told us about it," said Rosalie, eager to turn her mother's attention.

"Oh, just some people who wanted to know about our family tree."

"Family tree?" said Rosalie, full of curiosity at once. "Have we a tree? How I'd like to see it!"

"She doesn't mean a tree that grows in the ground, Rosie," explained Phyllis, "she means our line of ancestors. I'll tell you about it after breakfast. We must hurry now, and you'd better run up and call Bob. He'll be late to school."

"But what did those lawyers want to know about our ancestors for, Mother?" continued Rosalie when she came back from rousing her brother. Rosalie never dropped a subject until she had exhausted it utterly, or the people who knew about it.

"I'm sure I don't know," said Mary Challenger wearily, going to the window for the third time since she had come down stairs, to look for a car that did not come. "They are probably writing a book on the family lineage, or some client of theirs is, and has set them to find out about everybody. I only know I wasted two good carfares and a whole morning going down there and waiting for them to look up their papers, and then answering their questions. I had to tell all about my grandmothers, and my great-great-grandfathers, and your father's family too. It is all utter nonsense anyway. What difference does it make who your ancestors were?"

"But aren't you going to open this letter, Mother?" asked Rosalie anxiously.

"No, I can't be bothered with such trivial things now. It's likely only to tell me that the book will soon be ready and that I can have a first edition reserved for me if I will forward five or ten dollars to-day. That's the way those things go. I don't want the book. What would we do with it? And where would we get the five or ten dollars to pay for it?" She spoke bitterly, looking down the empty street, and trying to force back the tears that had somehow got the habit of slipping slowly down her cheeks.

"May I open it, Mother?" asked Rosalie, still engrossed with the letter.

"Yes, if you want to," said the mother indifferently.

Rosalie tore open the envelope with curiosity.

"Oh, Mother! You'll *have* to go," she exclaimed, "It says they have something very important to tell you. Listen:

> Dear Madam:
>   We have compared the data which you gave us the other day and find it to be in all particulars correct. We have instructions to ask you to come to our office as soon as you can conveniently do so, and learn something which will be very greatly to your advantage.
>   Very sincerely,
>   HAPGOOD AND WRIGHT,
>   Attorneys at Law

Rosalie was all eagerness.

"Now you'll go, won't you, Mother, and see what it is?"

But the mother turned a sad smile on her little girl. "No, dear, I shan't bother about it. It's just a way of advertising. You don't understand. They want to sell a copy of the book and they feel sure if they get me into the office they can persuade me that I must have the whole story of the Challenger and Langdon families. That's all it can possibly mean."

"But Mother," said the little girl, disappointed, "Wouldn't you just *try* it? It *might* be something nice, mightn't it? A job for Phyllis or Melissa perhaps?"

"Not possibly, little dear," smiled the mother sadly. "Jobs don't come that way."

"Let me see it," said Phyllis with a sudden idea. "It might be a place where I could find a job."

"Oh, Phyllis!" sighed the mother, "To think you have to go

around in men's offices hunting a job. I don't like it!" and the slow tears came again.

But Phyllis read the letter through thoughtfully and put it into her pocket for future reference. She might even go to those lawyers who were so much interested in her family and ask for a job, if her other places didn't pan out.

But Phyllis did not go job hunting that day. She was too anxious about her mother who would not rest nor eat, and who stood at the window continually looking out. She half expected to see her fall fainting from sheer weariness.

Breakfast made a diversion for a few minutes for the rest of them, and Phyllis helped Bob and Rosalie to get off to school with lunches and everything. Then she cleared away and washed the dishes, and made a nice little piece of toast and a cup of hot coffee for her mother.

"Come, Mother dear," she coaxed, "let me feed this nice brown bite to you. See it's all buttered and lovely and hot. And now take a sip of the coffee. Listen, I've got a suggestion to make. You know this waiting time is rather hard, but it's pretty sure that you'll probably have to go to Steve *some*time soon, if not to-day. I've been thinking we ought to get you all ready so you could go at a moment's notice. You see Melissa might come at any minute now, and she'll like as not want you to go right back. You'll have to eat to have strength."

"But, how could I go, Phyllis?" asked the mother as she swallowed the coffee obediently. "I haven't any money—"

"Are you quite sure? We've got to plan for it somehow. Let's get out all our money and see how much we have. I still have eight dollars left. How much have you? Where is your purse?"

"Up in my bureau drawer. But Phyllis, you've got to have something to live on while I'm gone. And there would be other expenses besides just my fare."

"There'll be a way to get enough," said Phyllis. "Let's find out first how much we have, then how much we have to have, and then where to get the rest, see?" and she hurried off upstairs after her mother's purse.

"Bob will have his pay to-night you know," she reminded as she came back and emptying out the purse began to count.

"But what would you live on?"

"Well, I'm to have another day's work Monday. It won't likely be ten dollars this time of course but it will be something. And we have quite a lot of things in the pantry. We wouldn't starve right away. Anyway if it came to that Mr. Brady wouldn't let us starve, you know that, and while I hate to take things from a stranger, still we can pay him back with interest some day you know, and he likes us."

"*Can* we?" said the mother hopelessly.

Nevertheless she began to help count up possibilities, and the tears were staunched for a time at least.

"Now," said Phyllis, "I'll call up and see what the train fare is, and the time table and so on. I'll run down to the butcher shop to do it. It doesn't cost Mr. Brady anything on local calls. He told me to use his phone whenever I needed to. And while I'm gone you go upstairs and get together the clothes you will need to take along. You'll have to go prepared for a week or two in case you should have to stay."

"But what would you say to your father?"

"Why, I'd tell him Steve has a broken leg. He won't be scared at that. Steve's an athlete. Things like that happen to athletes every day you know," said Phyllis airily. "Father won't think a thing of it. I'd just tell him we got a telegram and we don't know the particulars yet. You wouldn't need to worry about that. I know Father. I could keep him satisfied all right. Then you could write funny little letters about the things Steve says and all, and he'd not miss you so much if I went to see him every day."

"You're a dear child," said the mother, with a shadow of a smile.

"So, now, Mumsie, you just go up and pack, and I'll run

out and get the information we need about trains and so on, and don't you worry. I won't be gone fifteen minutes."

Phyllis had actually succeeded in turning her mother's thoughts from the immediate trouble over Melissa, and giving her something to do to make the time pass. But she was wise enough not to wait to do the telephoning herself. She did not want to leave her mother alone so long. She asked Mr. Brady to get his errand boy to find out train times and prices and send her word when he came over with the order of cheap meat she needed for broth for her mother. Then she hurried home.

Mary Challenger went up to her room to gather together a few necessities as she had promised, but left alone, her mind at once reverted to Melissa again; and she went around her room saying out loud. "O, God. Find my little Lissa! O, God, you needn't do anything for *me,* if you'll only find my Lissa and keep her safe!"

Phyllis hurried upstairs and entered into her preparations exactly as if she were sure of starting in an hour.

"You'll want at least one extra dress, Mother. It will be safer to have it along," she suggested as she folded the old black crepe that had done duty for best for quite a while.

"It's lucky I won't want three!" said the mother with a twinkle of her own dry humor that usually kept the family so heartened and merry when all went well, "because, if I wanted three, it would be just too bad!" She mimicked her children's tone as she said it and Phyllis had to laugh at that.

The morning wore on to nine o'clock and still no word from Melissa. Phyllis felt that she should go crazy if something didn't happen pretty soon, yet she maintained an outward calm and kept her mother's mind busy.

"Now Mother, tell me exactly what you want said to Father. I'll write it down," she said, and that occupied a few more minutes.

When the butcher's boy arrived with the timetables and information Phyllis almost fell downstairs in her hurry to get to the door quickly, and she was so frightened that she could hardly speak till she recognized him.

"Phyllis," said her mother sharply when she came back with the timetables, "I've *got* to do something about your sister at once! Your father will blame me severely and justly if I don't. In fact I don't see how I could have let it go so long. I should have done something last night."

"But—what could you do, Mother? I'm sure Melissa must be all right somehow."

"Your being sure doesn't make it so," said the mother, with a look of agony on her face. "I've got to telephone somewhere. We should find out when she left the hospital. Why didn't we do that last night?"

Phyllis tried to keep her lips closed, but her mother's searching eyes were upon her, and suddenly she knew she must tell the truth. It would only mean a few moments' delay even if she did not.

"Well, Mother, I may as well tell you now. I telephoned early this morning. They started yesterday about ten thirty the nurse said. I didn't tell you before because I thought it would only make you worry more, and I thought surely some word would come from Melissa pretty soon."

Her mother looked at her quietly, with a tense control of herself. Phyllis could see that she felt the news was momentous. Then she said in a low steady voice:

"We should telephone those people who took her and find out if they are home. What was that name? Do you remember?"

"Yes, Hollister. Mr. Brady wrote it down for us. He looked up their address in the city too. He's remarkably thoughtful for a stranger."

"He's a very unusual man," said Mary Challenger. "We shall never forget his kindness. Now, Phyllis, will you look up their number and run out and telephone?" Mary Challenger's lips were white but she kept that steady self control, and after she had spoken she went into her room like one who goes to a last resort and quietly knelt down beside her bed.

So Phyllis with that feeling of utter goneness and despair, more frightened than she cared to own at this unnatural calmness in her mother, hurried off to the butcher shop again to telephone.

It was only a maid with a foreign accent who answered:

"Naw, they bayn't coom hum yet. They goes about a greaddeal an' they never tells me. I dono when they coom. Mebbe ta-day, mebbe next week. I cayn't tell."

When Phyllis got back she found her mother on her knees with the door quite unlocked. She lifted a white anguished face and read in her daughter's face that there was no news yet.

"I'm afraid we ought to put it in the hands of the police, Phyllis," she said quietly. "I'm sure your father would say so. I've asked God to help about it, and He doesn't, and now I think we'll have to call in the police. Your sister must be found."

It was just then that they heard a step on the porch and a knock at the door.

Phyllis turned and hurried down to answer it, a terrible fear upon her. Perhaps this was a telegram to say that Melissa had been killed in an accident! Her sister Melissa! Pretty little frail Melissa! Her throat contracted and her eyes filled with apprehensive tears as she flung open the front door.

14

THE tall young man who walked down the platform that morning in the mists before the dawning had no idea when he set down his suitcase and folded his arms to lean back against the station wall and await the early milk train, that he was not entirely alone in that part of the town.

Everything was as still as things usually are at that early hour when people are deep in their late sleep before waking. The houses lay along the streets beyond the track like a deserted village. The milk man and the bread man had not yet started on their rounds. There were no birds so early in the season to break the silence with their matins. Not even a dog, nor an old gray cat, was abroad to skulk eerily across the still, dark road. The very street lamps seemed blinking low, as if their time had almost come to sleep now, too.

The air was keen and sharp and clean after the storm. The young man shivered and pulled his coat collar up, yawned and changed his weight to the other foot. He did not enjoy rising so early as this. It seemed ridiculous to spoil a good night's sleep. But it had been necessary to meet his appointment for the day.

He yawned again half audibly and was startled to hear a

softly breathed moan as if in answer. He turned sharply in the direction from which it had come and saw something lying on the platform, a heap of papers perhaps, or merely a burlap bag. Some freight that had not been too valuable to leave outside. He turned away and thought the sound had been his imagination, but presently his thoughts turned back to it, and he walked slowly toward the dark object, eyeing it carefully in the dim light of dawning to try and dispel his illusion that it was a person. As he drew nearer it took even a more human form. Could it be a person lying there? Some drunk perhaps? Or—some one—*dead*—it might be!

He stopped and then went forward cautiously, his footsteps scarcely audible. One must be careful these days, there were so many murders about. The form was utterly still. Perhaps he ought to go back and rouse some one to investigate. A murder would be a serious business and he would not want to get mixed up in any such thing. It might delay him too, and his business was urgent. He turned and walked away again. Perhaps it was all imagination. If not he had better not know.

He went back to his suitcase and stood with his back to the huddled form at the other end of the platform, yet he could not forget it, and presently knew that he would not all day, no matter how urgent his business. He must dispel this phantasm. Perhaps it was only a box with a pile of old newspapers on the top giving a semblance of a person.

He walked slowly up the platform again and came nearer, and now he saw that it was surely a person, a girl, huddled up as if she were cold. Her hands were slipped up inside her sleeves. Her hat had fallen off behind her, her head was pillowed on a shabby satchel. Could she be drunk? He stooped lower and saw that her face was delicate, pretty, and very sorrowful. There were tears upon her white cheek. Or were they rain drops? Was she breathing? She lay so still that it almost seemed she was not living.

He walked away silently again, strangely disturbed. Was there something he ought to do about it?

He went to the extreme other end of the platform, around the corner of the station and stood there looking up the track. If the train came now it might easily be that she would not be seen at all. People were all sleepy on a train at an hour like this. But if she were seen it would be extremely embarrassing to be connected with her in any way. It might look bad both for her and for himself. Not that he would let that weigh with him if she were in any need of his ministrations of course. But she seemed to be as comfortable as one could be taking a siesta on a dark platform in the open in the middle of the night. And anyhow, what had he to do with it?

Yet he could not get away from the thought of her, puzzling what had brought a pretty little sorrowful girl like that to be sleeping there all night. There had been no smell of liquor on her. She did not look like a girl that stayed out all night on purpose.

The train was late. He grew more and more uneasy. Perhaps she was ill, out of her head. To reassure himself after he had listened for the hundredth time for a sound of the train, he walked back again slowly and viewed her from afar.

The light was coming stronger now. Things were looming out of the darkness with a ghostly unreality, a house here, a shed there, the water tank not far away, the track spinning away like spider webs. The street lights were beginning to look sick. Was that the sound of a train coming? He listened and heard a humming on the track. It was some distance away, but still, coming at last. Why didn't he walk away and get out of sight behind the station so that if anybody did notice the girl he would not be in the picture at all?

What was that sound across the tracks? A truck? Was it perhaps coming to the station with milk for the train? Why, of course.

The humming of the tracks was more distinct now, but it did not disturb the sleeper. Could it be possible that she had come down early to catch the train herself, and fallen asleep waiting?

He ought to get away now before that truck driver came near enough to see where he was standing. Yet he lingered uncertainly. Ought he perhaps to waken her? He could see the loutish form of the driver slumped in his seat as he passed a street lamp on the other side of the track. Would a nice delicate girl like that—if she *was* a nice delicate girl such as she looked—relish being found sleeping there when that fellow came down the tracks with his milk cans to the high milk platform, as he undoubtedly must come pretty soon?

The humming sound was very clear now, and the girl did not stir. Suddenly the distant darkness became illumined by a great headlight. The train had swept around a curve. It would be here in a moment and the girl had not stirred.

Quickly he stepped to her side and stooping, touched her shoulder gently.

"I beg your pardon!" he said clearly in her ear, "but, is it possible that you meant to take this train? It is almost here."

Melissa started up looking around wildly in the dim morning light, her face full of fright.

"Oh, the train? Is there a train coming? Yes." She tried to rise but fell back with a moan, yet started up again.

"I must have hurt my ankle when I fell in the field," she said aloud, as if speaking to herself, "but—I must get up! I *must* get this train. Mother will be so worried."

He helped her up and steadied her against the wall of the station.

"If you will just wait here until I get my baggage," he said courteously, "I will help you on the train."

He picked up her bag and handed it to her, and Melissa stood there like a little child just wakened out of sleep, rubbing her eyes, not rightly remembering how she came there, only very much frightened.

The young man was back in a moment, and taking his own bag and her little one in one hand, he put his other hand under her slender arm and guided her to the trian which was coming to a halt before them now.

They had to walk back two cars to reach the passenger coach, and she limped so that he had to help her, and almost lift her up the steps . She was stiff and sore from the cold, and lying on the wet boards all night. She was half sick, too, from her long frightened walk in the fields, her fright, and her nights spent on the hard hospital couch.

He seated her in the only section that was unoccupied, the seat by the door which had been vacated by a laborer who swung off for the day's duty at the station they had just left. There was a bunch of red lanterns standing on the floor in the aisle, and the young man guided her around them, and put her down in the seat, then looked around for a place for himself. But everything else was filled by laborers going to their work, some sprawled over a whole seat, their heads back, their mouths open, fast asleep, snoring. Then he looked down at her and laughed pleasantly.

"Would you mind if I sat here?" he said, "There doesn't seem to be any more parking space left in this car."

"Of course not," said Melissa reassured by his courteous manner, and his merry eyes. "I am very grateful to you. I am afraid I should still have been sleeping on that platform if you hadn't been kind enough to waken me. I was pretty tired."

"You certainly looked it. I'm glad I made no mistake. I didn't know but I was being a little presumptuous."

The train had started on by this time, after backing up to the milk landing and taking on a great many enormous cans, and now it was well under way. The conductor with a red lantern swung on his arm came in, slammed the door, and looked them over curiously.

"Fare!" he said snappily.

The young man handed out his money, and Melissa slipped her hand under her coat and quickly unfastened the safety pins, with a deep gratitude to Brady for his thoughtfulness. Suppose she had not had this money! What would she have done? She would have had to walk all the rest of the way home and it would have taken her days! A sudden unexpected sense of security enveloped her. Somebody had been looking after her in spite of all the trouble, even if it was only a butcher; she had not had to go out into danger without some provision. Yet what made Brady so kind? He was only a stranger who had taken a notion to Bob. There must be some Power beyond just human whims to make people do nice things.

"Now," said the young man, when the conductor had passed by, "since I'm wished on you for a while it's high time I introduced myself. My name's Ian Jenifer. I'm taking a graduate course in the university in your city—at least the city where you told the conductor you are going—and I've been out here last night at a Bible conference, and visiting my aunt. Do you know many people in Cliffordsville? My aunt is Mrs. Merton on Maple street. Perhaps you know her and that would introduce us nicely."

"No," said Melissa, "I don't know anybody in Cliffordsville. I didn't even know it was Cliffordsville. It was too dark to read the signs when I got there. I didn't have any idea where I was except that it was a railroad station and there would likely be a train sometime. I was so tired I must have fallen asleep. I can't thank you enough for waking me. I don't believe I would have heard the train at all; I was just all in. I had been through a pretty awful experience and I'd been out all night in the storm."

"Oh, I'm sorry!" he said sympathetically, giving her a keen quick look. "I thought your dress felt damp. Aren't you going to catch a terrible cold?"

"Oh, I hope not," she said looking down at her wrinkled coat, "I didn't get so very wet. You see I took refuge in an old barn by the roadside during the worst, but afterwards the trees were wet, and the grass in the fields where I had to walk. Oh—this sounds queer, doesn't it? I guess I'll have to tell you about it, if it won't bore you."

"Of course not," said the pleasant voice and he gave her another keen look.

"Well, you see my brother at college got hurt in an accident and I went out to see him. I didn't know the people who offered to take me. They were the family of one of my brother's classmates, and their son had been hurt too. They were to take me one day and bring me back the second day after.

"I hadn't been long on the way before I wished I hadn't come with them. I was sure my mother wouldn't have approved. The young man was rather fresh, and his mother went to sleep part of the time, and I felt very uncomfortable. But it was worse the day we started back. I wouldn't have gone with them only I wanted to save the money. I knew we couldn't afford the carfare, and I thought I had to stick it out. But when I got in the car I found that a queer kind of girl was going back in place of the mother. She had on a great deal of make-up, she smoked cigarettes all the time, and I didn't like the way she acted at all. I was glad she was in the front seat with the man this time, instead of myself, and I thought it was going to be much better than on the way out. There was another thing that troubled me, too, we had started five hours late and I knew my mother would be worrying about me. Then after about an hour of driving we turned into the woods, and came to a sort of cabin, and there was another young man there waiting on the porch with a case of liquor beside him. They loaded the case into the car right in front of me, and put the young man in the back seat. I saw right away that he must be drunk. He was awful. He kept putting his head on my shoulder, and I couldn't get away from him. The people in the front seat didn't do a thing but laugh. They thought it was a good joke. Once when he tried to kiss me I screamed and then they turned around and threatened to gag me if I made another sound. You see by this time they had all been drinking a good deal, and they were mad because I wouldn't. And besides they were afraid they were being chased. The young man who got in with the liquor told them the state police were around, and by and by we heard shots behind us."

The gray eyes were watching her as she told her story.

They had an angry light in them as the story went on.

"And a thing like that can go on in a civilized country!" said Jenifer indignantly. "Do you know their names? Could you locate that cabin in the woods?"

"Oh, I wouldn't want to try!" said Melissa shivering and putting her hands before her eyes. "Yes, I suppose I could perhaps find it. I am sure I would know it when I saw it. And of course I know their names. But oh, I don't want ever to see any of them again. Ought I to? Father would feel so dreadfully to know I had been through all this, and I wouldn't dare tell Mother all of it. She would never trust me out of her sight again. She would be frantic. She is probably frantic now. You see I sent her a telegram that I would be home yesterday at three o'clock in the afternoon. She will think some awful thing has happened. But there hasn't been a chance to send another. I hoped the station would be open before the train came so I could let her know I am all right."

"Why, we can do that at the Junction," he said looking at his watch. "We're due there in half an hour, and we have three quarters to wait for the express to the city. It's early yet. She won't be awake will she? Or we might telephone."

"I'm afraid she won't have been asleep at all yet," said Melissa with trouble in her eyes. "But, you see there isn't any telephone. We're only there temporarily, waiting for Father to be well enough to come home, and we're hoping to find some place in the country."

"I see," said Jenifer. "Well then the wire is best. It will go through quickly so early in the morning. If this were an express we could send the telegram right away from the train, but I guess the Junction is the best we can do."

"You've been wonderfully kind," said Melissa. "I don't know why I have bothered you with all my worries. I never talk to strangers, but somehow you don't seem like a stranger. I guess I'm kind of upset and silly with all I've been through."

"Of course!" said Jenifer, "I'm glad I could help. I think it is always easier to have a friend by when things go wrong. I certainly would like to go out and hunt down those brutes that made your night such a wild experience. But perhaps we'd just better forget them and let you get some rest. Wouldn't you like to put your head back in this luxurious milk train and take another little nap before we get to the Junction?"

He spread his overcoat over the back of the seat for a pillow, and Melissa lay back and closed her eyes. But she could not sleep now. Her mind was alert again and on a tension. She was thinking of her mother and what they all would say to her when she got home, thinking of the narrow escapes she had had, dozens of them in the night that was past, and also in the days that were past since she left home. Then it occurred to her that something had seemed to be about her, preserving her at every turn. Though she had suffered with fright and exposure, from indignity and mortification, yet none of them had actually destroyed her, nor even really harmed her any, except to destroy her peace of mind, and hurt her pride. It really was wonderful how she had escaped from her unpleasant traveling companions, how there had always been some kind of shelter when it rained the hardest, some help in every crisis; that barn when the storm was at its worst; the young man when the train was coming and she asleep.

She looked at the young man by her side through the fringes of her lashes, studied the lines of his lean pleasant face and compared him to Gene Hollister. Here was a man that one could trust. Here was a man her father and mother would honor. She had no question in her mind about confiding in him. He was honorable. That was written in every line of his expression.

Jenifer had taken out a book and pencil and was at work. Melissa dropped her veiled glance to see what he was doing and found to her amazement that he held a small limp covered Bible in his hands and was writing in minute script little notes along its margin. She tried to make out the words without really opening her eyes, but could not. What could it be he was doing?

He took out a little notebook from his pocket, and copied things into the margin of the Bible here and there, fluttering the leaves over as if it were a familiar and beloved book. There was no mistaking the look of deep interest in what he was doing. He was not studying this from duty. It was something he earnestly desired to do, and his look was as of one delving deep in a chest of treasure and discovering new jewels the deeper he went. Melissa had never seen any one look that way about a book, not even her father when he was deep in scientific study, or had found some literary treasure in a musty tome. She marveled at it. What sort of young man was this one who had come so unexpectedly into her life, just apparently to save her from a trying place, and help her on her way a little while?

Then in the midst of her meditations the conductor came through waving his unnecessary smoky red lantern and calling out to the sleepy passengers:

"Next station, Marwood Junction! All change cars! This train goes no farther!" And all the sleepy passengers stretched and yawned and looked about them.

Ian Jenifer closed his book almost reluctantly it seemed with a last lingering look at a verse he had just marked and slipped it into the bag at his feet. Then he turned toward Melissa and finding her wide awake he smiled. She noticed there was a kind of radiance behind his eyes that seemed to come from some hidden source. It seemed somehow that it was the look with which he had been reading the Book, as if the Book itself had reflected something from its words into his face.

"Rested?" he said, and smiled again. "Now we can send our telegram. Have you thought what you want to say?"

"Oh! Yes," said Melissa, starting up. "I thought I'd say" she tapped the words out on her fingers, " 'Unavoidably delayed, no telephone. Am all right. Home to-day.' "

"Nothing could be better," said the young man. "That tells

everything without telling a thing!" and he grinned genially. "Well suppose you write it out with the address. I think there'll be time before the train stops. Here, take my pencil and write it in my notebook and then I'll look after it for you as soon as we are landed and lose no time."

Melissa wrote it and handed the book back. He read it and looked up at her interestedly.

"Challenger!" he said. "That's a striking name. I don't believe I ever heard it before, but it has a distinguished sound that I like. Then you're Melissa Challenger. I like that too. You know I haven't been introduced to you before. But come, we'd better get out of here and not let this mob get ahead of us. We'll need some time to get a bite to eat too." He steered her to a small wooden room with a bench running all around and left her with the baggage while he went to send the telegram. Then he returned and piloted her outside and around to another door where a long counter was flanked by a row of high stools which were fast filling up.

Jenifer found a seat for Melissa, and himself stood just behind her waiting for the laborer who occupied the next stool to finish his coffee.

The menu was simple and substantial, sausage, hot cakes with sirup, and coffee. Melissa fell upon hers with a relish.

"I hadn't much lunch yesterday," she laughed, "I was afraid I would miss my escorts."

"And no dinner at all, I can guess."

"No dinner!" said Melissa, "I ran away just as dinner was about to be served."

They found that they had to eat rather hurriedly after all for by the time they were served the train was almost due, so there was little opportunity for talk.

When they were seated at last in the express Melissa looked up suddenly and asked:

"Are you a minister, Mr. Jenifer?"

She was still puzzling over his Bible study and the look on his face while he was reading.

He looked up with a smile.

"No," he answered, "I'm a construction engineer. That is, that's the way I earn my living."

Melissa looked puzzled.

"I don't understand," she said. "You were studying the Bible and I thought scholars, real scholars, college people, didn't believe in the Bible any more—unless of course they were ministers."

"And why ministers?"

"Well, of course, that's their *business*."

"You mean either that ministers aren't scholars, or else they are not honest ministers?"

Something in his tone brought the color to Melissa's cheeks.

"Well—er—when I went to college my professors thought, that is they said that the Bible was a beautiful piece of literature of course, but they didn't accept it as the book of God."

"No?" said Jenifer, "Well, were they Christians, Miss Challenger?"

"Christians?" said Melissa. "What difference would that make, if they were scholars?"

"All the difference in the world," said Jenifer earnestly. "The Bible itself says: 'But the natural man receiveth not the things of the Spirit of God: for they are foolishness unto him: neither can he know them, because they are spiritually discerned.' To a man who is spiritually dead the Bible would mean nothing. He couldn't understand it. It would be full of contradictions."

"But isn't it full of contradictions?" asked Melissa.

"No," said Jenifer, "To one who is born again and 'has received the Spirit which is of God' that he might 'know the things that are freely given to us of God,' there isn't a contradiction from beginning to end. It is like a great picture puzzle that fits together perfectly to form the picture of the God-

Man, Christ Jesus. But it is a great subject. One cannot explain all that in a few minutes."

"Yes," sighed Melissa, "I can see it must be. You used several phrases I never heard before and don't understand. I guess I must be one of those 'spiritually dead' ones," and she gave a little embarrassed laugh, for indeed it was to her as if he were talking in an unknown tongue.

He turned eager eyes upon her.

"What were they? I'll be glad to explain."

"Well, that about receiving the Spirit of God. Is that a sort of Spiritualism?"

"No," he said gently. "The Holy Spirit is a Person of the Godhead, Who 'takes the things of Christ and shows them unto us,' makes them plain to us. He dwells in every child of God."

"Child of God?" said Melissa wonderingly. "That's another strange phrase. That must have something to do with the being 'born again' that you spoke of!" She ended with a little laugh as if it were some queer kind of joke.

"It certainly has," answered Jenifer heartily. "You see, everybody born into the *world* is dead in sins. One must be born again to be fit for *heaven*."

"How on earth could that be?" asked Melissa, now thoroughly astonished and bewildered.

For answer Jenifer reached for his worn Bible once more. His fingers seemed to caress the pages as he turned them quickly and pointed to a few lines.

"But as many as received Him, to them gave He power to become the sons of God, even to them that believe on His name," read Melissa.

"Now, you tell me," smiled Jenifer, "how does one become a child of God?"

Melissa's eyes went back to the verse.

"It says, by 'receiving Him,' 'believing on His name,'— whose name?" she asked sharply.

"The name of Jesus," Jenifer answered tenderly, "and 'Jesus' means 'Savior.'"

"Then I'm to believe that Jesus is my Savior? Is that it?"

"That's all," said Jenifer with a ring to his voice as he noted the quick way in which the girl applied the truth to herself. "And this is what makes Him your Savior and mine." He turned the pages again.

"But He was wounded for our transgressions, He was bruised for our iniquities: the chastisement of our peace was upon Him; and with His stripes we are healed. All we like sheep have gone astray; we have turned every one to his own way; and the Lord hath laid on Him the iniquity of us all."

"Oh!" cried Melissa, "That's what I did. I went astray and I went my own way! And yet," she went on, tears of wonder standing in her eyes, "God didn't punish me for it! He took care of me by sending you! And, do you mean He punished *Him* for what I did?"

"That's exactly it," said Jenifer watching her eagerly.

There was silence for some time then as Melissa read over the words again and pondered the wonderful truth she had discovered, while a strange new joy mounted in her heart, and a song of thanksgiving arose beside her from the heart of the young man who had led her to his Lord.

Then she began to ask questions and the time sped away as they talked till suddenly they were at their journey's end before they knew it.

"I'd love to tell you more," said Jenifer eagerly, as he gathered up their baggage, "For while I earn my living at engineering, my real business in life is to witness to others about my Lord Jesus. Might I come to see you sometime soon and may we talk more?"

"Oh, I wish you would," said Melissa earnestly, "I never heard anything like this before. I don't believe my mother knows either. If it is true it would be wonderful! To just live and trust everything, day by day, and know it would be all right. It is too good to be true. It is not—earthly. It does not seem natural."

"No, it is heavenly," he smiled. "But here, we must get off."

"Now," said Jenifer as they reached the station, "We are going to get into a taxi and drive straight to your home. Your mother is not going to have to wait an extra second to know that you are safe. Since God sent me to look after you I consider it my right to be sure that you are safely landed in your mother's arms."

He smiled down at her and Melissa's face grew rosy with the pleasure of it. It was wonderful to be taken care of that way after her wild experience.

"Oh, thank you," she said, "You have been wonderful to me!"

"Not in the least. I'm quite selfish in this. I want to see you safe, and I want to see where you live so that I can come again if you will let me, and come soon."

"That will be lovely," said Melissa, "I somehow feel as if I had known you ages. And I do want you to meet my mother and the family."

So he put her into a taxi, and Melissa, well escorted, started on the last brief stage of her journey back to the little Brady house.

15

WHEN Phylis threw open the front door and found the messenger boy standing there with a telegram in his hand she fairly fell upon him and snatched the envelope from him. Bob and Rosalie had come home early on account of a short session, and Bob signed for the message, for Phyllis had torn open the envelope and was reading.

"Oh, Mother, she's all right," she called as she rushed upstairs. "She says she was unavoidably detained where there was no telephone, but she is all right and she'll be home today. Hear that? There! Read it for yourself."

Mary Challenger with a great light breaking in her face took the paper holding it with shaking hands and read. Then she looked up to where her children stood in breathless eagerness about her and said as if she were just thinking aloud:

"Then He does answer prayer. God does answer prayer! Even my poor prayer!"

Phyllis looked at her in amazement for an instant and then threw her arms about her and crushed her in a big hug.

"Of course He does," said Rosalie radiantly. "He began with the beefsteak and onions, and He's going to do all the rest I'm sure."

"Aw, gee! Didn't ya all know that? What's all the excitement about?" put in Bob.

"And now," said Phyllis, "Mother, you've got to lie down and rest. Yes, you have. There are no two ways about it. Rosalie and I are going to get a dinner ready that can be served as soon as Melissa gets here, whenever that is. We have chops. Mr. Brady just sent them over, lovely ones, and chopped potatoes creamed, they'll keep and warm up indefinitely, and we'll open a can of stringed beans. Melissa likes those. Then there are six tomatoes, and two stalks of celery. Rosalie will make tomato surprise for salad, and how would a cottage pudding do for dessert? That won't spoil with standing. Or no, chocolate blanc-mange. There is quite a little cream. I saved yesterday's and to-day's from both bottles. How's that for a fatted calf, Mother dear?"

"It sounds good," said the mother with a trembling smile.

"And Mother, do you think we ought to ask those Hollisters to stay for dinner, or couldn't we afford it? Rosalie and I would let them have our chops."

"Why, yes, of course. We must ask them even if we can't afford it when they have been so kind to Melissa. We certainly can't repay them any other way. We must be courteous. And of course they'll be hungry after such a long ride."

"We can't make the table look very grand," said Phyllis with a thoughtful look toward Rosalie's three dandelions.

"That doesn't matter. We'll just give them what we have. I somehow feel that things are going to be brighter now dear, perhaps the bank will open to-morrow—or *some*thing." Her voice trembled off into silence.

"Go lie down Mother," commanded Phyllis again. "You know you *may* have to take the evening train."

But Phyllis as she went about her dinner preparations was silently wondering how her mother could take a train even if she had to, for all her mathematical calculations had served only to show that there was not quite half enough money in the family to cover what would likely be necessary expenses of such a trip. She sighed heavily as she went out into the kitchen and began to peel potatoes.

"Why do you sigh, Phyllie? Aren't you glad now, Sister, since Lissa is all right?"

"Glad? Sure! But I'm wondering what's coming next."

"You mustn't, Phyllie."

"Well, I don't know where the money's coming from to send Mother to see Steve, and I'm just sure she's got to go, and soon."

"But if God can answer one prayer, can't He answer another?"

"I suppose so," said Phyllis trying to smile. "Bob, what time is it in there by the cuckoo? I wonder if I've got plenty of time to make blanc-mange and get it good and cold before they come?"

"Aw, gee! This old clock has stopped again!" answered Bob. "I wonder what's got inta her. Guess I musta forgot ta wind her last night. She ain't acted right since that Barkus woman monkeyed with her."

"Why, Bob, she didn't touch the clock."

"Yes she did too. Put her old paw on the tail piece and pulled real hard. I saw her do it. I bet she did somepin to her. I'm gonta get up on a chair and see. Do you havta know the time right this minute? Cause I'd rather get her going first and then I can set her when I get back from asking Brady."

"That's all right Bob, only don't break that clock. You know how Father feels about it."

"Aw, whaddaya think I am?" said Bob as he mounted a chair and began to examine the inner workings of the fine old clock.

Five minutes later the girls in the kitchen were startled by hearing the cuckoo cooing out vigorously, one! two! three! and then an exclamation from Bob and a clattering sound of something metal falling and rattling on the floor.

"Aw, gee! Now whaddaya think of that!" came Bob's voice, and both girls rushed to the door in consternation.

"Did you break it, Bob? I told you not to bother with it!"

"Naw, I didn't break it, grandma!" responded Bob wrathfully. "I just put my hand up there ta see what was getting in the way of that clapper and stopping it right in the middle of a coo, and out that thing tumbled. Whaddaya think of that now? Somebody went and put a tin box inside that clock. Isn't that the limit?"

"It's a part of the works of the clock of course," said Phyllis with a worried tone. "You ought not to touch a clock. Nobody but a clock maker knows how to fix a clock."

"Aw, cut it! You're only a girl if you are older'n I am. I didn't touch the old clock!" said Bob, as worried as herself, getting down with a thump from the chair and bending over the thing on the floor. It isn't a piece of the works I tell ya, it's a *box*. See! There's an advertisement on the cover. A little thin box. Quinine pills it says, plain as day. They don't use quinine pillboxes ta make the works of a clock do they? I *ask* ya!"

The girls came and stood gazing curiously while Bob picked up the box, but as he lifted it the cover came off with a ring and went spinning across the floor, and out of the box fell what looked like a wad of colored paper, green and yellow and white.

"Why, it's money, Phyllis, look!" said Rosalie picking up the little packet. "Where do you suppose it came from?"

Phyllis took it in wonder and unfolded it, her eyes growing wide and startled.

Two one-hundred-dollar bills and a fifty dollar bill. She held it in her hand and stared at it. The two children were speechless with wonder. Then Bob rallied.

"Aw, I bet Brady put that in there. I bet he put that money in that box and hid it in that clock for us. I bet he knew we hadn't much and he fixed it so the clock would stop, and so it would fall out if we tried ta fix it. I bet that's it. I'm goin' down ta the shop and tell him he can't put that over on us."

"*I* think God sent it, if you ask me," said Rosalie with conviction.

"Wait!" said Phyllis sharply, "Here's a paper with writing, a
note perhaps."

She smoothed out the bit of folded paper and read:

> First payment of two hundred and fifty dollars made
> by Clarence Stuart to me, to-day, on the money (one
> thousand dollars) loaned by me to him, with the old
> cuckoo clock for security, the money to be used by him
> toward his university course abroad. It is understood
> between us that the clock, an heirloom in his family, is
> to be returned to him (or his heirs) when the final pay-
> ment is made.
>
> John F. Challenger

The date was the day that Mr. Challenger had been taken
to the hospital, several months before.

The children stood and looked at each other, and then at the
clock.

"Why do ya 'spose Dad put the money in there instead of in
the bank?" asked Bob practically.

"Because he knew if it was in the bank he would be likely to
spend it," said Phyllis. "I think he wanted to get it all together
at once for some reason. Perhaps he thought that was a good
way to save it."

"H'm!" said the boy contemptuously, "I don't think much
of that for a hiding place. It doesn't seem like Dad."

"Perhaps he didn't want us to know about it," said Phyllis.
"You know how he always was about the confidence of his
students. Perhaps the boy didn't want it known that he was
borrowing money or something, and you know Father had
been sick for a week before he went to the hospital. He
couldn't take it to the bank. If he had asked Mother to she

naturally would have asked where the money came from, wouldn't she? I expect he just thought he would be back in a few days and he would stick it up in there and it would be all safe. That explains why he was so insistent that we keep the clock. The boy wants it back again."

"But 'spose we'd a sold it that day when Barkus kicked up such a row?"

"Mother wouldn't sell it you know without his permission, and when she asked him about it he said we mustn't part with it on any account. You see he felt it wasn't really his. It belonged to this Clarence Stuart."

"Gee!" said Bob. "Well, the money's his all right any way. I don't expect he'd want us not ta use it. Whyn't ya tell Mother?"

They suddenly all sprang together toward the stairs and hurried up.

"Hush!" said Phyllis, "she may be asleep."

But Mary Challenger was not sleeping. She was kneeling by her bed, and still kneeling, she lifted a startled face and looked at her children.

"See! Mother! We've found the money for your trip!" said Rosalie with shining eyes. "It was in the cuckoo clock. Isn't it wonderful?"

And then they gathered around her on the edge of the bed while she sat with them and read the paper, and handled with wonder the clean new money.

"I feel as if it came straight down from heaven!" said the mother, a new look in her delicate face.

"And now I guess Melissa Challenger won't say those things she did any more about not believing in God," said Rosalie triumphantly, "not after we've told her all that has happened. My! I wish she'd come!"

It was just at that moment that the taxi drew up before the door. Melissa had started to explain that this house was only loaned to them for a few weeks till they could find something they could afford, but she hadn't got two words out before

Bob threw wide the door and yelled with all his might and main:

"Here they come! It's a taxi. They musta had a flat tire! Ur a smash-up! Anyhow here they are!"

Then Rosalie came flying out with her curls blowing and her cheeks glowing, and Mary Challenger came swiftly down from her bedroom and folded her eldest daughter in her arms. There were tears on her cheek when finally she released her daughter to the rest of the family.

It was not until then that any of them saw the tall young man who stood smiling in the doorway surrounded by bags.

It was Melissa who recovered first and introduced him.

"This is Mr. Jenifer, Mother. He's been wonderful to me. I want you to thank him. I don't know when I should have got home if it hadn't been for him. I certainly wouldn't have been here yet."

Then the mother turned her attention to the young man, and taking his hand thanked him as only a mother who has been through a night of agony and anxiety can thank her daughter's rescuer.

"Jenifer!" said Bob, "But I thought his name was Hollister!"

"No, it's not, thank goodness," said Melissa. "Those Hollisters were unspeakable, Mother. They got drunk and tried to take me into a roadhouse for dinner and a dance. But I got away from them, and found my way back to a railroad station in a village. It's a long story and it can wait. We are *awfully* hungry. Have you got anything in the house to eat? And can't Mr. Jenifer have some too? He lives away up town and it will take him so long to get there!"

"Oh, no, that's all right. I couldn't think of intruding now," said Jenifer smiling, "I'll just run in some other time if you'll let me, some evening perhaps, and see if you are any the worse for your trip."

"You are staying now, please," said Mary Challenger taking his two hands in both of hers. "I cannot let you go this way."

"All right," said Ian Jenifer, "If you say so I'll stay now. It's really what I want to do, if you just won't take any trouble for me."

"We won't," smiled Phyllis waving the knife with which she had been paring the cold potatoes, "We're almost ready to serve dinner. I've only the chops to broil!"

"And there are two more chops than you ordered, Sister," added Rosalie in a stage whisper. "You can give Mr. Jenifer two, and none of us will have to go without either."

Everybody heard it of course, and everybody broke down and laughed hilariously, to the utter confusion of sweet Rosalie, who rallied however and laughed with them.

Jenifer insisted on being allowed to broil the chops. He said he knew how, and proved that he did by doing them to a lovely brown, and presently they were all seated around the table eating a delicious meal and all talking at once. And while they were in the midst of it Brady appeared at the door, beamed upon them, was introduced to Jenifer, whispered in Melissa's ear: "That's a *regular* guy you've brought home this time!" and then vanished.

Just the joy of having Melissa safe and home again was enough for the first few minutes. Then suddenly the mother's face grew sober and she asked:

"But you haven't told me about Stephen. Just how is he dear? Should I go to him to-night? You needn't be afraid to tell me the truth."

Melissa's face grew troubled at once.

"Oh, Mother, I'm not sure, but I think so!" and then she told as well as she could just how he had seemed to her and just what the doctors and the nurses had said to her.

"I think I should go at once," said the mother, rising. "If you will excuse me now I'll get my things ready. We have been looking up the trains and there is one at six o'clock."

"Mrs. Challenger," said Jenifer rising, "Wouldn't you like to have me get a later bulletin on your son's case before you leave so that you will not have to be wondering and anxious all the way lest conditions have changed since your daughter left?"

"Oh, that would be very kind," said Mary Challenger, "but I don't like to trouble you further. Perhaps Phyllis could do it."

"I would like to do it for you," said the young man earnestly.

"But Mother, he's already missed a very important appointment to bring me home," said Melissa. "I don't think we ought to hinder him any longer."

"It doesn't matter," said Jenifer "It really doesn't. I shall call up the man and explain and I can just as well see him this evening. Please let me go."

"I'll go with ya and show ya the way," offered Bob importantly.

"Yes, do," said Jenifer cordially, "then we can get acquainted and you'll be able to set me right if there's any question I don't know about."

They went off together, Bob looking up at the young man adoringly, and in his heart remembering what his friend Brady's opinion had been. Yes, he surely was a "regular guy," Bob thought.

The rest of the family rushed upstairs to help Mother get ready for her journey, Melissa to tell more in detail some of the things that had happened to her on the way. But they had not time for connected conversation. One was hunting handkerchiefs, another gloves, another was polishing her shoes, Phyllis was repacking the bag to get everything in, and they all were interrupting each other with eager questions.

It was in the midst of this that there came a knock on the front door.

"You run down, Rosalie dear," said Phyllis, laying her mother's best dress in smoothly. "It's probably just a peddler."

Rosalie came back in a minute.

"It's a man to see Mother," she announced. "He's a nice

looking man. He has a shiny car out in front."

"Well, I can't possibly spare the time to see anybody. It's likely that Refrigerator man that came yesterday and Phyllis told him I was out. Run and tell him dear that your mother is trying to catch a train and she doesn't want anything any way."

"I did," said Rosalie, "and he said he wouldn't keep you but a minute, but it was very important. I think he said a name that was on that letter you got this morning."

"Oh, well, tell him, dear, that Mother couldn't possibly buy any book at this time, she hasn't got the money."

Rosalie went downstairs and accosted the man who still stood on the front porch waiting. He was a nice looking man as Rosalie had said and she hated to disappoint him about the book.

"Mother is sorry," she said sweetly, "but she just can't take the time or she will miss her train. And she says tell you she couldn't possibly afford to buy a book now anyway."

The man smiled.

"Oh," he said, "you're mistaken. I'm not a book agent. You tell your mother I'm from the firm of lawyers she visited the other day. Tell her it's about her inheritance. And it's very important that I see her at once. There is a paper she should sign to-day."

Rosalie eyed him uncertainly but went back upstairs. "It isn't the book, Mother. He says he wants to see you about your inheritance."

"Inheritance?" laughed Mary Challenger. "Whatever does the man mean? I suppose it's some more of those silly questions that he asked me the other day. Tell him, dear, that there never was any inheritance in the Challenger family that I ever heard of and I have told him all I know. He'll have to get the rest of his facts somewhere else."

Rosalie traveled down again.

"Mother says there never was any inheritance that she

knows of. She says she can't tell you any more facts for your book."

"Book what book? I really don't know what you mean, child."

"Why, aren't you the man that is writing a book about our family tree?"

"Not at all!" said the man. "My dear, there is some mistake. I am quite sure your mother does not understand or she would at least take time to sign her name to this document which is all she has to do. I have the keys to the property here—"

Rosalie with a bewildered look went upstairs again.

"He says you don't understand, Mother. He says you would come down if you understood. It's not about a family tree nor a book nor anything. It's an inheritance, and property."

"Phyllis, for pity's sake do go down and see what the man means. He has probably got the wrong house."

Phyllis went down and said coolly,

"Who did you want to see?"

"Mrs. Mary Challenger," said the man. "Isn't this where she lives? I'm quite sure this is the number she gave me."

"Yes, she lives here," said Phyllis, "but she is really in too much of a hurry to speak with you. My brother has been hurt in an accident at college and she has to take the six o'clock train. Can't you give me the message?"

"You are Miss Challenger?"

"I am Phyllis Challenger. Yes."

"Ah!" said the man, "Phyllis! I believe that is the name mentioned in our client's letter, Miss Challenger. Your mother has been left some property by a distant relative. It is not a large estate of course, but still it is a fairly comfortable one. We had first to establish your mother's identity before handing it over to her, but everything is quite all right now, and we are anxious to get the matter settled up and out of our hands. I have brought the keys to the property with me, and the necessary papers to be signed, together with all data about the investments. I wish you could persuade your mother to at least sign this paper. Mr. Wright feels that it ought to be attended to at once. The rest of the business could await your mother's return if necessary, or perhaps she could delegate you to attend to it."

In a daze of wonder Phyllis invited the man in and went up to report.

"Mother, the most amazing thing! I think the man must be out of his mind. He says you've been left some money by a distant relative. At least he said property. I guess you'll have to go down and see him for a minute. He says if you'll just sign the paper he can hand over the keys. He didn't say what to. It may be a warehouse or a chicken coop, but for sweet pity's sake if we own some property let's find out what it is. This seems to be a day of surprises."

But before Phyllis had finished speaking Mrs. Challenger had swept her aside and gone downstairs.

Rosalie lingered near Phyllis for a minute.

"I think this may be going to be an answer to one of our prayers, don't you, Phyllie?" she whispered eagerly.

"Better wait till you see, dearie. It may turn out to be a family tree after all, or at least a branch."

Five minutes later the girls, listening at the top of the stairs, heard Jenifer and Bob come in, and they slipped down to tell their mother it was time for her to start, but they found their mother signing a big official looking document with a great seal on one end and Jenifer standing by to sign his name as a witness. The insistent gentleman stood smiling above the table, and as the last name was written he accepted his fountain pen from Jenifer's hand and said to Mary Challenger:

"That's all, Mrs. Challenger, that's quite all for to-day. Thank you for coming down. Mr. Wright was anxious to get the matter settled up. The rest of the papers are down at the office in our vault, and are perfectly safe until you call for them when you get back. I hope you will enjoy your property. Of course it isn't really an estate, just a modest comfortable home, but I think you'll like it. Oh, and here's your bankbook. You'll find the entries there of all interest that has accrued while the estate was being settled. And now, I'll bid you good afternoon, and sorry to have bothered you."

He bowed himself out of the door, and the family stood staring at one another, until Bob, who didn't know at all what it was about announced that the taxi had come to take his mother to the station.

Then they began to pour out questions, but Jenifer stopped them.

"I'm sorry," he said, "but you haven't much time, Mrs. Challenger, if you really want to catch this train."

"All right! I'm ready. Bob get my suitcase. It's upstairs. Phyllis, what did you do with my hand bag? Sorry, children, but Phyllis heard it all. She can tell you what she knows. I don't know much about it myself. I've been left some property by a cousin I never saw, who died in England. He's only a fourth cousin. It sounds like a fairy story but if it's anything worth while we'll enjoy it when I get back. Now be good children and don't any of you get lost. Phyllis you won't forget what I told you to tell Father—"

She was gone, with Jenifer sitting beside her in the taxi smiling and waving his hand as if he were an old friend of the family.

Phyllis stood on the sidewalk twirling a couple of keys tied together with a string, waving her hands joyously, and Melissa in the doorway was thinking how handsome Jenifer looked as he took off his hat especially to her when they drove away.

It seemed very strange to have their mother gone, just at night too that way, and all this excitement; Melissa home with a long tale to tell, and then these mystical keys, and the strange story of the inheritance. The girls were so excited they could hardly get the table cleared off. They talked and talked while they washed the dishes.

"And Lissa," said Rosalie with shining eyes, "you can't talk that way any more about God not answering prayer. Wait till you hear about the money in the cuckoo clock. Phyllis, you tell her about the cuckoo clock, and how we prayed for money for Mother to go and see Stephen."

Melissa listened in wonder as the three told together, first one, then the other, about how Bob found the money in the clock, and then she turned to Rosalie who was watching her with happy eyes.

"That's wonderful, isn't it, Rosy dear? But I've been finding out some things too. I prayed myself when I got in that terrible storm alone, and some while I was in that car and was so frightened. And then I prayed when I found I'd got to stay alone out on the railroad platform. I tell you I was afraid when I lay down. And I was cold and wet too, and so tired. And God heard me, I'm sure of it."

She was still just a minute, and they all stood watching her in some embarrassment. It didn't sound a bit like the old Melissa. Then she began to speak again.

"I've found out something else," she said in a low voice, lifting shy eyes to theirs. "I've found that I've been a sinner, and I've taken Jesus Christ for my Savior. I guess you'll think it's queer, the way I've been talking lately, but I've learned a lot of things since I went away, and—I'm very happy this new way. I don't know if I can be very different, but I want to be."

There was a great silence in the kitchen. Bob turned his back and looked out the dark window, beginning to whistle softly. Rosalie went and laid a soft kiss on the back of her sister's neck as she sat at the table wiping silver, and Phyllis spoke up at last.

"I guess we all have a lot to learn! I know I had. We've all been praying. Bob and I, too, haven't we, Bob?"

"Sure thing!" said Bob with his back still turned and a queer soft sound to his voice.

"And Mother's been praying too," went on Phyllis,

"but,—somehow I didn't know how you'd feel about it. You've been so—since you went to college,—you know—"

"I know," said Melissa, "I was all wrong. I'm glad I found out. But isn't it kind of queer how we all found out at once?"

"Well, we all went through a lot of hard things together. I used to wonder how there could be a God and let us suffer so, and be so humiliated, but Mr. Jenifer says that God has sometimes to let the people He loves suffer really hard things, because they won't listen to Him any other way. I guess that's the way we were."

"I guess we were," said Phyllis. "I wonder what Father will say to it. He doesn't know what we've been through of course. And Steve. He's had it pretty soft. I just wondered what they'll think to know we feel this way."

"I wonder!" said Melissa softly.

"Now," said Phyllis, flinging her dishcloth on the line to dry, "I promised Mother I'd put you to bed at once, Lissa. You've got a lot of sleep to make up. Come on, here goes! No more talk to-night."

The matter of the inheritance had made little impression on the rest of the family excepting Phyllis who had heard the lawyer's announcement. It was to the others an unknown quantity, very pleasant to dream about, but not at all real. They referred to it gayly several times as a joke.

"When we get our millions," Melissa had said as she wiped a bent fork, "I move we buy a dozen new forks."

"Aw, gee, I'd like a new sweater," said Bob. "Mine's ripped all across one shoulder."

But Phyllis thought a great deal about it after every one was in bed. She lay there wide awake and planned about it. Would it be a little cottage with a yard around it somewhere in the country? And in the morning before any one else was up she took out the keys and looked at them wisely. She meant to go and see that house before anybody else, just to find out if there was anything they could do with it. It couldn't be sold, there had been a proviso in the will to that effect the lawyer said.

The cousin had wanted his home to stay in the family. Queer. Why did he care after he was dead? There was a letter from him among the papers. Mother had taken that with her to read. That would likely tell all about it. Then her thoughts drifted off to Melissa and how wonderful it was that she too had prayed, and felt she had been answered, and she fell asleep at last praying for Steve, and that her mother might not find him worse.

16

SUNDAY morning the children all slept late, for they were worn out with excitement and anxiety. While they were eating a combination meal of late breakfast and early dinner, Brady came in with a message from their mother that had come over his telephone. She had arrived safely and had found Stephen's condition slightly better. The cerebral symptoms were not quite so strongly present. The doctor thought that the next two or three days might see a marked improvement. The children were to be very careful and not take risks in any way. She sent her love, and reminded them not to worry their father with anything.

That lifted a heavy load from Melissa's mind for ever since she had left him, she had been depressed by the thought of her brother tossing in delirium and fever.

Melissa took charge of the house and sent Phyllis off to visit her father.

It was the first time Phyllis had been to see her father for two months. The doctor had wanted him to see nobody but his wife if possible. His eyes lighted up at sight of her.

"Why, how you've grown, daughter!" he said, "and how pretty you are. I'd forgotten what a charming family I have and thought of you all just as babies. But where is your mother? She isn't sick is she?"

"No, but she's gone to visit Steve. We had word he had broken his leg,—now don't get worried!" she added quickly as she saw the look on her father's face. "He's much better, but Mother thought she better go and cheer him up a little," said Phyllis, according to the plan that had been agreed upon between herself and her mother.

"Oh, but that's hard for him now just at the end near commencement!" said the father. "Athletes will take such risks! I hope it won't affect his marks. Of course a broken leg will mend,—you say he's really better?—but it's hard to have to suffer and keep still so long. Poor Steve! How long did your mother plan to stay? When did she go?"

"Just last night, Father. She decided quite suddenly. She wasn't quite sure just how long she ought to stay. She said it would depend somewhat on Steve's state of mind. If he was cheerful and satisfied she might come back soon, though she thought she ought to stay long enough to go over his clothes and put them in shape. He'll probably need a lot of darning."

She was making out quite a good case she thought, and her father did not seem much upset by it.

"How did he break his leg? Was it a fall?"

"Well, we haven't had the details," said Phyllis vaguely, "Mother can tell you more when she comes. Or maybe she'll write you. She didn't like to be away from you long."

"Oh, I'm all right. I'm fine. They'll be dismissing me soon. By the way, I'm to have another examination to-morrow, and after it they want me to sleep, so you better plan not to visit me until Tuesday for they won't likely let you in."

Phyllis felt very happy when she finally came away. It was great to see her father looking so well, and there was a gentleness about him that was so different from his hurried days when he was a busy professor rushed from morning to night and no time for his children to get acquainted with him. It thrilled her heart. Oh, that inheritance of Mother's surely would have something in it that would help them to find a solution to the matter of a home where Father would have the right conditions.

Phyllis found Jenifer at the house when she reached home. He had come to tell them that their mother got off safely, and to see if Melissa was all right after her journey. They asked him to stay and have supper with them, and he agreed if they would go to evening church with him. He had his car and there was room for everybody.

Bob would have wriggled out of such an invitation ordinarily, but he had "fallen" for Jenifer as he said, and he went without a murmur.

"Gee, I wouldn't mind going to church every Sunday if it was like that!" said Bob who had listened intently. "I never heard a guy preach like that. That was real!"

And so the first day of their mother's absence passed happily.

There was a letter from their mother in the morning mail next day. It came after Melissa had gone out after a job that Jenifer had told her about, and Phyllis read it alone.

Dear Children:

It seems a long time since I left home. I can hardly believe only one night has passed. This is just a line to let you know that your brother is really better to-day. He opened his eyes this morning a few minutes and seemed to know me. I'm glad I came. The doctor says it may make all the difference in the world in his recovery having me here. Tell Father not to worry and you be sure to let me know if he needs me for I can always come and send one of you back here to Steve.

Everybody here is telling me how sweet Melissa is, and it makes my heart very proud. But when I saw the hard little couch where she slept for two nights with only a pillow it made my heart ache. She was a brave girl.

I am enclosing the letter from that cousin of mine four times removed! I thought you would like to see it. Keep it carefully. I wouldn't say anything to Father about it yet until we know more about it. Don't lose those keys. We'll hunt up the house. It might be a place to go for a while, though I don't suppose from what the lawyer said that it can be much. Still, it can't be much more humble than where we are now, and if it is in the right location it might be a great help. You see by the letter that there'll be some money too and that will be a help. I haven't an idea whether he was well off but I judge not. I never heard much about them. They lived in the west when I was growing up, and I never met any of them. But it's a nice letter, isn't it?

Now I must go to Steve for a while. The nurse said I might sit by him if I wouldn't speak a word. Keep on praying and be good children.

Lovingly,
Mother

Phyllis put her head down on the table and cried a few tears before she read the other letter. It was so strange to have Mother away, so sweet to get a letter from her so soon. Phyllis felt a heavy burden upon her.

The other letter was written in a cramped trembling hand.

My Dear Cousin, (it read)

You do not know me at all I suppose, and I know very little about you, but when I found that I had only a few months to live I began to wonder what I should do with the few things of this world that have fallen to my share. I didn't exactly want to leave them to public charities, especially the house I built about ten years ago for my dear wife and myself to end our days in,—she died in France soon after its completion and never saw it finished—and I never went back after that. I couldn't bear to. So I set about trying to find some relative, to leave my house and what else I had in some friendly hands. After several months the lawyers into whose hands I had put the matter wrote me of having found trace of a Mary Challenger. Then I remembered my mother having spoken of you, of having attended your wedding, and later of your having several children. I remember the name of one of them was Phyllis, which was my mother's name and I had always liked it. So it pleased me that I had got trend of some one who even in a distant way belonged to me.

You see the house was just finished before we went abroad, or nearly so, and we had our furniture and things moved in by the storage people after we left. I had been called abroad suddenly on business. That is the reason I am putting a proviso in my will that the house shall not be sold by the legatee for at least ten years after inheriting it. My dear wife's personal effects are there, packed just as she left them in preparation for her trip. There will be her clothes and private letters, and her little personal treasures. I would like some friendly person, some relative to go over those things. I cannot do it myself for I am a sick man, and could not stand the journey, but I don't like the idea of several old cats on a Charity Board doing it, to maul over Hilda's silks, and fine laces, and speculate about her private affairs. I would like you, Mary Challenger, to do that for me.

And if so be that Mary Challenger is not living, then I would like the house to go to that little Phyllis if she is alive. If not, then some other member of the family, with the same request that they do to my wife's personal effects what they would want done to their own in a similar case.

If your circumstances are such, that it is convenient, I should be glad if you and your family would make my house your home for at least a part of every year for a time, for I would be glad to have the house loved by some one, we put so much thought and happy anticipation into it. I am leaving you money enough to keep up the house in the way that we would have done if we had lived there, and so I hope that may not be an objection to your keeping the place. But in any event I would like it kept up in the family for at least ten years.

And now in closing may I wish you all best blessings, with whatever dear ones you have with you.

I have a firm belief in the faith of my Fathers, and I expect to join my wife in the house of many mansions, so that your enjoyment of the earthly home I am leaving behind need not be hampered by any sadness on my account. I am glad there is some one of my own family to whom I can leave my belongings when I go.

Your fourth cousin on your mother's side,
Nathan Osgood Forsythe

When Phyllis had finished reading the letter she put it carefully away in her mother's handkerchief box in her bureau drawer, and then put her hat on. She had intended going out again to hunt a job, but she was too excited about that house now. If a person who could write a nice letter like that, a good Christian person, had intended living in the house, it must be good enough for them for at least a little while. It might be small, but what did that matter? They could even get a tent to supplement it if there weren't rooms enough for them all. It would be summertime soon. It would be fun to sleep in a tent. And perhaps if it seemed wise they could build a cheap addition. Maybe Steve could work at it with a carpenter, or—weren't there such things as patent houses all ready made to be set up? Well, she'd better not be planning till she saw where it was. Of course ten years was a long time, and the neighborhood might not be pleasant nor healthy. One could never tell. She would just go and see, for Mother might get her hopes all up about it and then be disappointed. Besides the last thing Mother had said to her was, "See if you can't find us a house outside the city. Maybe there'll be money enough to pay for it pretty soon."

So Phyllis went to the traffic cop on the avenue and asked how to get to Lynwood. It was a pretty name, Lynwood! She said it over several times as she rode along in the trolley, Rosedale Lane, Lynwood. It sounded sylvan and restful. What if it should be a little white bungalow—it wouldn't be a stone one, that would be expecting too much of course—but a little white one with green blinds and an apple tree in the yard perhaps. They could have a garden of poppies and lilies and delphinium. Maybe there would be more trees, an elm would be wonderful but they belonged with estates, and the lawyer had distinctly reminded them that this was not an estate.

She dreamed her day dreams as she rode, studying interestedly the people who were her fellow travelers, till by and by they all got off, and then the car wound around between pleasant houses, large lawns, smooth roads, an occasional gateway covered with vines, and a little stone church a block away covered with ivy. It was pretty out this way, but of course it might not be beautiful like this in Lynwood.

Suddenly the conductor came to her and told her that Lynwood was the next stop. She got off, her heart beating as wildly as if she were about to seek her fortune.

There was no one about at Lynwood station, a little vine covered stone structure pretty as a picture. There were woods all about and a road that wound across the tracks, down into the woods and up a hill. She wondered which was Rosedale Lane. Then she spied a flagman and went to ask him. He pointed her down the hill and through the woods, and she started out half fearfully. Perhaps she ought not to do this all alone. Perhaps she should have waited for Melissa. Nevertheless she hurried on.

She crossed a little rustic bridge and passed the more closely wooded district, and now she came out on a broad way with high hedges on either side, that almost hid the houses behind them. The road wound on and presently there was a sign at a turning "Rosedale Lane," and she knew that she was right. But there were no numbers. How would she know when she came to the right house? In fact she must be out of her way somehow for these were all large fine houses. Probably estates.

And now the way wound up a hill, decidedly up and up. Her city bred feet were tired and her back ached. The sun was growing warm, and perhaps she was going the wrong way after all, who knew?

She heard a car coming and stepping aside to let it pass looked at the driver with a half hesitant appeal. Dared she ask the way?

It was a young man driving a smart little roadster. He wore no hat and had the air of a college boy. She ventured and he slowed down and looked at her interestedly.

"Would you tell me if I am on my way to the Forsythe house?"

"The Forsythe house? Sure. You're right. I'm going right there. I live across the road. Hop in and I'll take you. This hill isn't so good on a hot day."

Phyllis hesitated.

"Oh, is it far? I needn't trouble you. You're very kind I'm sure."

But the youth had jumped out and was opening the other door of the car for her. Phyllis was troubled. Ought she to get in? Wasn't this exactly the same thing that Melissa had done and got into loads of trouble? Getting into a car with a strange young man? Why, it wasn't respectable. It was what they called being "picked up." Still he said he lived across the road, and if he was to be a neighbor why it was probably different.

"It's about a quarter of a mile farther," said the youth with another engaging smile. "Better hop in. I'll have you there in a second."

And against her worst convictions she got in. She wondered as she did so whether all the Challengers were weak-minded when it came to refusing rides in beautiful cars. It couldn't be that this young man had told her the truth, for he looked far too opulent to live across the road from any house the Challengers would be likely to inherit.

But by this time they were whizzing up the hill in great shape, and the engaging smile was turned on her again.

"Are you one of the Forsythes?" he asked.

"Why, no, not exactly," said Phyllis, "we're relatives."

"Say! That's great! It's been closed so long I certainly would like to see that house open."

"Did you know the Forsythes?" she asked timidly.

"No, I was just a kid when that house was built, but I remember my mother watching it and talking about the time when the people would come there. She wanted some neighbors. She was awfully lonesome here."

They topped the hill and he pointed to a large light gray stone house, ornate and lovely, set on the top of a little hill, its lawn sloping down to a miniature lake at the foot that Phyllis suspected was a swimming pool.

"That's where I live," said the boy, pointing with a wave of his hand. "It's still lonesome. Nobody in it but me and my kid brother now. And the servants, of course."

"Oh, isn't your mother—" she stopped dismayed. She ought not to ask personal questions.

"No, she's dead," said the boy gloomily. "Died three years ago. I haven't been here much except vacations since. I've been mostly in prep schools, and college. I've been one year to college. But I don't like where I was. I'm thinking of staying home this winter and going into the city to the university. My dad doesn't care what I do. He's in Europe. He got married again, and they live abroad. I don't like her so I stay here."

Phyllis looked at him in dismay.

"Oh, I'm sorry!" she said. "I don't see how you do without

a mother or a father either! I have both, and they're wonderful!"

"Say! That must be great!" said the boy. "I'd like that. I haven't really had a home since Mother died. Say, you're different from most girls I see. Are you coming out here to live? I wish you would. We could have some great times. But then if you've got a father and mother like that they wouldn't let you have a look at me. You see my father was divorced from my mother when I was only a kid. That's not so good you know. But I can't help it."

The boy settled into gloom for a moment again, but then roused to point to the other side of the road at a stone house, long and low, with wide arched stone porches, set against a background of hemlock and plumy pines.

"There's the Forsythe place!" he said, "I'll drive you up to the door. It's always been kept up pretty well. I know the caretaker, but he's away in the city to-day. I took him down to catch the car. Have you a key?"

But Phyllis was looking in dismay.

"Oh, there must be some mistake. That couldn't be the house. It's only a small house I'm very sure. That's an estate. The lawyer distinctly said it wasn't an estate."

"Oh, no, that's not an estate. That's just a house. There aren't more than three acres there. That's the house all right. You see I was born right here and I know."

"Oh, but—why it can't be. There must be some other Forsythes. Perhaps down at the other end of the road. Doesn't Rosedale Lane go over the other side of the tracks? I must have turned the wrong way."

"No, it just starts by the station and comes up here. And there isn't another Forsythe family within miles around here that I ever heard of. Why, here, didn't you say you have a key? Well, the proof of the pudding's in the eating, isn't it? Go try your key and see if it fits. If it opens the door it's your house, isn't it?"

"Well, but," said Phyllis quite bewildered, "I was only looking for a little house. I was afraid it wasn't going to be big enough for our family. There were only two of them in the Forsythe family you know. They wouldn't have had a great big house like this would they?"

"Why sure, why not? They must have had money enough to make it just as they wanted it. They're the right Forsythes all right. They had only one son and he was killed in the world war. That was just when they built this house. They were expecting him home and then when he got killed they went abroad and never did come back. Mrs. Forsythe died and he stayed over there. That's the last I heard of them. Nathan O. Forsythe, that's the name. Same people aren't they?"

"Yes, that's the name, but it doesn't seem possible."

"Do you know if Forsythe is coming back?" asked the young man.

"Oh, he's dead," said Phyllis sadly. "He's left the house to my mother."

"Great!" said the boy. "Are you coming here to live?"

"Oh, I don't know," said Phyllis. "It seems too wonderful. My father is a college professor. We haven't usually lived in such large houses. But it would be—well, I can't tell anything till Mother comes back."

"Say, I hope you do come here to live," said the boy wistfully. "It would make life less lonesome just to see some lights on that other hill. I stay home at night sometimes and wander around the rooms and think what it would be like to have folks, and then I look out the window. There's the game room down in our basement, and the swimming pool, and the tennis court, but somehow I hardly ever use them. You don't do things like that alone. Once in a while I get some of the fellows from college on to stay a day or so, but they think it's slow out here."

"Oh, how can they?" she said. "I think it's the most beautiful place I ever saw."

"Well, what do you say? Want to try your key?"

"Oh, I'd like to see in there, but it seems almost like house-breaking."

He laughed and swung his car into the drive. They swept up under a porte cochère to a wide oak door set about with many thick hemlocks.

17

PHYLLIS got out and whirled around on the landscape, looking off to the beautiful hills and then to the great massive stone house across the way, quite on another little hill by itself.

"It would be wonderful to live here and look over to a great beautiful palace like that," she said.

"Palace nothing, but I hope you do. I like you. If the rest of your family is just half as good it would be wonderful!"

"We've all been praying for a house in the country," mused Phyllis almost forgetting the presence of this nice boy, "but we never expected to have God hand us out a place like this. I can't believe it!"

The boy stared at her.

"Do you pray? Do you believe in praying?"

Phyllis brought her gaze back from the scenery and looked at him thoughtfully.

"I didn't till lately. But we had a lot of trouble, and—well somehow we got started to praying through my little sister. We all prayed and—things happened. This is one of them. I couldn't help believing in it now."

The boy continued to stare.

"I never did care for girls much," he mused. "But—well—I certainly hope you come here to live! What do you say, shall we go in now?"

Phyllis took out her keys and the young man opened the door. It let them into a wide hall, oak paneled and floored. There was a glass door at the other end through which the sunlight poured, and the grass crept close to a wide stone paving just beyond.

On either side of the hall were two wide oak-beamed paneled rooms, reaching comfortably the depth of the house, and arched windows with deep window seats suggested cushions and a book. The room to the left had an immense fireplace and bookcases from floor to ceiling with glass doors across the whole outside wall, except for the windows. The room to the right had two great windows with another fireplace between, and at its end a wide arch gave a view of a dining room with its built-in china closets and bay window.

Phyllis lifted her eyes to a noble oak staircase sweeping up a wide curve.

"This is perfect!" she breathed. "But—it looks as if somebody was just moving in."

"That's it," said the boy gloomily. "They were when they went away. All these are their things."

"I know," said Phyllis softly. "It seems too bad."

She walked quietly up the stairs, touching the dusty hand rail and marveling at its beauty of line.

There were six bedrooms on the second floor, beside a room which the boy designated as the servant's room, though it looked palatial to Phyllis. They all had views that were breath-taking in their loveliness. Phyllis looked and at last covered her face with her hands and rubbed her eyes.

"I just can't think it's real!" she said, her eyes shining. The boy beamed also.

"Say, it's great having you like it that way. My, I'm glad I met you on the road. I wouldn't have missed this for anything. Say, how about coming over to my house and having a bite to eat? We always have plenty of cake on tap."

"Oh no, thank you," said Phyllis in alarm. "I must go right home now. It's time to get dinner, and my sisters will wonder where I am."

"Have you sisters? Are they like you?"

"I have two, but they're not like me. They're both pretty, and have golden hair, especially Rosalie the youngest. I'm the dark one."

"Pretty! Oh!" he said in a tone that made Phyllis' cheeks glow at his admiration. Then he asked, "Is your name Forsythe?"

"Oh, no, my name is Challenger, Phyllis Challenger."

"That's a story-book name. I like it. I never knew a girl named Phyllis. Well my name's Garrison, Graham Garrison. Say, come on over and see my house."

"Oh, I really couldn't this time," said Phyllis. "I'd love to but I know Mother wouldn't think I should. Perhaps, if we come out here to live, sometime when Mother gets here I could come. But now I must hurry right back to Melissa."

"Who is Melissa? Your sister? And Rosalie you said your little sister was. Well, why don't you bring the whole bunch out then?"

"I'm not sure," said Phyllis. "We may have to wait till Mother gets back. She went to see my brother who is in college. He got hurt in an accident, has a broken leg, and she went last night. I don't suppose we can do anything till she gets here."

"Say, I hope she comes back soon. How about letting me take you back to the city?"

"I mustn't," said Phyllis shaking her head. "I've got to be square with what Mother would like. If she were here it would be different. She might say yes, but as it is I can't."

"Well I'm taking you down to the car anyway. I'm sure she wouldn't want you to walk alone." He grinned and Phyllis said: "Well, perhaps."

When Phyllis was back on the trolley speeding toward the

city she began to wonder at the ease with which she had conversed with the attractive young stranger. Wasn't that just what Melissa had done and got into trouble? Yet he seemed only a nice boy. Well, anyhow, he hadn't done or said a thing out of the way except to try and tell her she was pretty, and that of course was only kidding. She put any uneasiness she had felt out of her mind and began to work out a plan of action.

Melissa had not come back yet when she reached home and it was not quite time for the children to come from school. She got herself a bite of lunch and sat down to write to her mother:

Dear Mother,

I went to see Father yesterday, and he was delighted to see me. I was surprised how well he looks. Isn't it going to be wonderful to have him home again?

When I got home Melissa and Rosalie had the dishes all washed—we had slept late so dinner was late,—and Mr. Jenifer was there with his car. He has a nice car. And he stayed to supper with us and took us all to his church. We liked the minister very much. Bob liked him too.

This morning I went out to see your "inheritance" house. I think it would do very nicely for us for a while. It has a fireplace and bedrooms enough so we could get along, and there is a nice room for Father to rest. There would be room enough for a garden too.

I was thinking, Father says he will soon be allowed to come home, perhaps sooner than you expected. Would you like it if Melissa and I were to go out and clean the house and get things in some shape so we could go there in a hurry in case Father is ready to come home sooner, or in case Steve has to come home? We could do that, and then if you didn't like it we could look around for something else later. There seem to be beds and things enough for us to get along a while without getting the storage ones. Let me know at once if you would like us to dust it up a little in case of an emergency.

We all miss you very much but we hope you are having as happy a time as you could under the circumstances and we send Steve our love and hope he is much better. Father says don't mind him, he is almost well, and he's glad for Steve to have you for a while. He says tell Steve it's tough luck but it will all come out right pretty soon he hopes.

Lots of love. I must put the potatoes on for hash now,

Lovingly, Phillis

P.S. Rosalie has just come in from school. She got a hundred in her spelling. She sends you a hug.

Melissa and Bob came in soon and as they were all hungry they decided to have dinner as soon as they could get it on the table, but they had scarcely got seated before Jenifer arrived.

"I'm going to try not to be a pest," he said, "but I had to go out to one of the suburbs to leave some blue prints for a man and I thought perhaps you folks would like to go along seeing you are all alone. I haven't anything else to do this evening and we can stay out till you get sleepy, ride as far as you please. Perhaps you'd like to stop at a road house somewhere and get a drink?" He looked at Melissa and grinned mischievously.

They all laughed and accepted the invitation with delight.

It was Phyllis who proposed that they leave the dishes and go at once while it was still daylight.

"Yes, it will not be dark soon to-night. March is almost over you know. It is spring," said Jenifer. "It couldn't be better weather for a ride. But get your coats. It may be cool before we get back. There's going to be a wonderful moon. Is there any place you'd like especially to go? I don't have to be five minutes in Glen Park and then we can tour anywhere."

"Oh, anywhere will be lovely, it doesn't matter," said Melissa happily.

"But yes, there is," said Phyllis. "There's a place I very much want to go. I was wondering how I was going to get you all there. It's a house I heard of."

"Oh, Phyllis," said Melissa, "don't let's go house hunting the only chance we have to take a ride!"

"That's all right, we'll get the ride in too," said Jenifer, smiling assurance at Phyllis.

"That's all right," said Phyllis with a toss of her head and a grin. "It's a pretty ride all right. I've been there! No, I'm not going to tell you where it is. I'll tell Mr. Jenifer alone, and he can be the judge whether we shall go or not."

They hurried upstairs for their coats and Phyllis had a moment's conference with Jenifer. Then they all piled out into the car joyously, just as if there never had been a time a few short days ago when they were almost starving and some of them were sick and all of them were sad.

Jenifer had Melissa beside him, Phyllis and Bob with Rosalie between them were in the back seat, and Phyllis was dimpling and smiling to herself as they skimmed along the road out of the city and into a beautiful countryside. Occasionally she slipped her hand into her bag to make sure a couple of keys were quite safe, but she said nothing more about house hunting.

"Isn't this wonderful here!" exclaimed Melissa, as they drove along into the finer suburbs, and delved down into a road that went straight through the woods. "Oh, I love it here!"

Phyllis was watching the way happily, but she only gave a smiling assent to Melissa's eagerness.

And then came the great hedges, and the hidden palaces in the distance, and they all exclaimed over those. Finally they climbed the hill and there on the left was the big stone mansion with its towers and turrets, and the lovely pool at the foot of the lawn.

"That certainly is a wonderful house. Fancy living in a place like that! Fancy living where you could look at houses and lawns and drives like that! And oh, that beautiful pool!"

Melissa was most enthusiastic. And then, she discovered the other wide-spreading house off to her right.

"That's prettier yet," she said. "That's my idea of a house. If I ever get very, very rich I'll build one like that. I like the rough stone better than the face stone. I like the casement windows and the arches. Look at those vines! How I'd like to see what it's like inside!"

Jenifer had turned his head to the back seat and raised his eyebrows, and receiving a mysterious signal from Phyllis, he said quite casually,

"Well, why not? Suppose we do!" and drove his car around the curve straight into the driveway.

"Oh, do you know them?" asked Melissa in awe.

"Yes, a little," he said with a covert grin. "Well enough to ask them to let us look through their house."

"I'm not very dressed up," said Melissa beginning to straighten her hat and push back her hair. "My shoes are rather shabby."

"They won't mind," said Jenifer with assurance, and he swept up under the porte cochère and brought the car to a stand still.

"They aren't home!" announced Bob, "there isn't a curtain at any window."

"I see a light in that window," said Rosalie eagerly.

"Aw, that's only the sunset reflected in the glass, Silly!" said Bob.

"Let's find out," said Jenifer, getting out. "Phyllis, have you those keys?"

"Phyllis Challenger, you haven't been foolish enough to look at a palace like this have you? You couldn't touch it unless you were a millionaire," said Melissa crossly.

"Are you going to get out Miss Challenger?" asked Jenifer, "or do we wait outside?"

Melissa, smiling, allowed him to help her out.

"You see your sister got a chance to look at this house and she thought we all would enjoy it. It certainly has nice lines doesn't it? Look at those arches. They couldn't be better!"

He unlocked the door and they all stepped inside and gasped their appreciation.

Bob looked around for a minute and then glimpsed something through a window.

"Gee! There's a garage too! And a dog kennel! I'm going out ta look."

He came back pretty soon and announced in a loud tone that there was a car in the garage. "It's a big, shiny one," he said. "Looks swell. It's up on jacks. Whaddaya 'spose that's for?"

"Are you sure we aren't intruding?" asked Melissa, looking about uncomfortably. "It seems rather impudent, looking around on people's private possessions. Just look at that desk! Isn't that lovely? My, wouldn't it be fun to live in a house like this!"

Phyllis said not a word, just walked around enjoying herself. She let them go all through the house and exclaim over every delightful feature, and comment on the views from the window, especially the one through an arched window where the sun was setting behind a distant hill, and sit down before the fireplace enjoying an imaginery fire; and then finally, just as they reluctantly got up to go, and even Bob and Rosalie had simmered down in their enthusiasm a little, she turned about and said,

"Well, Challengers, friends, what do you think of it?"

"Think of it!" said Melissa. "Do you have to ask?"

"Do you think this would do for us to live in for a while?"

"Do!" laughed Melissa, "well, rather!"

"Well, we can," she stated quietly.

"Can what?" asked Bob sharply.

"Live in it."

"You're crazy!"

"No, I'm not crazy," said Phyllis. "I mean it. I know the owner, and we can come here and live if we want to."

"Who is the owner, Sister?" asked Rosalie, her eyes wide with wonder.

They were all very still, looking toward Phyllis, expecting some joke, except Jenifer who stood in the background and watched Melissa's lovely face with the sunset glow shining on it touching up the rings of gold hair that escaped about her forehead and cheeks from the trim little hat.

"Who is it, Phyllis," coaxed Melissa, "don't tease us, who owns it?"

"Our mother!" said Phyllis quietly in a voice that carried sudden conviction to the entire group. For even Jenifer hadn't known the whole secret.

"What?" said Melissa, jumping up and gazing around to see if it wasn't all a dream. "Our Mother owns this? Phyllis, there's some terrible mistake. Somebody is playing a joke on you."

Phyllis laughed.

"I thought so myself at first, but it's no mistake. It's all true. This is the property the lawyer made her sign for just before she left. He gave her the keys then. But she doesn't know herself how wonderful it is. She thinks it's a little cottage somewhere."

Then into the midst of the excitement of the moment there sounded a quick knock on the open door, and a fresh young voice called:

"Is there any admittance? Are these the Challengers? Because if they are I'm coming in. I want to meet them. Phyllis Challenger aren't you going to introduce me?"

Then Phyllis with very red cheeks stepped forward and said, "Oh, good evening! Melissa, this is Graham Garrison. He lives across the road and he'll be our neighbor. And this is

Mr. Jenifer our friend, Graham; and these are Rosalie and Bob, my sister and brother."

"Well, I'm certainly glad to meet you all. How soon are you moving in? Because I'm keen on having some neighbors right away. How about dropping in on me for a few minutes since the light is fading and the electric light isn't turned on here yet. I tried to get Phyllis to come over this morning but she seemed to think she hadn't time."

Then Melissa gave Phyllis a look of quick inquiry and turned back to look the boy over more carefully.

When they had finally locked the door and all climbed into Jenifer's car, with Garrison in the front seat with Jenifer and Bob, and Melissa in the back seat, Melissa leaned over and whispered to Phyllis.

"Phyllis Challenger, where in the world did you pick up that good looking cherub of a boy?"

"I didn't pick him up, he picked me," said Phyllis gayly. "He picked me up and rode me up the hill this morning when I thought I'd lost my way."

"Does Mother know him?" asked Melissa.

"No, but she will," said Phyllis coolly. "Isn't his house gorgeous? I'm crazy to see inside of it. It must be lovely. But of course I wouldn't go over this morning alone.

"But what will his people think of us all dropping down upon them?"

"He hasn't any," said Phyllis. "His mother is dead and there's only himself and his kid brother, and he's off at school most of the time. He has a lot of servants I guess from the way he talked."

They went into the house while the boy owner showed them about, and they got wonderfully chummy with him. They all voted him most interesting. It was growing late when they tore themselves away to take the blue prints to Jenifer's man.

"Well," said Melissa when they got home at last and began to prepare for sleep, "aren't things different! Who would have believed the night Mrs. Barkus made such a fuss about the rent that all this would happen inside of one short week? Life is queer isn't it? Phyllis, I wonder if God meant to do this all the time for us, and was only waiting for us to pray for it?"

"Ask Ian," said Phyllis with a twinkle in her eyes. "I heard you calling him that to-night. If you have got that far you ought to be able to ask him a lot of things."

"Well, he asked me to," said Melissa, blushing.

"It's all right," said Phyllis smiling, "but about that other question, I think myself that God was waiting till we got done trying to do everything for ourselves, and being proud of it, and got to where we knew He was the only One who could give us anything. We'd been forgetting God, Melissa Challenger. In fact we never paid the least attention to whether He existed, and we had to be taught better."

"I guess that's so," said Melissa. "I know I got to the end of myself that night."

"Well, now, Lissa, what shall we do about this house? Shall we clean it up and get ready a surprise for Mother and Father?" and she told her what she had written in her letter that afternoon.

"Oh, Phyllis. Wouldn't that be wonderful!" said Rosalie. "Could we really do that? And are we really truly going to live in that wonderful house?"

"I think we are," said Phyllis.

"Gee! Then we won't have ta go ta that old stick-in-the-mud school any more, will we? Gee! I'll have rabbits and guinea pigs! Gee! Graham Garrison said we could swim in his pool as much as we liked!"

By the time they got to bed the Challengers were too excited to go to sleep.

And then, they had to get up and read the letter from their distant cousin before they could quiet down again. After they had been still for a long time, Melissa said sleepily:

"Say, Phyllis, I didn't get any job to-day, but it won't matter so much now, will it? I think I can get that library position in the fall. I heard the girl that was after it was going to be married. And now that Mother has money enough to keep up this house it won't matter if I do have to wait a few weeks."

"No," said Phyllis joyfully, "it never mattered, because I guess God knew what He was going to do with us all the time."

18

MARY Challenger had been more than three weeks with her son and she was getting uneasy about her husband and the rest of her family. She felt she ought to be back in the city planning somehow for her husband's home coming. It was far beyond the time that had first been set for him to leave the hospital. She was afraid the delay might be worse for him.

And yet when she suggested going home, her boy was like a spoiled child. He looked desolate and forlorn.

She had watched beside him during his fevered hours that first week of her coming enough to learn the whole story of the wreck. She heard his varied opinions of one Sylvia Saltaine, and her heart was wrung by her insight into temptations that had come to her oldest son in college. On one occasion she met this Sylvia when she visited Jack Hollister's room with a message from Stephen about some fraternity matter. She heard the details of the wrecked car and her son's full part in it from his own delirious lips, and was both anguished that he had been mixed up in such things, and rejoiced that he had not been more fully involved in the shame of it. It was good to know that her boy had not been drunk when the car went over the precipice.

She even had a long talk with the college president and the dean, and found food for thought, for regret and for some pride too. But most of all in those lonely hours after the patient had gone to sleep, she had learned to pray. It was her only solace during those first anguished days of waiting to see what was coming.

Stephen was no longer delirious. He was very weak, and could talk very little, but one day after discovering that he had let out a good many things while he had a fever, he had a heart to heart talk with his mother. They came closer than they had done since he was a little boy, and went deep into one another's souls. Then was Mary Challenger glad that she had come and glad that she had stayed with her boy.

The children had written very little of what was going on at home. Since Phyllis' unenthusiastic letter about the house, her mother had given up hope that the legacy was going to give her much help for her difficulties though she had told Phyllis to clean it up if she thought it was worth while.

The talk in their letters had been mostly of what they cooked for dinner, what happened in school, or what Father said the last time they visited him, and how he was walking around his room quite like his old self. Once or twice they mentioned taking a ride with Mr. Jenifer and described the scenery. She wondered at their lack of news. They often filled a whole letter with the kindnesses of Mr. Brady.

But one day right out of the blue, the doctor walked into Stephen's room and asked him how he would like to go home the next week. He outlined how easy the journey might be made, an ambulance to the station, a berth in the train, one of the nurses to go with him till he was settled in his own home.

When Mary Challenger saw the look in her boy's face she knew it must be managed in spite of all difficulties. After a long wait in the telephone booth she managed to get Phyllis on the wire by the kindness of Mr. Brady.

"Phyllis," she said, realizing that she must not make a long expensive conversation. "The doctor wants me to bring Stephen home. He thinks it will be better for him now. Can you find a room at some quiet hotel where there is good elevator service for a few days while I can look around and find a proper house? I think we may be able to manage the expense. You know that lawyer told me there was some money in the bank for me. I'll have to go down to the bank and find out about it as soon as I get there, and then we must get right to work and find some kind of a home."

Phyllis' voice lilted over the wire with joyful sound. "Lovely, Mother! When are you coming?"

"Well, the doctor said he might go day after to-morrow if all goes well. But we'll have to wait till you find a place for your brother that will be really comfortable. We'll have to bring a nurse for the journey you know."

"All right, Mother! I think I know a good place. Wire us what train you will be on and we'll be at the station with a car. Mr. Jenifer offered his for him when he was ready to come home. Shall I say day after to-morrow then? Will you take the day train or the night? All right. We'll meet you day after to-morrow at the evening train. I think it's around six. You can let me know."

"But Phyllis you must be sure to find a comfortable place—"

"I know Mother. I will of course!"

It was as easy as that! After the mother had hung up the receiver she felt she had only half said what she intended and she sat down and wrote a long laborious letter, telling it all over again, and sent the letter by air mail. It seemed too simple, as if Phyllis had known this was going to happen and had the hotel all picked out for him. The mother couldn't understand it. They were altogether too casual at home. But then they were young of course.

She found she was a trifle disappointed in the back of her mind about that inheritance house. Phyllis hadn't said a word about it. She had hoped so that it might turn out an abiding place at least for a time, but if Phyllis had thought it worth anything she certainly would have mentioned it now when there was such a stress. Well, at least there was much to be thankful for, and perhaps there would be some money left over from the regular upkeep of the little house to help out. Melissa would get that library job in the fall perhaps. She seemed to be hopeful in her last letter. And Phyllis would be able to find a secretarial place by summer. Anyway, there was nothing she could do till she got home but pray, and prayer had brought her thus far. She must not forget the great deliverances of the past.

So she packed her boy's scanty, tattered wardrobe, wept a few tears into his trunk to think she had not been able to dress him better in his last college year, and prepared to take him home.

There was great excitement among the Challengers, little and big, during the next two days.

Melissa and Phyllis had been working like beavers for the last three weeks. They had cleaned "Heritage House," as they laughingly called it, from top to toe with the help of Bob and Rosalie after school. They had burrowed into bureau drawers and trunks of which they had discovered the keys, and found sheets and blankets and pillows and spreads. They had made up the beds with hand embroidered linen pillow cases, and handsomely initialed sheets, and everything was in apple pie order. They had had more solid pleasure out of the work than they had ever had in their lives before.

Of course they had to make daily trips to see their father, one or the other of them, and there were a few little things that they had to do where they were living, but for the most part they managed to spend a good deal of each morning at Lynwood working hard.

Graham Garrison discovered their presence, and fell into the habit of coming over to help. He really was a great help moving heavy pieces of furniture into place, hanging out heavy blankets to air, even helping to wash windows. It is safe to say that he had never in his whole life together done as much work as he managed sometimes to get into one morning now.

He hunted up the caretaker, too, and nagged him into helping. He took the car to the garage for a good overhauling. He had his cook make up delicious lunches to bring over to the girls as they worked. And then he insisted on driving them home day after day in his car. He said he had to go in town to inquire about courses at the summer school. He made up excuses to do this every day in spite of their protests, and sometimes when they started out in the morning they would find his car standing before the door ready to take them, or lurking around the corner, sneaking up on them just as they were about to take the trolley car.

In the evening they often went back to Lynwood with Jenifer who managed to drop in three or four times a week and worked with them joyously as if it were his home he were preparing.

Once Brady and his family drove out in the evening to look the house over and beam in every room with unselfish pride and pleasure in what had come to the Challengers.

"You better have that there 'lectric ice box looked over and running pretty soon," he told them the first night he came up. "'Cause the first night you're up here, I'm goin' ta send up an order an' fill it up so your mommie won't havta bother her head fer two ur three days."

So Phyllis came home from her mother's telephone call with shining eyes and a happy heart.

"Well, they're coming day after to-morrow," she announced gleefully to Melissa who was washing out stockings. "Stephen is coming! The first thing is to talk to the hospital people and see if Father can come too. I think we had better bring him over the night before and let him get used to things and rested don't you? Then he'll be there to surprise them, sitting down by that open fire in that wonderful room with the books all around! Won't that be great?"

"Rare!" said Melissa smiling joyfully.

"Lissa, you go over to the hospital and talk to Father, and see if he feels he can stand it, and I'll phone his doctor and explain it all. I think they want him to come. They feel it will be better for him. I think they wonder why we haven't brought him home before. Lissa, I wouldn't tell him at first anything about our moving till we're on our way. He won't notice which way we're driving, perhaps."

So they plotted lovingly and carried out their beautiful plans. It was Jenifer who brought the invalid from the hospital. Melissa went with him and introduced him to her father as a new friend they had found while he was sick. The two men took to each other at once. Jenifer knew just how to make things comfortable in the car for the invalid, and how to treat him as if he were not an invalid at all.

It was in the bright morning that they took him to his new home, and when they were half way there he said to Melissa,

"Why, child, have I forgotten the lay of the land? It seems to me you are not on your way home."

So Melissa broke it to him very gently that they had not been in Glenside for many months. It had been sold and they had had to move. But now, Melissa explained, just before Mother went away she had inherited some property from a cousin and they were going to that house. Even Mother herself had not seen it. It was to be a surprise to her too.

He watched as eagerly as if he were a child for a sight of the new house, and when they turned into the beautiful sweep of the drive-way he murmured:

"Beautiful! Beautiful! Nothing could be lovelier. Oh, I'm glad my Mary is to have a real home at last!"

They would not let him talk much, and they put him to bed at once in the long room on the right of the hall.

It was Jenifer who had suggested that there would have to be a hospital room downstairs for a time till the two invalids were well enough to walk upstairs. So the girls had established two beds, one at either end of the great sunny room, and it was here they put their father to bed to rest after the ride.

They fed him with broth that Phyllis had made, and left him to rest, but when they came tipping in to see if he was all right, they found him lying happily, looking off across the beautiful rolling hills that were just putting on their lovely spring foliage. He seemed very happy, and not at all excited.

After he had had his dinner they told him more of the surprise, all about Stephen coming too, and how they were going to meet him.

Young Garrison came over in the late afternoon with a great sheaf of roses, a whole hundred of them, and some pots of hyacinths and daffodils. He went in to see the invalid, and be introduced, though indeed Phyllis had told her father of him two weeks before. She stood by watching Graham's face as he was talking with her father, and she could see he admired the scholarly professor.

"Say, he's all right," he said to Phyllis as he went out. "Boy! What wouldn't I give if I had a father like that! Now, when your mother gets here I'm going to be happy."

Phyllis loved it that he said such things about her father and mother. It made him fine in her eyes. She watched him down the driveway, walking with his head up, and thought how nice it was to have a friend like that, and how good God had been to her. Then she turned back to her cooking, for there was to be a real company supper that first night. Chicken with the little biscuits and gravy that were a tradition in the Challenger family for any festivity. Mashed potatoes, onions,—Rosalie insisted on them—and snow pudding that the invalids could eat.

Melissa was gone to meet the train with Jenifer and bring Mother and Stephen home. It was almost time for them to come. The table was set with the best Forsythe china, and everything was ready. In a few minutes now Bob and she would help Father into his best dressing gown, and get him to the big davenport before the fire in the library. There he would be among the book cases, which were filled with many books now, for the girls had delved into boxes and barrels and brought them out and shelved them. Oh, it was a wonderful day for the Challengers!

But before Bob came back from getting another bottle of milk from the farm half a mile away, Graham came in again.

"I thought perhaps you'd let me help some more," he said wistfully. "I'd awfully like to be here when they come if you don't mind. It seems as though they sort of belonged to me too," he said with a funny little wrinkle around his engaging eyes.

So it was Garrison's strong arm that helped the professor to his couch before the fire, brought him his medicine, and a rug to lay across his feet, and hovered about telling what he knew of the old Forsythe house till Rosalie announced from her perch in the wide window seat. "There they come! I can see Ian's car just coming up over the hill. The greyhound on the front shines red in the setting sun. Oh, Mother's coming back! Mother's coming back! I'm glad, glad, glad!"

Then all was bustle and stir for a few minutes while they helped carry Stephen in to his bed.

But Stephen was like one revived. He looked around everywhere, and smiled, and when he passed through the wide hall he looked toward his father on the couch and waved his hand gayly.

"Hello, Dad! Isn't this great?" he shouted as he was borne past; and then he protested.

"I'm not going in another room to bed yet. I want to go in there with Dad and see everybody together. There's another couch on the other side of the fire. Why can't I go there?"

And so he had his way, and the Challengers gathered around the fire just as Phyllis had dreamed they would when she first saw the room.

When they were settled on the two couches Mary Challenger took her first look around the great beautiful room.

"Phyllis! Phyllis! No wonder you said you knew a lovely place. But my dear, isn't this going to be very expensive? It looks like a wonderful private home. This is not a hotel!"

"No, Mother dear," laughed Phyllis, "it is a private house. I know the lady who owns it. She's lovely and she won't charge us anything. We can have it as long as we like."

"Oh my dear!" said the mother looking wistfully about. "It's very wonderful, but you know we can't be under obligation like that. We must look for something right away the first thing in the morning. You know Father will never stand for being under obligation to any one."

Phyllis' eyes were dancing.

"He will this time though, Mother, for he happens to be married to the owner. Mother haven't you really suspected at all that this is your own house that you inherited from your cousin?"

They all stood there watching her with broad grins of delight on their faces, and their eyes dancing with fun, Rosalie dancing and clapping her hands, Bob with his eyebrows up to his hair his eyes were so wide with merriment, Melissa smiling in the doorway with Jenifer just behind her, and Graham peeking in around the other corner of the opening.

Mary Challenger stood and stared at them all, then up at the oak beams of her palatial home, down at the beautiful hardwood floor, out through the vistas of the arched windows toward the dying sunset, "Not *this!* This can't be my house!" she said, and then the tears trembled into her eyes, bright tears, and she took one step and knelt beside her husband's couch, and buried her head on his shoulder. "Oh John, and I've been so untrustful!" she said, "so worried and afraid lest God wouldn't take care of us, and here He has given me all this!"

The professor-invalid laid his thin hand on his wife's head like a tender blessing and said feelingly:

"You deserve it all and more, Mary—beloved!"

It was after supper had been served in various places, to the invalids in the library, and to the rest of the family including Jenifer and Garrison in the dining room, that they gathered again around that open fire for just a few minutes before the invalids were put to bed.

The nurse had been sent away in the Garrison servants' car to catch the evening train back to his hospital. They were together at last as a family, for Jenifer and Garrison had succeeded in making themselves a part of it somehow already, and a sweet silence hovered over them all. Phyllis had turned out the lights and was sitting on the floor by her father's couch with the flicker of the firelight on her face, and Garrison stood by the big mantel watching her surreptitiously. Rosalie was curled in her mother's lap in deep peace, Bob in one of the window seats with his chin on his knees looking out at the stars, Melissa on a little stool beside her brother's couch, and Jenifer around the other corner of the mantel watching her.

Suddenly the master of the house spoke.

"Children, this has been a wonderful day. The blessedest day of my whole life except my wedding day," and he smiled across at his Mary. "I've been thinking before we part I'd like to say a little word while we're all together. No, don't go away you two," he said as a little stir in the shadows of the mantel showed the two young men about to withdraw, and leave the family to itself. "Jenifer, Garrison, you have helped to make this happiness of ours possible. You are one with us to-night. And what I have to say I want to say to you too.

"No, Mother, don't you stop me. I'll not be but a minute. It won't tire me. It's the crowning of the day. I want to give a testimony this first night in this new home before I sleep.

"I want to say that I have to thank the Lord for sending my illness to me. I do believe He did it in kindness. I was getting so far away from Him that I scarcely believed in His power any more. And when He laid me low He began to teach me again to look to Him. For a time I was in despair. I thought I should lose my mind, to see my attainments, my family, my ambitions all in the dust; to see myself a failure, sick and ready to die.

"Then the Lord sent a servant of his, an old minister to visit me one day. He was there in the hospital with a sickness worse than mine. A painful sickness that racked his body sometimes till he almost fainted. He was there to die, because his disease was a fatal one. And yet he wore such radiance constantly, and went about whenever he was able, telling others of His mighty Lord and what He had done for him, that I was ashamed, and one day I asked him to pray for me and he did. Such a prayer as brought me close to the throne. Every day after that he came in to my room when he was able and read the Bible with me, and prayed. I never knew what a Book that was before. Oh, it's a great book!

"Now, Mary, the thing I want to say to you, and to my children, and to these other two friends here who have been so kind to you all, is this. I'm a new man now, please God. The Lord Jesus is to come first in my life henceforth. I believe I've been born again, and I'd like to go on record this first night in the world again, in our new home, as saying that I want our house to be a house of prayer. Yes, Mother, I'm not going to talk any longer. I'm just going to ask Jenifer here, to read a few verses from the Book of books, and pray a short prayer with us before he goes. Can you see by the firelight—Ian?"

"All right, sir!" said Jenifer with a ring to his voice, and he had his Testament out of his pocket and was stooping to the firelight, fluttering the leaves over as if he had known this was to come to pass.

It was a sweet stillness that hung over the little group. The boy Garrison stood in awe and watched it. It was like no experience that had ever come to him before.

Jenifer read: "I will bless the Lord at all times; his praise shall continually be in my mouth . . . I sought the Lord and he heard me, and delivered me from all my fears. They looked unto him and were lightened: and their faces were not ashamed. This poor man cried and the Lord heard him and saved him out of all his troubles. The angel of the Lord encampeth round about them that fear him and delivereth them . . . O taste and see that the Lord is good. . . . The Lord is nigh unto them that are of a broken heart; and saveth such as be of a contrite spirit . . . none of them that trust in him shall be desolate."

There followed such a prayer as brought the Lord Christ down into their very midst, and in the hush and quiet of the room no heart was unmoved. Stephen's head was turned away toward the back of the couch and there were tears upon his cheeks. Even Bob rubbed the back of his hand across his eyes, and Graham Garrison stood with bowed head in wonder and an awe he did not know he could feel.

After they rose from their knees they were very quiet about their good nights. Phyllis turned on the lights in the hall and the young men lingered to help the invalids into the other room.

Graham Garrison took Mary Challenger's hand in goodnight, and said in a voice that was all husky with feeling:

"You Challengers are a great bunch. I shall never cease to be thankful I met your daughter and got to know you. I appreciate being here to-night."

Jenifer took Melissa's hand for a moment at parting. "Our God is a great God!" he said quietly.

"Wasn't it wonderful!" said little Melissa. "I'm so happy to-night I don't know what to do! And to think I wondered how Father would take it! Oh, I'm glad God sent you to us!"

"So am I!" said Jenifer and then pressed her fingers with a quick clasp and a bright smile and was gone.

Out under the starlight Garrison was waiting for Jenifer.

"Come over and stay with me to-night, Ian!" he said, "I'd

like to hear more about this thing. How do you get that way?"

Ian Jenifer threw an arm across the other's shoulder, "All right, Graham, I'll come. I'd like to," and then added thoughtfully, "Aren't those Challengers a dear people?"

"They certainly are," said the younger man. "I never saw any one like them before. I'd like to belong to that family."

"So would I!" echoed Jenifer heartily.

About the Author

Grace Livingston Hill is well-known as one of the most prolific writers of romantic fiction. Her personal life was fraught with joys and sorrows not unlike those experienced by many of her fictional heroines.

Born in Wellsville, New York, Grace nearly died during the first hours of life. But her loving parents and friends turned to God in prayer. She survived miraculously, thus her thankful father named her Grace.

Grace was always close to her father, a Presbyterian minister, and her mother, a published writer. It was from them that she learned the art of storytelling. When Grace was twelve, a close aunt surprised her with a hardbound, illustrated copy of one of Grace's stories. This was the beginning of Grace's journey into being a published author.

In 1892 Grace married Fred Hill, a young minister, and they soon had two lovely young daughters. Then came 1901, a difficult year for Grace—the year when, within months of each other, both her father and husband died. Suddenly Grace had to find a new place to live (her home was owned by the church where her husband had been pastor). It was a struggle for Grace to raise her young daughters alone, but through everything she kept writing. In 1902 she produced *The Angel of His Presence*, *The Story of a Whim*, and *An Unwilling Guest*. In 1903 her two books *According to the Pattern* and *Because of Stephen* were published.

It wasn't long before Grace was a well-known author, but she wanted to go beyond just entertaining her readers. She soon included the message of God's salvation through Jesus Christ in each of her books. For Grace, the most important thing she did was not write books but share the message of salvation, a message she felt God wanted her to share through the abilities he had given her.

In all, Grace Livingston Hill wrote more than one hundred books, all of which have sold thousands of copies and have touched the lives of readers around the world with their message of "enduring love" and the true way to lasting happiness: a relationship with God through his Son, Jesus Christ.

In an interview shortly before her death, Grace's devotion to her Lord still shone clear. She commented that whatever she had accomplished had been God's doing. She was only his servant, one who had tried to follow his teaching in all her thoughts and writing.

*You'll be thrilled with
the romance and adventure of
America's best-loved author!*

—

*Don't miss all the
Grace Livingston Hill
romance novels!*

—

Tyndale House Publishers, Inc.